THE PRISONER

The City of Dreams
Book Three

The Scottish novelist Joan Fallon, currently lives and works in the south of Spain. She writes both contemporary and historical fiction, and almost all her books have a strong female protagonist. She is the author of:

FICTION:
Spanish Lavender
The House on the Beach
Loving Harry
Santiago Tales
The Only Blue Door
Palette of Secrets
The Thread That Binds Us
Love Is All

The al-Andalus series:
The Shining City (Book 1)
The Eye of the Falcon (Book 2)
The Ring of Flames (Book 3)

The City of Dreams series
The Apothecary (Book 1)
The Pirate (Book 2)

NON-FICTION:
Daughters of Spain

(all are available in paperback and as ebooks)

www.joanfallon.co.uk

JOAN FALLON

THE PRISONER

SCOTT PUBLISHING
(ESPAÑA)

ACKNOWLEDGMENTS

My sincere thanks to my editor Sara Starbuck for helping me to create an exciting novel out of a turbulent period in history, to Angela Hagenow for her excellent proof reading and to Lawston Designs for the cover. Their advice and support have, as always, been invaluable.

REAL HISTORICAL CHARACTERS
Ali ibn Hammud al-Nasir Khalifa 1016 -1018
His eldest son:
Yahya ibn Ali ibn Hammud al-Mutali, Khalifa Yahya 1 1021-1023 & 1025-1026 & Khalifa Malaqah 1026-1035
His second son:
Idris ibn Ali al-Mutaayyad Khalifa Idris1 Malaqah 1035-1039

Eldest son of Yahya I and Fatima:
Hasan ibn Yahya ibn Ali Khalifa of Malaqah 1040-1042
Second son of Yahya I and Fatima:
Idris ibn Yahya ibn Ali (Ben-Yahya) Khalifa Idris II Malaqah 1042 -47

Sons of Idris I:
Muhammad ibn Idris ibn Ali ruler of al-Jazira
Yahya ibn Idris (Yahya II)

Abu al-Qasim Muhammad ibn Abbad, Abbad I ruler of Isbiliya
Badis ben Habus sultan of Garnata
Samuel ibn Nagrilla a Jewish scholar & politician, grand vizier to rulers of Garnata
Joseph ibn Nagrilla his son
Naja al-Siqlabi an ex-slave who became tutor to the sons of Yahya I
Ibn Baqanna grand vizier to Idris I
Zuhair, sultan of Álmeria
Abu Mansur Isa ruler of the Barghawata tribes in Sebta

FICTIONAL CHARACTERS
Makoud ibn Ahmad
Abal and Basma his wives
Umar ibn Makoud his son
Ibrahim ibn Makoud his son
Dirar ibn Makoud his son

Aisha bint Makoud his daughter
Bakr ibn Assam his son-in-law
Avi   Jewish merchant and friend of Makoud
Salma   Makoud's cousin, a scribe
Simon   Married to Salma, a translator
Zara and Layla   daughters of Salma and Simon
Iqbal   husband of Zara, an alfarero
Jabalah   warlord
Yusuf al-Basir   chief librarian
Marwen   assistant librarian
General Rashad
Labib   grand vizier
Qusay   a servant
Uday   a servant

PLACE NAMES
Al-Andalus the Islamic name given to Moorish Spain
Alboran Sea the part of the Mediterranean near Málaga
Al-Jazira the city of Algeciras
Garnata the city of Granada
Isbiliya the city of Seville
Écija, a town between Córdoba and Seville
Jebel al-Tarik Gibraltar
Maghreb the region of North West Africa bordering the Mediterranean Sea
Malaqah the city of Málaga
Middle Sea one name for the Mediterranean
Qurtubah the city of Córdoba
Sea of Darkness one name for the Atlantic Ocean
Sebta the town of Ceuta in North Africa
Tanja Tangiers

A book is like a garden you carry in your pocket.

Arab proverb.

The Prisoner

Malaqah 1040 - 1042 AD

CHAPTER 1

At first Ben-Yahya didn't know where he was. He opened his eyes expecting to see the sun streaming through his bedroom windows, their muslin hangings fluttering in the warm breeze, to smell the sweet scent of orange blossom and hear the call of the imam as he did every morning. Instead he could see nothing and the smell that assailed his senses was of excrement and putrefaction. Was he in hell? Had he been struck blind? Gradually his sleep-stopped eyes adjusted to the gloom and then he remembered. A tiny glimmer of the pale dawn squeezed through the slit in the wall and lighted his dingy cell. Instead of his soft bed of silk-covered cushions, he lay on a stone floor with straw for a mattress. A burst of anger overwhelmed him as he remembered how he had come here, and he leapt to his feet and kicked the straw pallet to one side. Why, in the name of Allah, had he been arrested? But, more importantly what was he doing in this hell-hole? And how was he going to get out? He'd seen enough of the dungeons to know that they were unassailable. He'd never escape without help. His mind was racing; whom could he trust? And how on earth was he going to be able to contact anyone?

He felt in the pockets of his robes. Yes, his purse of money was still there. That filthy quaid may have taken his dagger but he hadn't the wit to take his money. He had two hundred silver dirhams in his purse and another two hundred gold dinars sewn inside his djellaba. He took the purse and tucked it inside the straw pallet for safety.

The beam of light had grown stronger and now the voice of the imam began calling the faithful to morning prayer. All at once the door of his cell opened and the gaoler came in, carrying an earthenware bowl of water and a cloth.

'Here you are, my fine friend. Clean water and something to dry yourself on. You must be someone important to warrant such special treatment.' He put the bowl and towel on the floor, and backed out of the room. Once more the door slammed shut.

Ben-Yahya bent over the bowl and began to wash himself. At least he could still perform this part of his morning ritual. Once he was clean he placed his cap on his head, knelt and began the Fajr prayer. Allah wouldn't abandon him. He'd always been a good Muslim, went to the mosque regularly and never missed a prayer-time. True he occasionally drank wine, but only in moderation. Allah wouldn't condemn him for that. Allah would save him.

The gaoler must have been waiting outside because the minute Ben-Yahya finished praying and sat back on his heels, he opened the door. 'All done?'

'Tell me something, friend. Who is Khalifa at the moment? I have only just arrived in this land and would like to know by whose authority I have been arrested.'

The gaoler hesitated for a moment. Ben-Yahya could see that he wasn't a cruel man; he was just obeying orders and he could feel no ill-will towards him. The prayers had stilled his anger.

'Well, I don't suppose it can hurt if I tell you. All they said was no visitors. They didn't say I couldn't speak to you. It's a lonely life I have here. It'd be good to have someone to talk to, and you've travelled, I can see that; you'll have some interesting tales to tell, most likely. You see, most of the prisoners have been in here a long time, and those that haven't gone off their heads by now, well they don't have anything new to talk about. I can understand that. They just have the four walls to look at and that would make anyone go mad. Some of them turn to religion and they pray day and night and believe Allah will save them. Others rant and rave about being innocent and how someone is going to realise their mistake and set them free. All nonsense of course. Nobody ever leaves here.'

'So, who is the khalifa?' asked Ben-Yahya, trying to hide his impatience.

'It's a new man. When the old khalifa died, his son was supposed to take over. They say he was too young to be a good khalifa, so his uncle deposed him. But he's dead now and the son has claimed his inheritance. He's the new khalifa now. But of course who knows how long he will last. I can't count the number of khalifas I've seen come and go in my lifetime. We live in unsettled times,' he added, nodding his head wisely.

'His name?'

'Just a moment, let me get it right. Ah, yes. Hasan al-Mustansir. As I said he's the son of the old khalifa. Yes, al-Mustansir. That's him.'

'Thank you,' said Ben-Yahya, feeling faint. His brother? If his brother had done this to him then he would never escape; he knew no-one here in Malaqah anymore, only Naja.

'I'll see you later with your dinner,' the gaoler said. 'Then maybe you can tell me a bit about your travels.'

'One more question, if you don't mind.' The gaoler stopped and looked at him. 'How long has Hasan been the khalifa?'

'This latest one? Must be almost six months now. It was just after Ramadan. I remember because…'

Ben-Yahya let the old man ramble on but said nothing, just went and sat on his pallet. So his brother had been on the throne for six months already and yet he had only sent word to him a week ago. He had this planned. It was no sudden decision on his part; Hasan had always intended to get rid of any opposition and now it seemed that he included his brother Ben-Yahya as part of that. He squirmed on the sharp straw and felt the money in his djellaba press against his leg. He had a lot to think about. He'd trusted his brother, loved him even. Why else would he have walked blindly into this trap? How could his own brother do this to him? How could he betray him? He couldn't believe that this was happening. He felt a black rage growing inside him. He would have his revenge, one way or another, maybe not today but one day. He just had to be patient and wait for the right opportunity. He would befriend the gaoler and win his trust then maybe he could persuade him to take a message to Naja for him. No matter what, he was going to get out of here. He was not going to rot in this filthy hole until he went mad like the other inmates. He would get out of here and then vengeance would be his.

CHAPTER 2

They had been travelling south for three days and the sea still seemed as far in the distance as ever. It glittered and shone on the horizon like a mirage, tempting them with the delights of a new future.

'Are you tired, dearest wife?' Simon asked. 'It can't be much further now.'

They had been walking through groves of orange trees all morning, along the flat and fertile valley of the Guadalhorce. Her cousin Rafa had offered to loan them two horses—since leaving Qurtubah all those years ago he had spent his time breeding horses and was well known in the taifa of Malaqah for the quality of his steeds—but Simon had refused. He said it would draw too much attention to them. People would wonder if they were royalty, or worse, if they had stolen them. Instead they borrowed a donkey from him to carry their few, but precious belongings. Iqbal had brought his mule, which he had loaded up with as many of his wares as it could carry. He wanted to sell some of his pottery in the small villages on the way. That was the reason they were taking so long to reach their destination. Salma wanted to hurry him up, but her son-in-law was very stubborn and he certainly didn't like taking orders from a woman, even if she was his mother-in-law.

'No. Not tired, just excited. I want to get there. I want to see little Makoud again,' she said.

Simon burst out laughing. 'Little Makoud? He's almost as old as us now, with two wives and four grown-up children. Hardly your little Makoud anymore.'

'I know, but I have been thinking of him a lot lately and in my mind he's still that fearless teenager who had to grow up too soon.'

'That was how it was for us all. So much bloodshed and death. It was enough to almost turn me away from God,' her husband said.

'Almost, dearest one. In the end you stuck to your faith despite the danger.'

'Hush. You don't know who might hear you.'

'Out here? There is no-one around for miles,' Salma laughed. 'We are quite alone.' Everything made her want to smile today.

Her husband nodded discreetly at Iqbal, who was slightly ahead of them, leading his mule. She knew he didn't trust him. They had never shared Simon's secret with anyone, not even within the family. Salma thought back more than twenty years to when they had miraculously escaped from the besieged city of Qurtubah. Simon had fled with them to Ardales instead of returning to the monastery in England, as his Abbot had instructed.

'Look at the sea,' she cried with delight. She felt like a young child again. Salma had never seen the sea, only occasionally from the highest point in Ardales when the light was right, where it appeared on the horizon as a tiny glint of blue. Now it lay, just out of reach, beyond a forest of sugar cane, but she could see that it was as immense as everyone said it was. It made her heart race just to look at it. It stretched ahead of them as far as the eye could see, and continued east and west until the mountainous coast hid it from view. 'Which way do we go now?' she asked, reluctantly dragging her eyes away..

'According to Makoud, once we reach the coast we just follow it due east until we come to the city walls. We will be in Malaqah before nightfall.'

They wound their way through the banks of sugar cane until they reached a path that ran along the sandy shore.

'Let's stop for a while,' Salma begged, once again more like a child than the fifty-year old woman she was. 'What do you say, Zara?'

Her eldest daughter dropped her bag on the sandy shore and plumped herself down beside it. 'Good idea, Mama.' She was expecting her first child and had found the walk difficult. Salma had suggested that she and her husband stay in Ardales until the baby was born, but Iqbal didn't want to wait; he had the idea that he was going to make his fortune in Malaqah and was in a hurry to get started.

Salma heard a squeal of pleasure and looked up to see her youngest daughter, Layla, with her skirts tucked up around her waist, paddling in the waves.

'Come in. It's lovely,' the girl cried. 'So blue. So clean. Oh, Mama, it's wonderful. This must be what heaven is like.' She kicked her feet to see the water splash and dug her toes in the sand. 'And there're fish. Look. Look at that one, the silver one.' Excitedly she bent down and tried to catch it but it slipped through her fingers and was away.

'You'll need to be quicker than that if you want to catch something for our supper,' her father said, with a laugh.

The donkey that Makoud's brother had loaned them, stopped abruptly; it too had decided that it needed to rest. 'Well it looks like the women and the donkey have made the decision,' he said to Iqbal. 'We'll rest here for a short while.'

'But we're almost there,' moaned Iqbal. 'You can see the mosque glinting in the sunlight.' He glowered at Simon but didn't argue, and sat down beside his wife.

Zara pulled off her sandals and rolled up her trousers. 'I need to cool my feet,' she said, getting up and gingerly walking through the sand and into the shallows. The waves lapped lazily around her ankles.

'It's so calm and peaceful,' Salma said, a touch of surprise in her voice. She'd always thought the sea was a terrible place, rough and stormy, a place of danger, with pirates and immense depths where sea monsters lurked. Instead this reminded her of the millpond where her neighbour ground his corn, only a hundred times larger. It was like a giant mirror reflecting the mottled sky above. She lay back and stretched her aching limbs on the sand.

This was a big step they were taking, going back to a city to live, but she couldn't turn down her cousin's kind offer. When he learnt of his mother's death he had immediately sent word to Salma, inviting her to bring her family to Malaqah and live with him. As she read his words she realised just how much she had missed the bustle of living in a city; Ardales was a quiet town and the pace of life was slow and gentle. Her aunt and uncle had loved it there. How could they not love it? It was a safe haven for them all. There they were out of reach of the marauding soldiers; there food was plentiful and they could resume their normal lives without fear. At first she'd settled down to life in the country. She and Simon had married and then she had children. It would have been enough for most women but not for her. She never spoke of it, but she longed to work again. When she thought of her days in the library in Qurtubah—and she thought of them often—and the books she had transcribed, it was with a mixture of hope and sadness. Hope that the libraries had survived the repeated onslaughts of the zealots and the ignorant Berber soldiers, and sadness because she doubted that they had. What little news reached them told of death and destruction; her beloved Qurtubah was but a shell of its former glory. But now she would have a second chance. She would look for work in the libraries of Malaqah. Her cousin Makoud had told her that the new khalifa was a cultured man and wanted his city to gain the reputation for learning that Qurtubah had once had. She hadn't hesitated. Now that her cousin Fatima was dead, there was nothing to hold her in Ardales and she persuaded Simon that it wasn't too late to make a new life for themselves and their family in Malaqah. So she had brought all her calligraphy tools with her, wrapped carefully in a piece of sacking and tied to the donkey.

She must have fallen asleep because the next thing she knew was that Simon was shaking her and whispering, 'Wake up Salma. I think there's someone hiding in the sugar cane, watching us.'

She opened her eyes and saw that Iqbal had unsheathed his sword—her cousin Rafa had insisted that at least one of them was armed, even though she'd protested that it was futile because neither Iqbal nor Simon were warriors. Zara was standing white-faced beside the mule, holding the reins in her hand. What was happening? Layla, where was Layla?

'Layla?' Salma sat up, now wide awake.

'It's all right Mama, I'm here.'

'Just get up slowly, Salma, and act as if everything is normal. If we can get across the bridge, we should be safe; I can see some fishermen's houses on the other side.'

She did as her husband asked, and with Simon leading and Iqbal following at the rear they set off along the coastal path. She could see the bridge that Simon spoke of, but it seemed a long way in the distance. Who were the people watching them? Was there even anyone there? She knew her husband could be a bit paranoid at times—understandable after all they'd been through—but this time he looked genuinely worried. Now she was glad that Rafa had insisted on Iqbal taking his sword. She hoped he knew how to use it.

'Can we walk a bit more quickly?' Iqbal was beginning to look jumpy. In fact they all were nervous now.

'It's probably nothing,' Salma said, more in an attempt to calm her daughters than from genuine belief. 'Probably an animal, a goat or something.'

At that moment two ragged individuals stepped into the path in front of them. 'Stop,' one of them bellowed, wildly waving his dagger at them. His companion was a good bit shorter in stature, a gruesome creature with a livid scar down the side of his face and he carried an enormous sword in his hands. Salma recognised it at once as a cleaving sword, the type used by soldiers in battle and capable of slicing through armour, but this one appeared to be far too heavy for their opponent. At first she thought they must be mercenaries, but then she decided they were probably just runaway slaves.

'What have you got in that sack?' the one with the sword asked.

'Just some food for our journey,' Simon said quietly.

Salma saw her husband draw his dagger from the folds of his robe and hold it behind his back. But would he use it? It was against his beliefs to take a life, but could he do it to save his family?

'She's a pretty one,' said the taller man, looking at Layla. 'Sweet as honey, I expect. I think I'd like a taste of her.' He stepped towards Layla but Salma was too quick for him.

'I don't think so,' she said, stepping in his way. 'My daughter has the sickness. That is why we are taking her to Malaqah to see the doctor.'

'What sickness is that?' asked the shorter one, stepping back involuntarily.

'I don't know what they call it. But they say that the rats brought it from the East, on the sailing ships. Most of our neighbours are dead and those that have survived, have run away. We couldn't stay in our village any longer.'

'She doesn't look sick.'

'Come closer and see for yourself,' invited Salma, 'but be careful not to touch her. It is very infectious.' She saw that Layla had pulled her scarf over her head, covering most of her face.

The man hesitated then said, 'Rubbish. Your lies aren't good enough to deceive us, old woman. Forget the girl, Pablo; we can find better than her elsewhere. Now bring me that sack, woman. Full of gold and jewels, I shouldn't wonder.'

'My wife speaks the truth. My daughter is sick, and we have no gold and jewels. We are just poor people trying to make our way to Malaqah to save our daughter's life.'

'Shut up, old man. Who are you anyway? You look like a foreigner. A Christian are you?'

'Maybe he's a spy,' said Pablo. 'We could get good money for him in Malaqah.'

'We have nothing that would be of use to you,' said Iqbal, who up until then had been very quiet. Now he moved towards the men. 'Get out of our way and let us pass. We have business in Malaqah and must get there before nightfall.' He held Rafa's sword in front of him. It was smaller than the cleaving sword, curved and slender and easier to handle. A sword for speed, capable of slashing and slicing your opponent, and was used mostly by the cavalry. How would he fair on foot, in a fight against this ruffian with his enormous sword?

'Oh, business in Malaqah, is it?' sneered the one called Pablo, waving his dagger under Iqbal's nose. 'Well we have business here, don't we Juan. We'll start by getting that old crone to cook us some food. Then we'll see how sick that girl really is.' He turned to grin at his companion.

And that was his mistake. To everyone's surprise, Iqbal's sword swept through the air and sliced off the man's arm. The robber turned and gazed vacantly at Iqbal, stunned by his action, then watched as his arm fell to the ground, the hand still clutching his dagger. A howl escaped from his throat as he collapsed to the ground in a pool of his own blood. Juan snarled and immediately turned to face Iqbal, slowly lifting his heavy sword to strike but Iqbal was too quick for him. Once more the scimitar flashed in the sunlight as it descended towards the attacker and sliced through his neck. With a groan, he dropped to the ground, dead.

'Get their weapons,' Iqbal ordered Simon, who stood there astounded, looking at the blood dripping from his son-in-law's sword. 'What? Do you disapprove? A man is entitled to protect his family, isn't he?' Iqbal was shaking but whether from fear or excitement, Salma couldn't tell. It had all happened so quickly; one moment they were being threatened by two thieves and the next, one was dead and the other dying. She felt numb. Iqbal had saved them.

Simon bent down and prised the bloody dagger from the severed hand, then picked up the cleaving sword. 'What are we going to do with him?' he asked, pointing to the injured man. He was writhing on the ground, moaning, his blood pumping into the sand.

'Nothing,' said Iqbal.

'We can't just leave him there in agony. Show some compassion.'

'A few minutes ago he was about to take you to Malaqah and sell you as a spy. He was going to rape your daughter and only Allah knows what he had in mind for Salma and Zara. Why should I have any compassion for him?'

'Here, let me bind his wound and then we can leave him to make his own way to wherever he's going,' said Salma, bending over the injured man. She felt the nausea rising in her throat; Iqbal's actions had brought back memories she would rather forget.

She took a strip of leather from her bag and wound it around the man's arm. 'Here, help me pull this tight, Simon. At least we can stop him from bleeding to death.'

Iqbal was right; a few moments ago she had been praying for someone to stop these men, kill them, disable them, whatever was necessary to protect her family, but despite that she couldn't walk away from a wounded man, whoever he was and no matter what he'd done. In Qurtubah during the civil war, she'd stabbed a man in self defence. Then she'd run away, not knowing if he was alive or dead. Although she knew she'd had no choice, it had been hard to live with that on her conscience; there was no way she was going to make the same mistake twice.

Gradually the bleeding slowed and finally stopped, and she was able to cover the raw wound with a light sprinkling of their precious dried hare's blood. That would help it to heal and prevent infection. Next she wrapped it in clean muslin. 'There, that should do until you can reach a doctor,' she told the barely conscious man. She had done what she could for him but there was still the chance he'd die from shock or from an infection.

'Right, can we go now?' asked Iqbal, glaring at her.

They resumed their journey in silence, the women averting their eyes as they made their way carefully around the dead body. Their earlier, light-hearted mood had dissipated as quickly as an early morning mist. Death and destruction was still all around them. Salma felt fear grip her heart. Had they made a grave mistake leaving Ardales? Ahead of them was the bridge over the Guadalmedina river and beyond that the high stone walls of Malaqah and their future. But what kind of future awaited them in that city?

CHAPTER 3

Hasan al-Mustansir stretched his long legs along the full length of the bed. It was time he rose and went to meet his ministers. He let his hand rest for a moment on the pale-skinned arm of his new wife, Jamila. She was his cousin, and unlike her rather podgy brother, Yahya, she was a real beauty. She was also a delight in bed; he felt a rush of passion towards her and would have pulled her towards him again, but at that moment the door to his bedroom opened and a small stout man appeared.

'Your Majesty. Forgive me, but the grand vizier is becoming impatient. He says he has news for you,' the old servant said, bowing obsequiously.

His new love forgotten, Hasan pulled back the silk sheets and leapt out of bed. He was the khalifa now; he had to attend to his duties. He clapped his hands and another servant entered.

'Make haste. I must get dressed and go to see my ministers. Why did you not wake me earlier?'

The slave, little more than a child, dropped his head and muttered something incoherently, which Hasan took to be an apology.

He followed him through to the bath house and stepped into the warm, scented water. As he lay there, letting the child wash him with the sweet-smelling soap that came from Aleppo, he began to think about his family, and his cousin in particular. True, Yahya had put up no resistance when Hasan had arrived in Malaqah to claim the throne; he hadn't even objected when Hasan told him that he wanted to marry his sister. He had been very compliant about it all. Maybe too compliant. Perhaps he was just biding his time. After all, his brother Muhammad was ruler of al-Jazira, maybe he expected him to come to his aid. Maybe they were both thinking about deposing Hasan when the time was right.

'The water is cold,' Hasan complained. 'Help me get out.' He stood and pulled a cotton towel around himself, impatiently.

'Let me dry you, Sayyad,' his slave said.

'No. You are too slow. I told you we must hurry. I can't spend all morning lying in the bath. And in future, address me as Your Majesty. I am the khalifa now. Don't forget it.'

'Yes, Your Majesty.'

He pushed the child away and towelled himself down, vigorously. The idea that his cousin Yahya might be plotting something was beginning to take hold. He would have to deal with it, and quickly.

'Bring me my white robes,' he commanded brusquely.

The child pulled a white silk djubba over the prince's head and smoothed it into place. It was Hasan's favourite. He stroked the folds, feeling their sensuous warmth. His mother had warned against him continually wearing silk and recommended he choose cotton instead; she said it was forbidden by the Quran, that it led to false pride and vanity. But Hasan didn't believe her; he had never read anything about it in the Quran and, like every good Muslim boy, he had learned its words by heart at an early age. So now that he was the khalifa he would continue to wear silk tunics and djellabas, and his cushions and the covers on his bed would also be made of silk. What was the point of being Khalifa if you couldn't enjoy the good things of life? And anyway his mother was not here; she was in Sebta and if he had anything to do with it, that's where she would stay.

The grand vizier and General Rashad were already waiting in the throne room by the time Hasan arrived. They bowed and waited until he was seated.

'What news do you have for me, my friends?' he asked, leaning back and stroking his sparse beard. He was in a good mood. His plans were turning out well; there was only one cloud on the horizon. His lily-livered cousin Yahya. He had gone scuttling down to his brother in al-Jazira and promised never to return but could he rely on that? Did it really matter? The only true heir to the throne, his brother, was securely locked up and couldn't harm him from a prison cell. On a military front, he had renewed the alliance with Badis ben Habus, the ruler of Garnata. He should feel invulnerable, but he didn't. He looked around him at the richness of the room, with its marble floors and pillars, its stucco covered ceilings painted in reds and blues and greens, the Persian tapestries hanging on its walls. It was certainly a room fit for a khalifa. Along the walls stood the Palace Guards, resplendent in their green and gold uniforms. Every one of them under his command, and loyal to a man.

'You have heard the news from Morón, Your Majesty?' asked General Rashad.

'What news? What is this about Morón?' Instantly his tranquility was shattered. Morón was becoming a constant irritation to him; with its own governor, it was nonetheless allied to his enemy, Abbad I, ruler of the kingdom of Isbiliya.

'Abbad I is massing his troops in the area, Your Majesty. I believe he plans to attack Malaqah,' began the general. 'The easiest route would be through the taifa of Morón; after all it is under his protection and it lies on our north-west border. You can be sure that the governor of Morón will do nothing to prevent him.'

'Why did I not know of this before?' Hasan exploded, his good mood disappearing fast.

The general looked down at his feet and replied, 'We only received word this morning, Your Majesty. I immediately sent a message to the grand vizier.'

Hasan scowled at his chancellor and said, 'So? What do we do about this power-hungry bastard? Is the enormous taifa of Isbiliya not enough for Abbad I? Well, he is not getting his hands on Malaqah. I'll see to that.' They were brave words but the news had unsettled him. Abbad I had ruled Isbiliya for twenty years; he was a clever man and a ruthless leader. His mighty army was well armed and supported by numerous allies, and besides which, Isbiliya and Malaqah had been in constant dispute for years. He would not be easy to overcome. Hasan's uncle had defeated him only the year before but it had made no difference to Abbad's ambition or strength; his army was as formidable as ever.

'Indeed, Your Majesty, he must be stopped but how? Our troops were greatly depleted after the Battle of Écija,' replied the general.

'But his army must be weakened too; after all they were the ones who were defeated,' said the grand vizier.

'We won, that is true, but we were lucky; they underestimated us,' replied the general. 'Your uncle, Idris I, was a brilliant military tactician, Your Majesty. We had…'

'Enough of this. We are not here to gossip over historical battles. The question is, what are we going to do to stop this despot from taking over our territory?' He was not in the mood to hear anyone extolling the virtues of his dead uncle.

'His expansion through al-Andalus must be halted, Your Majesty. I have watched Abbad's progress over the years, and he will never be satisfied until he has control of all of the south, from the Atlantic to the Middle Sea. If Malaqah falls, then next it will be Garnata and Álmeria, and maybe even Murcia,' said the grand vizier.

'So, what do you advise?'

'We must do as he does,' said General Rashad. 'We must make alliances with others, so that we are stronger.'

'We have an agreement with the Zirads of Garnata. I spoke with their ambassador just a few weeks ago. We agreed to support each other in the case of an attack from the Christian infidel,' Labib said.

'But what about an attack from another Muslim taifa? Did you mention that?' asked the general. 'Did you specify Isbiliya? The Zirads fought alongside us at Écija. Are they prepared to do so again?'

Hasan looked across at his grand vizier. 'Well? Did we?' he asked.

'Not specifically, Your Majesty. It was more a general agreement to send support if either of you were attacked. It didn't agree to making sorties against a threatening neighbour. Garnata lost a lot of troops at Écija, and according to ibn Nagrilla, their grand vizier, they are not keen on looking for fresh battles.'

'So what use is that? We have to sit here and wait until Abbad attacks us and then, maybe Badis ben Habus will send his troops to aid us? No. We need something more. What about Qarmuña and Álmeria? They fought with us at Écija.'

'No. Qarmuña is too frightened of upsetting Abbad, and Álmeria is having problems with pirate attacks. Neither of them will support us in this battle,' said the grand vizier.

'We could ask Ferdinand for his support,' suggested the general.

'Ferdinand I of León? A Christian king? Why would he help us?' Hasan asked, astonished at the suggestion. Ferdinand was their enemy. He above all others wanted to wipe out the Muslims and take over their lands for Christianity.

'He has helped other taifas before. He may be a successful king, but he needs money. All the Christian princes are the same. They have spent so much money on their campaigns that now their coffers are empty. They need our gold. That is why he will help us. But we will have to pay him well.'

Hasan thought for a moment. It made sense. He knew his treasury was full of gold and silver—there was no shortage of wealth in Malaqah, only soldiers—and if Abbad conquered them he would have the gold anyway. He might as well spend some of it on mercenaries who could help him to defend his realm, as leave it for Abbad to take.

'Very well. Send a messenger to Garnata first of all. Make it clear to Badis ben Habus that if Malaqah falls, then Garnata will be next and we won't be able to help him. It's in his country's interest as well as mine to stop this bastard while we can.'

'As you wish, Your Majesty,' said the grand vizier, bowing. 'And then? Will that be sufficient?'

'How do I know?' Hasan snapped angrily. 'Well General, what is your opinion?'

'The Zirads do not have a very strong army—I doubt if our combined forces would be enough to defeat Abbad—but it would be good to have him on our side. As the grand vizier has pointed out, there are few independent taifas left. It is time for us all to make a stand against Isbiliya.'

Those were his thoughts, exactly. If Isbiliya was defeated again by Malaqah—this time under his command—then it would be his name that everyone would be singing praises about, not his uncle Idris. It would be a magnificent show of strength from the new khalifa.

'Maybe there is another way,' said the grand vizier. 'We could hire a private army of independent mercenaries instead of approaching the Christian king directly. I hear that there are a number of such armies for hire.'

'Christians?'

'Yes, Your Majesty.'

'But could we trust them?' Hasan asked. He too had heard of these Christian armies who had no allegiance to anyone. Their soldiers fought for money and nothing else. So did that make them more trustworthy or less? Most soldiers fought for money; there were few who really felt any alliance to their country or their ruler. Times were too unpredictable for such lofty ideals. The composition of everyone's armies was changing. He only had to look at his own troops when they lined up for parade; true there were some religious volunteers who wanted to fight against the infidel, but mostly they were mercenaries and they came from all over: Christians, northerners, Berbers and militia recruited from the countryside. The proportion of regular soldiers was small now.

'If the pay is good, they will fight,' said General Rashad. 'Would I trust one of them with my life? Probably not. They would slit a man's throat for the price of a good meal, but for a bag of gold they will protect you to the death. Would you like me to make some enquiries, Your Majesty?'

'Yes, General. And in the meantime, put my army on alert. If the enemy is already in Morón we must be ready to defend the city in case they attack.'

He waved his hand, dismissing them both. He had a lot to think about. If he was going to have to pay for a private army, maybe it was time to speak to the treasurer of the Royal Mint.

He sighed. This was not what he had in mind for his first year as khalifa. He didn't want to gain just military prestige with the people; he wanted to be recognised for his cultural achievements as well. He wanted Malaqah to rival Garnata—and all the other taifas—in its intellectual and artistic accomplishments. His original plan had been to spend the city's gold on making Malaqah a more beautiful place, a cultural centre to rival the Qurtubah of the Omayyads. He had already spoken to the chancellor of the university and to the chief librarian about building up the libraries. It was his father, Yahya I, who had done much to improve the standards of both the literary and scholastic achievements of the city, and he planned to continue with his work. Only last month he had sent men to Damascus and Baghdad to find him poets and scribes. Good libraries needed many books and for that he needed good scribes; good libraries meant more students at the university and more visiting scholars. Good libraries meant greater prestige for Malaqah and for its khalifa. The usurper al-Mansor had gained notoriety more than forty years before for his destruction of the libraries. Hasan al-Mustansir would gain fame for his restoration of them.

CHAPTER 4

The apothecary could hear the women wailing from inside his tiny storeroom. What, in the name of Allah, was happening? Had someone died? Whatever it was, had terrified the women. Makoud put down the bowl and covered it with a damp cloth of fine muslin; he didn't want to waste a morning's work by allowing the new antiseptic cream he'd prepared to dry out.

'What is it?' he called, as he climbed down the steps from the shop. 'What's going on out there? Why all the noise?'

'Pirates,' said his son. 'They say there are pirates approaching the harbour.'

'Well crying and screeching like that won't scare them away.'

'It might do. I know those women terrify *me*,' Ibrahim replied with a laugh.

'Where are the guards? Aren't they supposed to protect the city?'

Makoud strode across the shop and stepped out into the street. His apothecary's shop was located inside the city walls, so he wasn't unduly worried about pirates, but others were more severely affected. Merchants said they were hampering their trade; three cargo ships had been attacked on the Middle Sea in the last month alone and it wasn't uncommon for his wives to come home from market complaining that certain goods weren't available because of the pirate raids; he'd had no pepper on his food for months now. Not only that, but some of these sea wolves were on the lookout for youngsters they could sell as slaves. One of his customers had lost a son. The lad had been out fishing with four others when they'd been attacked. The pirates had kidnapped them and taken their catch. At least that was the conclusion everyone came to when they found the empty fishing boat drifting off the coast. The year before, his own family had suffered at the hands of the pirates, when they had kidnapped his son-in-law. A sudden fear gripped his heart. Could it be that Captain Awar looking for revenge? Despite getting Bakr and his men back home safely, they had never captured the pirate who kidnapped them; he had disappeared. He had heard that he'd been drowned off the Barbary coast, but no-one knew for sure. Even if he was still alive, would Awar be foolish enough to come to Malaqah again? He had been forced to leaved Dragonera, his safe haven in the Balearic Islands, and his new ship had been burned to the ground; he had a lot to be angry about and he might think it was worth the risk. There was no doubt about it; these pirates were becoming a recurring nuisance for the city.

But right now he had to put that out of his mind; he was more concerned about his niece Salma. He had invited her and her family to come to Malaqah and live with them. They should have arrived a week ago and still there was no word from them. Perhaps he had been too hasty. He thought it would be a good opportunity for them because the city had entered a period of stability under the Hammudid rulers. Yahya I in particular had been an educated man who was anxious to strengthen the city's cultural reputation to equal that of the Qurtubah of old. When Makoud had first written to Salma, some time previously, suggesting the idea, everything was looking good for Malaqah. But since then they'd had three khalifas in five years. It reminded Makoud of those last few years in Qurtubah, when you never knew from one day to the next who was your friend and who was your foe.

So now, the new khalifa of Malaqah was Hussan al-Mustansir. 'What sort of a man was he?' was the question on everyone's lips. And would there be a future here for Salma and her family or had Makoud invited her into yet another war-torn city? He would never forgive himself if that was the case.

'I think it was a false alarm,' Ibrahim said, coming towards him. 'It looked like a pirate ship but it's sailed away now.'

'Well you can get back to work then, can't you?' He had no time for gossip and no interest in the new khalifa or his brother. His only concern was how long they would last before there was another coup.

'Very well, Baba.'

Makoud watched as his middle son dutifully went back into the shop. Ibrahim was a qualified apothecary now; he had been working with him ever since he left school. He was a natural herbalist and had taken to the role of apothecary's assistant as easily as Makoud had himself. It was in the family blood, this need to help the sick. Indeed it was his great-aunt Layla who had been the first to understand the healing properties of the plants and flowers that grew in the countryside. She had taught Makoud all she knew.

Makoud followed his son into the shop. He sighed. If only he would take a wife. Makoud had found two young women for him, both very comely and from excellent families but his son had stubbornly refused to meet either of them. Abal had said not to hurry him; that he had time to spare. But she wasn't his mother and although he always gave way to his first wife's wishes, the time would come when Basma would have her say. He knew his second wife wanted grandchildren. She had told him often enough. Three sons and not one of them married yet. What was wrong with the youth of today?

Salma could feel her heart pounding, not from fear but from exhilaration. Everything about this city made her feel alive. It was vibrant, colourful and everybody was going about their business peacefully. There were no derelict buildings, no shops boarded up against the soldiers, no empty streets and nobody frightened to leave their homes. The souks they passed were full of fresh fruit and vegetables, with stalls covered in more spices than she had seen in many a year: cloves, coriander, cumin, chilli, nutmeg, garlic, cardamom, cinnamon and saffron. Saffron. Her favourite. She hadn't been able to buy saffron since they'd left Qurtubah. The market was crowded; there were tall Africans with skin so black it sucked in the light, their white scarves wound around their heads in neat turbans, lighter-skinned nomads from the Maghrib with their long, flowing robes and their pointed-toe slippers, Jewish women with their yellow badges on their dresses, men with skullcaps, women with crocheted ghifaras on their long braided hair and veils around their shoulders, others in traditional djubbas, men with pale complexions and yellow hair, men from across the Narrow Straits, with flat red caps, men whose eyes were the shape of almonds and had no beards, Christians wearing the blue zinar. This was a cosmopolitan city, a port accessible to all parts of the world. There seemed to be nothing that one could not buy here: pottery, jewellery, carpets, clothes. There were men making sandals and belts, others who made harnesses and saddles, another selling baskets and ropes made from esparto grass, a woman selling pots of honey and another, pots of scented soap. There was even a soothsayer, her stall bedecked with bright beads and scarves. It was all so exotic and exciting. The smells and the sounds of the market alone made her want to smile. She felt at home here already.

'Where does Makoud live?' Simon asked.

'We must ask for the apothecary Makoud ibn Ahmad. It is close to the walls of the alcazaba. I'll speak to that woman over there. I'm sure she'll know where the apothecary lives.' She pointed to the soothsayer.

Simon raised his eyebrows and smiled. 'Well I suppose if anyone knows where he is, then she probably does. They're supposed to be clairvoyant, aren't they? Come on let's treat ourselves to some of that delicious smelling mint tea.'

While he and the others stopped and bought some tea from a nearby stall, Salma went across to speak to the woman.

'What can I do for you, my dear?' the soothsayer asked. 'Want to know your future?' Her eyes followed Simon and the others. 'That your family, dear?'

'Yes, it is,' said Salma. 'We've just arrived in the city. We've come a long way and now we're looking for my cousin, Makoud. He's an apothecary. Do you know where we might find his shop? He said it was somewhere near the alcazaba.'

'Yes, my dear. I know your cousin and his shop. A good man. It's not far; you're almost there. Just follow the road. You won't be able to miss it.'

'Thank you.' Salma turned towards the others, but the old woman put her hand on her arm to stop her.

'You've had a terrible experience, my dear,' she whispered. 'But Allah knows that you have a good heart. Don't worry, the man won't die and despite your broken dreams, life will go on.'

'What? What are you saying?' Salma stared at the soothsayer. She appeared to know what had happened to them. No. It was rubbish. How could she? Simon always said they were charlatans.

'Come on, Salma,' her husband called, finishing his mint tea and gathering up their belongings. 'What's wrong? You look upset.'

'Nothing. I'm fine.'

'Well. did you find out where we're going?'

It's straight ahead, just down there,' Salma said, pointing towards the huge walls of the royal palace. 'In the shadow of the alcazaba.' She didn't mention what the woman had said to her; Simon would only have scoffed and Layla and Zara would have run over there immediately to have their fortunes told.

'Thank Allah,' said Iqbal. 'My dear wife is exhausted.' He put his arm around Zara and helped her to her feet.

'I'm fine, husband. Don't make so much fuss,' Zara said, but the truth was she looked completely drained. The long journey and then the attack had taken their toll on her.

'My poor daughter. Don't worry, once we are in Makoud's house you will be able to rest,' said Simon.

'I shall put my feet up and not move until the baby tells me it's time,' she said with a laugh.

Salma knew it would be a miracle if that happened; Iqbal would soon be wanting her to run around after him. She wondered how he would be once the baby was born. Somehow she couldn't imagine him sharing Zara with anyone, not even their child.

Sure enough the pharmacy was exactly where the soothsayer said. Salma pulled back the curtain of the shop and went in, nervously. It seemed such a long time since she'd last seen Makoud. He'd only lived in Ardales for a few years before he began to talk about going to Malaqah to seek his fortune. His father had protested, saying he could be an apothecary just as easily in Ardales as anywhere; there was no need to go to a city. But Makoud was young at the time and craved adventure; in the end it wasn't until he was middle-aged, and his father had died that he finally made the move.

A noise from within made her stop. Someone was working in the back of the shop.

'Makoud?' she called. 'Is that you?'

A man straightened up and turned to face her. Even in the dim light, she knew it was him. His face had aged; deep lines were etched into his cheeks and his hair and beard were streaked with grey but the smile was unmistakably Makoud's.

'Salma. Welcome to Malaqah,' he said holding out his arms to her.

'As-salama alaykum, dear cousin. It is so good to see you.' Salma began to cry with happiness. Her beloved cousin had made a life for himself here, in Malaqah. She hugged him as though she never wanted to let him go.

'Wa alaykum e-salam, Salma. I was becoming worried about you. Were there problems on the journey? I expected you days ago.'

'I will tell you all about our journey later. It was not uneventful I must say, but I am here now and so very happy to see you. Where are your family? And your sons? I can't wait to see them again.'

'Come, let me greet your family and I will take you all to my home.'

She led him outside into the bright sunshine, where Simon and the others were squatting in a pool of purple shade beneath a carob tree, their belongings scattered beside them.

'Simon. You've lost your tonsure,' Makoud said, taking Simon by the shoulders and kissing him on the cheeks.

'As-salama alaykum, Makoud. Yes, I thought it best to look like a proper Muslim now I'm in Malaqah.'

'No regrets?'

Simon put his arm around his wife and said, with a broad smile, 'No regrets.'

'I'm so pleased to hear that. Come along then. We used to live here, above the shop but business has been so good lately, that I have bought a new house. It's much more comfortable and not far from here. My wives are so looking forward to seeing you again,' Makoud chattered on, happily, more like the young boy she remembered than the middle-aged man he'd become. Salma smiled to herself; it was good to be with family again. 'Today you will rest and tomorrow I will take you both to see the chief librarian. He is anxious to meet you,' he continued. 'The new khalifa has instructed him to employ at least twenty new scribes. When I told him of your work in the library in Qurtubah, he was delighted. Although I fear you may be disappointed with the size of this library; it is nothing compared to what you have seen.'

'If I can work as a scribe again, I will be content. We are both so grateful to you, Makoud, for this opportunity,' Salma said, her eyes shining with pleasure.

Simon ran his fingers through his thick hair. Makoud's comment about his missing tonsure had startled him; it had been such a long time since he had grown it out that he barely remembered what he'd looked like with it shaved. He hated lying to Makoud, or anyone else for that matter. When he'd made the decision to go to Ardales with Salma he had not intended to give up his religion—he could never do that—but neither had he intended to marry her. He thought just being by her side would be enough for him but he hadn't really understood the strength of his love for her and it soon became obvious that if he wanted Salma for himself, then he had to marry her. But here was the problem, a Christian man was not allowed to marry a Muslim woman. That was the law. So for the last twenty years he had been living a lie; he converted to Islam and married Salma but he continued to worship his own God in secret. He read his Bible and he prayed to the God of the Christians. He could do nothing else; Christianity was too much a part of him. But he was careful and, apart from Salma—and God—nobody else knew that he was leading a double life, certainly not his daughters; it would have devastated them to know that their father was a practising Christian.

'Simon. It's time to visit the chief librarian. Are you ready?' asked Salma. She was dressed in a plain green djubbah, with a white scarf around her shoulders and a green cap on her long black hair. Despite her advancing years, she still looked as lovely as the day he'd first seen her, in the library in Qurtubah. He felt a surge of love tighten his chest.

'I'm ready. Do I look like a real Muslim?' he asked with a smile.

'Not really. Your hair is too light and your beard too wispy, and no real Moor has eyes as blue as the sky. But you'll do. You are who you are. The chief librarian is looking for a translator. He will not expect you to be a native of Malaqah. Here, let me straighten your djubbah. That's better.'

'I hope I get the job,' he whispered. 'We have very little money left.'

'Don't worry. Makoud will look after us, for now.'

He didn't reply. He didn't want Makoud to support him and his family. It wasn't right. He was the head of his family and it was he who should provide for them. But the Muslims' sense of family obligation was so strong that he knew he could live there with them indefinitely and they would never complain. But that wasn't his way. The sooner he got a job and began to earn some money, the better.

'Ready?' Makoud asked, 'Good, then let me take you to the chief librarian. I warn you, he can be very particular, but he has a good heart. I've always thought that he has more love for his books than he does for people.'

Simon and Salma looked at each other and smiled; he sounded like someone they could grow to like.

CHAPTER 5

Ben-Yahya could hear the gaoler's shuffling steps approach his cell. Would he have news from Naja? It had been easy to bribe the old man to take a message. He was a simpleton. His instructions were not to let the prisoner have any visitors and he stuck to that, but he had no compunction about taking messages in and out of the prison.

He stood up in readiness, eager to hear from his friend, even if it was only a few lines. The iron key creaked as it turned in the lock and the heavy door swung slowly open.

'Well, what did he say?' Ben-Yahya asked before the old man had even entered the cell. 'Did he send me a reply?'

The gaoler shook his head. 'Can't find head nor hair of him. There was a man of that name. A tall man, grey-haired but strong. Carried himself with airs and graces, they say. Got off a boat one day and the next he was gone. Would that have been him?'

'What do you mean, gone?' Ben-Yahya felt sick. Had Naja deserted him?

'They say a fishing boat took him to the north African coast. Him and a little guy, his servant probably.'

Qusay. So he'd left Malaqah too. They'd both left him to rot in this bloody prison.

'They say he was a slave who'd been given his freedom. If that's the case, then I can't say I blame him. He wouldn't want to be locked up, or treated like a slave again, now would he?' mused the gaoler. 'Mind you, if the khalifa wants him in gaol then he'll have men out looking for him right now. Then they'll bring him here and you'll be able to exchange messages with him with no trouble at all. Unless they execute him, of course. They do that. Especially if the dungeons are getting full—as they are now. Or if it's a crime against the throne. That's always a beheading. You must have seen the heads rotting on poles by the main gate?'

Ben-Yahya stopped listening to the old man's ramblings and sat down on his bed of straw. Why had Naja fled? Maybe he hadn't deserted him; maybe he'd gone back to Sebta to get help to free him. Yes, it had to be that. Naja wouldn't betray him. Not Naja. Not after all those years of friendship.

'If you want anything else,' the old man continued. 'Just you let me know. Here's your message back.' He handed him a grubby piece of parchment. 'You never know, you might want to send it to someone else.'

Yes, so that you can get another piece of silver for achieving nothing, thought Ben-Yahya, but he took the parchment and thanked him. This dirty, smelly old man was his only link with the outside world; he mustn't antagonise him.

Naja al-Siqlabi was furious. He had travelled all the way to Malaqah only to be leaving it the moment he'd arrived, and worse still, as a fugitive. His first reaction to Ben-Yahya's arrest had been disbelief but then, when he remembered that the prince's father had died in inexplicable circumstances, he realised that this was no idle threat. If he and Ben-Yahya ended up in prison they would probably never see the light of day again.

'We must hurry, sayyad. They will be looking for us,' said Qusay. He looked as though he'd been snivelling again. 'How are we going to get past the guards at the Boveda Gate? And what's the donkey for?'

'Don't worry. The guards aren't going to stop a merchant who's just been to sell silks to the khalifa.' Qusay looked even more confused. 'A merchant has to have a donkey to carry his goods, idiot. Take his reins.'

'What if he bites me?' The boy took the reins gingerly, and added, 'He stinks.'

'So would you if you'd been sleeping where I found him. Now stop complaining and let's get going. Remember the Palace Guards are looking for the prince's servants; Hasan will have given them a description of us. We must try to look as inconspicuous as possible.'

Qusay nodded, and reluctantly began to lead the donkey towards the Boveda Gate.

Naja's escape plan was flimsy and had been made in haste; he'd never imagined for a moment that Hasan would turn on them like that. He had expected them to be greeted warmly, not to have to turn and run for their lives. Nevertheless he didn't anticipate too much trouble getting out of the alcazaba; after all, the guards were usually more interested in who was coming in than who was leaving.

Naja wound a turban around his head, in the style of the Maghrebi, so that it covered all his grey hair and part of his face. There was nothing he could do to conceal his sharp blue eyes.

'Come on, let's get out of here,' he said. He was beginning to feel nervous. Any minute the guards would realise that he and Qusay were missing. He hoped the quaid would think they were too unimportant to bother about and concentrate on Ben-Yahya. Nevertheless the sooner they were away from this place the better. Hasan wasn't stupid; he would track them down in no time. Naja adjusted his sword so that it didn't show under his djellaba; servants and merchants weren't usually armed but he couldn't risk being without a weapon, especially now, when he didn't know whom to trust.

They walked down the steps and across the parade ground. There were plenty of soldiers around, some lounging about drinking tea, others cleaning their weapons and some exercising their horses. Naja walked behind the donkey, his head slightly bowed, trying to avoid making eye contact with anyone; he could feel the adrenalin coursing through his body. He was a proud man; he had never forgotten that his father had been a king, and it was not in Naja's nature to hide away like a thief. One day he would make Hasan pay for this humiliation.

Ahead of him Qusay walked the donkey down a ramp and along the narrow alleyway; Naja could hear the sound of the waves crashing against the walls of the alcazaba. The guards walking along the battlements gave them cursory glances but were more interested in watching the harbour than looking at a merchant and his slave. At last they arrived at the Gate of the Columns. Ahead of them they could see the main entrance to the alcazaba, the Gate of the Boveda. Once they were through that it would be easier; they could lose themselves in the crowded city.

There were two guards at the gate, each armed with a long lance and a sword. As they approached the gate, the guards barred their way by crossing their lances in front of the gate.

'Halt. What's your business in the alcazaba?' asked one of the guards.

'Is something the matter?' asked Naja.

'Just answer the question,' said the other guard.

'I'm a merchant and I've just been to visit the Royal Buyer. I hope to receive a large order from him for some new silk wall hangings for the khalifa.' He rubbed his hands together and smiled, contentedly.

'And who is this wretched creature?' asked the first guard, poking Qusay with his lance.

'That's my servant. Deaf and dumb, but strong enough for what I want,' said Naja.

'What's in the sack?'

'Not a lot. The Royal Buyer was so enchanted by my samples that he kept the lot.'

One of the guards checked the empty sack. 'There's nothing here.'

'I told you. He kept them all.'

Ahead of them lay the entrance area to the alcazaba, a wide corridor with the Gate of the Boveda at the far end. Once through the gate there was a sharp left turn onto a cobbled ramp that led directly into the city and freedom.

At that moment a well dressed man on a fine bay horse shouted from the back of the queue that had formed behind them. 'What the hell's going on? We have work to do. Either arrest them or let them through. We can't stand here all day.' He looked like one of the khalifa's ministers and his words had an instant effect on the quaid.

'Go on then. Get out of here,' he said, standing back so that they and the donkey could pass through the gate.

Naja breathed deeply. The salty air was cold and fresh, and it carried the taste of freedom with it. Ahead of him loomed the Pillars of Hercules, the guardians of the gateway to the Middle Sea. Soon he would be back in Sebta and safe. It had cost him twenty silver dirhams and the donkey to persuade the captain to take him and Qusay to north Africa. He smiled to himself; it wasn't just Barbary pirates that robbed people on the Middle Sea. Still if it kept him out of prison, it was well worth it. He'd had enough of those shit holes to last him a lifetime.

Before he'd arrived in Sebta and become tutor to Ben-Yahya, he had been a prince in his own land. When he was only twelve-years-old he'd been captured during a raid by a neighbouring tribe and sold as a slave. His life had been one of pain and suffering until he'd been bought at the slave market in Sebta and taken to the prince's household. Then everything had changed: no more disgusting old men who used him for their pleasure, no more spells in gaol because he'd run off but had nowhere to run to, no more beatings, no more empty belly and scrabbling for a few mouthfuls of food. They gave him to Prince Ben-Yahya, who was a young child at the time, and Naja became his servant. The prince's mother, Queen Fatima, had suggested that he should convert to Islam. It was all the same to him; after what he'd suffered he didn't believe in any of their gods but he was shrewd enough to see the wisdom of her advice. Becoming a Muslim meant he was automatically given his freedom. He was a free man. He could have left, gone wherever he wanted, but he decided to stay with the prince while he thought about his future, and he became his tutor.

Naja still carried the name of a slave to remind himself of what he'd endured; Naja al-Siqlabi never wanted to forget how easy it was to lose the freedom he managed to regain. But already the tables were turning. It was brother against brother. Who could he trust now? Probably neither of them. No, he had no intention of ending his days in a prison in Malaqah, and he wasn't waiting to see what Hasan had in store for him. He would do anything to avoid being locked up again.

'We'll be landing any time soon,' the captain shouted down to him. 'Make sure you're ready when I say. We can't delay. We've just passed a school of tuna and I intend to catch one of them before we go back.'

'We'll be ready,' Naja called. Did the stupid man think he wanted to remain a moment longer than necessary on this stinking fishing boat?

He turned again towards the coast. The buildings of Sebta were growing visible in the brightening sky while the Rif mountains lay like a dark shadow behind them—the Mountains of the Seven Brothers, the locals called them. Soon he'd be home. But what was he going to do about Ben-Yahya? What could he do? It wasn't his fault. This was all Hasan's doing. He'd considered his young brother to be a threat to him and so he'd arrested him. But what was Naja going to tell Queen Fatima? And would Hasan send someone to arrest him too? He watched the fishing boat approach the harbour. Not long now. Once he set foot on north African soil he would be out of Hasan's reach. He'd be safe.

'Qusay. Get our bags,' he instructed the boy. The lad hadn't stopped snivelling since they'd left Malaqah.

'Yes, sayyad.' The child didn't move. 'Are we going back to the palace?' he asked.

'Yes, of course.'

'But the prince won't be there. What will I do? What will happen to me?' the child sobbed.

'You'll work for me. You'll be my servant.'

'But how can we live there if the prince is in prison?' he asked, his eyes round with bewilderment.

'Don't worry. Leave it to me. We will look after the palace for the prince until he is released. That will be our task.'

The confused servant gave a watery smile and went to retrieve their luggage.

Dirar watched the man standing in the prow of the fishing boat. They'd done very little fishing last night because the captain said they had to take some passengers to north Africa. This man was one of them, him and a timid, young lad who was his servant. When Dirar tried to speak to the boy, he had scurried away and sat down with their luggage. He looked hungry so Dirar had given him a slice of mojama and was rewarded with the briefest of smiles, although he still refused to speak to him.

The captain was being very secretive about it. From time to time they'd taken people across the Alboran Sea to Sebta and even once to Tanja. Normally they were people returning to their families for the festival of Eid, or merchants who needed to get across the Narrow Straits in a hurry. It didn't happen very often but it wasn't unusual. So why was the captain behaving so strangely today? Who was the tall man? He didn't look poor and he carried himself as though he were a prince, so why was he travelling in a fishing boat? Their boat was not large and had no sail, being propelled by only two sets of oars. It was a typical brightly painted fishing boat, which, if this man was running away from someone, was probably why he'd chosen it. It was unremarkable; there were dozens like it on the Alboran Sea.

As usual the captain didn't care who his passengers were; he just took their money and got rid of them as quickly as possible.

'This is as close as we can go,' he shouted at the tall man. 'You'll have to wade ashore now. It's not deep.'

Dirar could see that the man was angry with the captain, and rightly so. They were only just into the port and the waves were lashing against the harbour walls. The passengers would get soaked. He dashed forward to help them.

'Here, let me hold the bags while you climb down,' he said to the boy, who was shaking, either with fear or the cold. 'Give me your hand.'

While he helped the young boy lower himself into the water, the tall man jumped off the boat and strode through the waves towards the beach. He didn't look back once.

'Here, take the bags. You'll be all right. Just follow your master,' Dirar said, handing down the luggage. The child tried, in vain, to keep the bags dry, but the waves were too high and he was too short; within minutes he and the bags were wet through.

'What the hell are you playing at? Get back to your post. If we don't hurry we'll never catch up with that school of tuna,' shouted the captain.

Reluctantly Dirar took one last look at the child as he staggered onto the beach, dragging the sodden luggage behind him. The captain could be a real bastard at times.

Fatima was in the zenana, listening to a slave playing the oud, when her personal maid came rushing in to find her.

'Sayyida, Sayyida. Naja al-Siqlabi has returned. He says he must speak to you urgently,' the girl gasped. Her headscarf had slipped down her shoulders and her hair was dishevelled; she looked as though she'd run all the way up from the harbour.

'Calm down, child. Now tell me exactly what has happened,' Fatima said, trying to steady her own heart which had begun to beat rapidly. She signalled for the musician to stop playing and said, 'Naja is here, you say. On his own?' This was not good news. Naja should not have left Ben-Yahya in Malaqah alone. His orders were to protect her son. How could he do that from Sebta?

'Yes. He says it is important that he speaks to you right away.'

'Well send him in then. And straighten your hair,' she scolded.

No sooner had the maidservant left, than the door opened again, and Naja al-Siqlabi strode into the room. He stopped and bowed, before saying, 'Forgive me, Sayyida, for the interruption, but I have bad news. Your son, Ben-Yahya, has been imprisoned.'

It was as though a cold wind had blown in through the door with him. Fatima felt faint at his words. She motioned for her son's tutor to sit by her side.

'That is very grave news, indeed. Who has done this? And where exactly is my son being held?' she asked, trying to keep her voice as calm as possible.

'He is in the dungeons of the alcazaba in Malaqah, Sayyida. As soon as we arrived, Palace Guards arrested him.'

'And what of my older son? The khalifa? Why did he allow this to happen? Was it a question of mistaken identity? I told Ben-Yahya he should take more men with him. He looked like an itinerant soldier, not a royal prince. He should have had at least a hundred men with him, a retinue worthy of the brother of the khalifa.' She saw Naja hesitate. 'Well what is it? What haven't you told me, Naja?'

'It would have made no difference, Sayyida. The order came directly from the khalifa himself. From your son, Hasan.'

Fatima couldn't contain the strangled cry that leapt from her throat. Hasan had done this? To his own brother? It was unbelievable. She had thought they were always so close. Surely Hasan's new-found power hadn't corrupted him already? Hasan was supposed to support and protect his family, not lock them up. She gulped for air, trying to steady her racing heart. No, he couldn't do that. She had seen plenty of family treachery in her life, but she never thought her own son would turn on his brother. She would have to go to him right away.

'I came straight to tell you, Sayyida. We must rescue Ben-Yahya before his brother makes him disappear.'

'Disappear? Do you mean have him executed?' She struggled to maintain her composure.

Naja bowed his head and avoided her direct gaze. 'It's possible, Sayyida.'

'So how do we rescue him?' she asked. 'I have no army, not even my own palace guards.' Something wasn't right. 'Tell me, Naja, how is it that you were not arrested? Presumably you were with Ben-Yahya when you landed in Malaqah?'

'Yes, Sayyida. I was by his side all the time.'

'So why didn't they arrest you, as well?'

'We were not sure what was happening. I admit something didn't seem quite right. Ben-Yahya expected his brother to be there to welcome him, and was upset with what he took to be a disrespectful reception. At first, there was no show of force although the guards displayed a lack of respect for the prince. With hindsight, this should have alerted us.' He paused.

'So what happened?' Fatima snapped.

'It wasn't until we were inside the alcazaba that the soldiers became more brazen and when Ben-Yahya challenged them, the quaid ignored him. I'm sure they would have arrested me and Qusay if they had had the chance, but we managed to slip away while Ben-Yahya was resisting arrest. They were too occupied with restraining him to notice us. I think they'd been told not to hurt him.'

'How very convenient for you, Naja. My youngest son is arrested and thrown in a stinking prison but you and that child manage to escape. How very convenient. And here you are.' The irony in her voice would have made many a man shrink with embarrassment, but Naja was made of sterner stuff and simply bowed politely. She felt the rage building up inside her, against this treacherous servant and against her even more duplicitous elder son.

CHAPTER 6

Makoud's new house was not unlike the house she'd lived in in Qurtubah; the rooms were arranged around a central patio and there was a large, flat roof where the family sat in the evenings to enjoy the cool air. She realised at once that it was not really big enough for them all. Besides Makoud and his two wives, there was his oldest son Umar; he was a soldier and spent most of his time in the Dar al-Jund or away on campaign. Then there was Ibrahim, whom she'd already met at the pharmacy, and the youngest son, Dirar who spent most of his nights fishing and his days sleeping. Only Aisha, the daughter had left home; she was married to the owner of a shipyard and they lived with her husband's family. There was also a slave, who slept in the pharmacy at night, but ate his meals with them. Into an already crowded household she had brought two more men and three women, and very soon there would be a baby as well. As soon as they were settled she would have to look for somewhere for themselves.

'Are you ready?' Makoud asked.

'Yes. But we don't want to keep you from your work,' said Simon. He wore a ghifara on his head, covering most of his cropped blond hair, but it was still obvious that he was a foreigner. His fair skin had been burnt by the sun to a reddish brown and there was nothing he could do to disguise it.

'Ibrahim is looking after the shop. I will take you to Yusuf myself. I know him well. We have become good friends; his son works for my son-in-law.' Makoud replied.

Salma pulled her scarf around her head so that it partially covered her face, and picked up her bag of calligraphy tools. She could feel the excitement bubbling inside her as though she was a girl again.

'Shall I take it with us?' she asked her husband, stroking the cover of a book that she had rescued from the old library before it could be destroyed. It was entitled 'A World Study of Herbs and Healing Plants.' Her grandmother had used it as a reference book in her work in the pharmacy. On the old woman's death it had returned to her and now she could hardly bear to part with it again.

'Why not. It's not as though you stole it; you were just keeping it safe. Now it can go back into the library and be enjoyed by everyone.'

Sadly she picked up the book and slipped it into her bag. Simon was right but it would be hard to lose it.

The library was part of the university and lay to the north of the city, in a square, stone building topped with an enormous dome which was overlaid with blue tiles that glittered and glinted in the sunshine. Inside it was larger and more airy than the one she'd worked in before and the light was a great deal better for reading and working. Although the building was designed along the same lines as the one in Qurtubah, with separate rooms for the scribes and readers and even a similar garden for contemplation, unlike that library, where the rows and rows of high banks of shelving were always filled to overflowing with books, here many of the shelves were empty.

Makoud had left them in the communal area of the library, sitting on one of the low sofas designated for students, while he went to find Yusuf.

Salma breathed in the sweet smell of the wax candles, burned to hide the rancid smell of the iron-gall ink they used, and the heavy, musty smell of the books. It was perfume to her senses.

'Happy?' whispered Simon, touching her hand lightly.

'Yes.'

'No worries?' he asked, looking distinctly worried himself.

'No. What can go wrong? He will either give us work, or he won't.' She smiled reassuringly, but she knew why he was concerned. The law was strict. If he was found out, it could be death. At the very least he would be exiled. A pain shot through her chest. She could not bear it if either of those things happened.

An elderly man, wearing the clothes of a Jewish scholar, came in, nodded towards them in greeting, took a book from the shelf and sat down on the carpet to read it. He was followed by a group of chattering students who immediately became quiet when they saw Salma and Simon sitting there.

'As-salama alaykum,' one of them said, bowing his head slightly.

'Wa alaykum e-salam,' replied Simon.

The students sat on the sofas and took out their books to study. They didn't look very serious about it.

'Here's Makoud,' whispered Simon, getting up and giving Salma his hand.

'Is everything all right?' Salma asked. The students were looking on in interest. Even the old man had raised his head at the interruption.

'Yes. Everything is fine. Follow me. He can see you now,' said Makoud.

Yusuf al-Basir was an old man, with a beard as white as the snow on the sierras, but the chief librarian had a kindly face and his eyes twinkled with pleasure when he rose to greet Salma and her husband. Not so, the man sitting next to him. He was, she later found out, the assistant librarian, a man called Marwen, who had an ugly temper and a sly way of dealing with people. At the moment he was scowling at the chief librarian as though he couldn't wait for him to die so he could take his place.

'As-salama alaykum,' Yusuf al-Basir said. 'Welcome to the Great Library of Malaqah.'

'Wa alaykum e-salam,' replied Simon. 'We are honoured that you have taken the time to speak with us.'

'Your cousin, Makoud, tells me that you worked for many years in the famous library in Qurtubah,' he said, looking directly at Salma.

'Yes, sayyad. That is correct. At first I worked as a junior copyist but then I was promoted to a scribe.'

'So where have you been since you left Qurtubah?' he asked.

Salma began to explain how they had managed to escape the besieged city and had passed the last few years in the countryside. She pulled out her copy of 'A World Study of Herbs and Healing Plants' and handed it to him.

'This is an example of my work, sayyad. I managed to save it from the flames and have looked after it ever since. I thought you might like to have it for the library.'

'You stole it?' snapped the assistant librarian.

Salma felt herself tremble with rage, but she ignored him and continued to look at the chief librarian, saying as calmly as she could, 'I took it without permission, that is true, but I did so to save it from being destroyed. I hoped that one day I would have the opportunity to return it.'

'That was not your decision to make,' interrupted Marwen.

The chief librarian was barely listening; he was turning page after page in the book. 'Exquisite,' he murmured. 'Truly exquisite. You are a talented scribe, Salma. Your cousin was correct in his praise of you. I will be happy to accept this gift for our library.'

'But how do we know that this is her own work?' insisted the assistant librarian. 'Just because she stole it, doesn't mean she is the one who transcribed this book.'

'Enough, Marwen. If the woman is lying to me, I will know soon enough. You are aware as well as I that we have been ordered to find twenty new scribes. What would you have me do? Turn her away?'

Salma could see from the expression on Marwen's face that that was exactly what he wanted him to do.

'There is no place for women in this library,' he muttered, but the chief librarian didn't seem to hear him.

Instead he smiled at Salma and said, 'It would be an honour if you would join us in our work in building up the library here in Malaqah. I'm sure you noticed when you entered the reading room, that we have space for many more books. It is my job to find them. Some we will buy from countries in the east, others we will borrow, but many are being written here in our university. Copies must be made of them all, and the Latin texts we have must be translated into Arabic.' He turned to Simon and continued, 'You are a translator, I believe.'

'Yes, sayyad. I translate from Latin and Greek into Arabic and Hebrew.'

'You are not from here? Your fair skin gives you away,' he said with a knowing look.

'No, sayyad. I am a Muwallad. I came from the land of the Anglo-Saxons to study at the university in Qurtubah many years ago.'

'But you are a Muslim?'

'Yes, sayyad. I converted to Islam many years ago.' Salma noticed how her husband's neck reddened as he lied to the chief librarian. He was not a good liar.

'Well we need translators. You too can work here in the university.' Yusuf stood up. 'Splendid. I will expect you both here, tomorrow. When you arrive, Marwen will show you to your workplace and give you your first tasks. Something simple to get you started, I think,' he added with another smile. 'Alla ysalmak, my friends.'

'Ma'a salama, sayyad,' Simon said.

The assistant librarian said nothing, but his scowl grew even darker.

Salma felt light-headed. They had done it. Both of them could work now and that meant they would be able to afford a house of their own. Everything seemed to be going as they'd hoped. She was excited and couldn't wait to get back to Makoud's house to give them all the news.

As Salma was leaving she turned to have another look at her new workplace, and noticed Marwen arguing with the chief librarian. He looked very angry. Was it because of them? Surely not. He didn't even know them. Why would he be angry that they were going to work in the library? It was puzzling. She prayed he never found out about Simon.

CHAPTER 7

Hasan was furious. How had that slippery eel, Naja managed to get away? His instructions had been quite clear. Arrest his brother and detain his servants. But where were they? Neither Qusay, nor Ben-Yahya's tutor were to be found. He'd had men searching the city for them for weeks, and all in vain.

'Your Majesty,' said the head of the Palace Guards. 'We have news of the saqaliba.'

'Well? Spit it out, man. Have you found him?'

'No, Your Majesty. But we believe he has fled the country and taken the servant Qusay with him.'

Hasan jumped to his feet in anger. 'What the devil,' he shouted. 'Fled the country? That is the last thing I wanted. What the hell have you been doing all this time? I want the man arrested. Do you hear me?' General Rashad approached cautiously. 'Well? And what do you want?' Hasan snapped at him.

'I see you have heard the news,' said the general. 'We believe Naja al-Siqlabi got a fishing boat to take him across to north Africa.'

'Is that all you can tell me? Nothing else? When did this happen? Who took him across? And to where exactly? Find the fisherman and bring him to me.'

'Very well, Your Majesty but is it really worth it? He is nothing but a tutor. What threat can he be to you and the throne?'

'Possibly none at all but we can't be sure. I do not like uncertainty. Is that understood? Remember, Naja has been at my brother's side since Ben-Yahya was a young lad. He has taught him all he knows. I know my brother relied on him and he will have confided in him and looked to him for advice. Now that I am Khalifa I want to know exactly what my brother was planning and the saqaliba is the best person to tell me. So find him,' he commanded, his voice loud and angry. 'And remember I want him alive.'

He had to know if Ben-Yahya was a real threat to him. They had always got on well and he was actually very fond of his brother, but each had their eyes on becoming Khalifa. As soon as Hasan received news of his uncle's death, he didn't hesitate to claim the throne for himself. Now what he needed to know was whether Ben-Yahya was happy to continue being the brother of the khalifa or if he too was eager to get his hands on the kingdom. His little brother could be both impatient and headstrong. That was the reason he'd had him arrested, before he could cause any trouble.

'Very well, Your Majesty. I will send someone to the port to question the fishermen. One of them must know who took them across the Narrow Straits,' said General Rashad.

'Good. Now come and let us discuss what we are to do about the mercenaries,' said Hasan, leading the way into his council chamber.

The grand vizier was already waiting for them. Beside him, was the treasurer of the Royal Mint, a lugubrious man who never seemed to see the positive side of anything—too busy counting the money to see how it could be used, thought Hasan, as the two men rose and bowed to him.

'Be seated, gentlemen. Now I have already spoken to the treasurer about how we can pay for a private army, and he assures me that there is no shortage of gold in the vaults. So what we must discuss today is where do we find the right one? We need a well disciplined, well armed force, strong enough to help us to defeat Isbiliya. General, what have you to tell us?'

The general seated himself on the low sofa, next to the grand vizier. He crossed his legs, adjusted his cloak and then began. 'Your Majesty, as you know, there has been a lot of sickness in the countryside. Many people have died. So when our men went out as usual, looking for recruits in the Spring, they found few volunteers. Those men who had survived are needed to work on the land. And of course, as you are also aware, there were many casualties in the battle at Écija, which was only last autumn. So this year we are unable to swell the ranks of our army with volunteer militia men, which is why it is so important to consider recruiting troops from elsewhere.'

'Yes, General, we know all that. Get to the point. The mercenaries.'

'Yes, Your Majesty. Well, as we discussed previously, I counsel against speaking to King Ferdinand. I suggest we go straight to a private army of mercenaries and I have found just the one. It is led by a man called Jabalah.'

'Jabalah? The mountain?' asked the grand vizier, in surprise.

'Yes. That's what his men call him because he is a mountain of a man. His real name is Roberto de las Iglesias; he is from Toledo. You know of him?'

'I have heard men talk of him. They say he is fearless and a true warrior but he is not to be trusted. He fought for the Dukes of Toledo for many years, but then he betrayed them and joined forces with the taifa of Murcia,' said the grand vizier. 'Next he was fighting for the King of León. He changes sides more often than a ferryman crosses the Narrow Straits.'

'You are right. He is not to be trusted. He will not be fighting by our side because he is a Muslim, nor because he hates Abbad I of Isbiliya, nor because he wants to drive the Christians out of al-Andalus; he will fight with us for one reason alone, gold. And lots of it. If we pay him well, then we can rely on him to provide a strong, well-disciplined army to fight alongside us,' said Rashad.

'But what manner of man is he?' asked Hasan, uneasily.

'He is rich and powerful, and he has made a great deal of money by selling his services to the highest bidder. He is also unscrupulous and devious. He is someone on whom you must never turn your back because he will always try to outwit you.'

'So why do we want to join forces with a man like that?' asked Hasan. Jabalah sounded a little too ambitious for his liking.

'Because he has twenty thousand trained men. If we combine that with our own army and if Garnata can send another twenty thousand troops, we will have nearly a hundred thousand men, enough to rout Isbiliya once and for all,' replied the general.

'We have to make a decision quickly, Your Majesty,' said the treasurer. 'Their army is on the borders of Morón. It will not take them long to reach Malaqah. We must be prepared.'

'He is right, Your Majesty. There can be no delay,' said the general. 'We don't know when Abbad will make his move, but if he hears that we have the support of Jabalah he might think twice before attacking us.'

'How much does this Mountain want in payment?' asked Hasan.

'Ten thousand gold dinars and as much of the spoils as they can carry.'

Hasan looked at the treasurer. 'Well?'

'Your Majesty, that is a lot of money. But if you are determined to hire this army, then I can tell you that we have enough in the treasury to pay for it,' he replied, his face longer and sadder than ever at the thought of removing so much gold from the vaults.

'In that case, I leave it to you to negotiate with this man, General Rashad. In the meantime, despatch ten thousand men with one of your best quaids to reinforce the frontier with Morón. They are to send word if they see any sign of the enemy, but not to attack. Once we have all our troops gathered, we will cross through Morón and attack Abbad's troops. Is that clear?'

'Yes, Your Majesty. I will send a messenger to Jabalah right away.'

'And make sure you send a messenger to our friend Badis ben Habus. We need the support of Garnata as well.'

'Yes, Your Majesty.'

It was going to be a costly battle, but if it meant getting rid of the constant threat from Isbiliya, it was worth it. He waited until the others had left then called for his servant.

'Bring me some tea,' he instructed the young boy. He needed time to think about this campaign. Hasan was unused to battle but he knew how formidable Abbad's army was. He also was well acquainted with the land around Morón; when he was a young boy he had lived for a while in the taifa of Ronda, a mountainous region, rugged and wild, right next door to it. But Morón itself lay in a fertile plain that stretched back as far as the capital of Isbiliya itself. From their advantage point in the mountains that formed the frontier between Morón and Malaqah, Hasan's army would be able to see Abbad's troops coming from a great distance. One small doubt worried itself around and around in his mind, Jabalah. He knew he couldn't trust him. Rulers had used mercenaries for years to swell the ranks of their armies, but they were men employed by the khalifa and although they did not have the same loyalty to him as some of the other troops, they were under the command of the khalifa and his generals. This would be different. These men would be taking their orders from Jabalah, not from him.

Hasan walked slowly back to his private rooms. His thoughts had returned to the irritating problem of what to do about his cousin, Yahya. He had been too hasty in sending him away. He should have insisted that he stay in Malaqah for a while; he could have found many reasons to detain him there. He could have used Jamila as an excuse, saying that she would miss him; he knew that they were very fond of each other. Or he could have offered him a job as a minister. But he'd done none of that and now Yahya was in al-Jazira with his brother Muhammad, probably plotting how to get the throne back. Should Hasan send for him? But what then? He couldn't lock up his brother-in-law without antagonising Muhammad and upsetting Jamila.

As he entered the zenana, Jamila was sitting by the window gazing at the waves breaking on the harbour wall. She turned and when she saw it was him, she smiled and said, 'Husband. How lovely to see you again, so soon.'

'You look sad, dearest one. Is something troubling you?'

'No, husband. How can I be sad when I have everything I could want?'

'What about your brother? Don't you miss him?' he asked. An idea had come to him. He might have found a way of getting rid of her irritating brother for once and all, and nobody would know it had anything to do with him.

'He is my brother, so yes, I do miss him a little. But now I have you, husband; I do not need brothers and sisters. And soon I hope we will have a family of our own.'

Hasan bent down and kissed her gently on the forehead. 'That would be wonderful news, indeed. But I do not want to see my beautiful Jamila sad. Why don't you go to al-Jazira and visit your brother for a few weeks. I am going to be very busy with the campaign against Isbiliya and I will be forced to neglect my lovely wife for a while. I do not want you to be lonely.'

Jamila looked at him in astonishment. This was unheard of. No man allowed his wife to leave the country without him, least of all a man as important as Hasan. He could see the distress on her face as she listened to him telling her that she could take her servants and a corps of soldiers to keep her safe.

'Are you divorcing me?' she whispered, her voice filled with tears.

'No, dearest one. Of course I'm not divorcing you,' he said, enveloping her in his arms. 'I just want you to go and visit your family for a while. It will make me happy to know that you and your brother are reunited for a short time. Here, wipe your tears.'

Dutifully, Jamila wiped her face and smiled at him. 'When do you want me to go?' she asked.

'Whenever you want, my dear. As soon as possible, while the weather is fine but not too hot. I will send my personal slave with you as a bodyguard. He is someone I trust with my life, so he's the perfect person to guard my dear wife.'

She smiled at him and he felt his heart melt at the sweetness of her. 'Come, let us retire to my room,' he said, taking her hand and leading her into the royal bedroom.

Later that day, Hasan sent for his servant, Uday. This short, stocky man had originally belonged to his mother and as soon as Hasan was old enough to need his own slave, she had passed

Uday on to him. His mother, whose wit was as sharp as a knife, had called the slave Uday, 'Speedy', even though he was the slowest, most ponderous man in the palace. Now, ten years later, he was slower than ever, but he was meticulous and completely devoted to Hasan, who knew that Uday would do anything he asked him.

'Your Majesty,' Uday said, bowing low and waiting until Hasan spoke.

'My wife is going to al-Jazira to visit her brother. I would like you to accompany her,' he said.

If the slave was surprised at this news, he didn't show it, just nodded slowly and said, 'As you wish, Your Majesty.'

'And while you are there, I have a very important task for you. You must not mention it to anyone, and certainly not to my wife. Is that understood?'

'Of course, Your Majesty.'

'Good. Listen carefully to what I want you to do.' He knew that Uday would perform his duty meticulously, never questioning why he was being asked to do such a thing. 'And when it is completed I want you to send word to me that it is done.'

'Yes, Your Majesty.'

'Now, mark my words carefully and do not repeat them to anyone.'

CHAPTER 8

Hasan sat in the shade of a date palm, the book open on his lap. He looked up, irritated at the interruption; it was Labib, again, with more questions, he supposed, more indecisions. The grand vizier bowed and approached him, slowly.

'What is it this time, Labib?' Hasan asked, tearing his eyes away from the book.

'We have found the boat, Your Majesty. The slave escaped on a fishing boat.'

'Where is it? Bring the captain to me at once.'

'We don't have him, Your Majesty, but we know which boat it is. It left last night and by now they will have taken the slave to Sebta. He is out of our jurisdiction. There is nothing we can do until they return.'

'Do we know that for certain or is it another of your conjectures, Labib?' the khalifa asked. It irritated him how easily his grand vizier gave up on a task. 'Station some men down near the fishing fleet and when the boat returns, I want all the crew arrested. We will question them and find out exactly where they took this man. Is that understood?'

'Very well, Your Majesty.' He paused and added, 'You probably know him better than anyone, Your Majesty. Do you think he would just return to Sebta? Wouldn't it make more sense if he went somewhere where we could never find him?'

'You're right, Labib; I do know Naja al-Siqlabi, and I'm pretty sure that he will have headed straight back to Sebta because he will see an opportunity for himself in this situation, and he won't be able to let it go. He will want to ingratiate himself with my mother and turn her against me. But I don't deal in guesses and conjectures; I deal in facts. Find out where he is. Is that simple enough for you? Where the devil is he? And when you have found him I want him dragged before me in chains.'

He glared at the grand vizier as he was backing out of the room.

'And send the chief librarian to me. Right away.'

'Yes, Your Majesty,' Labib replied.

Hasan watched as his chief minister made his final bow and left. What a numbskull. If he didn't rely on him so much, he'd get rid of him; Labib was getting too old for the job. He should never have reinstated him after ibn Baqanna disappeared. Old men never took any chances; they liked to prevaricate, to wait and weigh things up before they made a decision. He needed a grand vizier who could act quickly and decisively.

He opened the book again. It was magnificent. The chief librarian had sent it to him only this morning but had not said where he had found it. It was a jewel among books but where was it from? Bagdad? Damascus? Constantinople? It was certainly better than anything they had in the library in Malaqah. This was exactly what he wanted for his library, books of this quality. He turned the page and the colours of the herbs glowed up at him as though they were living plants. It had been used; he could see that from the odd crease and stain on the parchment but nothing detracted from its beauty. Yes, this was the quality he was aiming for. Yusuf al-Basir would have to give up his secrets. He wanted more books of this standard.

The main library was not far from the alcazaba, so it did not take the chief librarian long to arrive at the palace. The khalifa was sitting in the garden reading the book that Salma had donated to the library a few days earlier. Yusuf hesitated, waiting for the khalifa to notice his presence. He had been used to treating the previous khalifa, Idris I, as the friend he'd become over the years, but he felt he would be expected to pay more attention to protocol with this one.

'Ah, Yusuf, as-salama alaykum,' said Hasan, closing the book carefully. 'Come here and sit beside me.'

'Wa alaykum e-salam, Your Majesty. I see you have been reading the book I sent you.'

'I have indeed. That is why I have summoned you.'

Yusuf felt his heart begin to race. He had noticed the odd stain on some of the pages, but he'd hoped that the beauty of the calligraphy would make up for them. Was the khalifa angry that he'd given him a used copy?

'Is there something wrong, Your Majesty?' he asked, nervously stroking his long beard.

'Wrong? Quite the contrary. The book is magnificent. I wanted to ask you where it came from. It is not a new book; I can see that. So where did you find it, or have you been hiding it from me?'

'It has only just come into my possession, Your Majesty. One of my new scribes rescued it from the library in Qurtubah, many years ago. She has presented it to our library in Malaqah.'

'Really. Are you telling me that she stole it?'

'No, Your Majesty. This was a book she was working on when the library was closed during the civil war. You will have heard that many thousands of books were destroyed during that conflict; she chose to save this one so that she could return it later, when the libraries reopened. Sadly that never happened in Qurtubah. But now she lives in Malaqah and recently she approached me for work as a scribe. She is a most talented woman; I was delighted to offer her a job in our library. She brought me this gem of a book. I thought you would like to see it straight away.'

'You were quite right, Yusuf. I've never seen anything so delightful,' said Hasan, his eyes shining with pleasure. Yusuf smiled; for once he could see the young boy that was still inside the khalifa. 'A woman, you say. Well I would like you to bring this scribe to the alcázar. I want to see more of her work.'

Salma could feel Marwen's eyes on her. No matter where she was or what she was doing, he was there, watching her. It made her feel very uncomfortable. Why didn't he get on with his own work and leave her in peace?

She dipped her pen into the inkwell, but it came out dry. That was strange; she had filled it with iron-gall ink only yesterday. Surely she hadn't used it all so quickly. She sprinkled a light coating of sand on her work to dry it and closed the manuscript carefully. Well, she would have to make some more ink, but the process was slow and it would takes weeks to be ready. Hopefully there would be some already prepared in the room which they all referred to as the kitchen, despite its awful smell.

One of the copyists was already in there, a youth of a similar age to her youngest daughter; he was an apprentice whose job was mainly copying and preparing tools, pens and ink for the scribes.

'Sa'id, I've run out of ink. Do you know where I can find some more?' she asked him.

'No Salma. I'm looking for it myself. I can't understand it; I make some every week, so that we will always have a fresh supply available and now all I can find is ink that won't be ready to use until next week.'

'So what can we do? I'm half-way through a manuscript that I wanted to finish today.'

'I'll make up another batch, but that won't help us right now,' said Sa'id, looking upset. 'I just don't understand it.' She could see that he felt he was to blame somehow. 'Don't worry. I'll go and see if anyone has any they can spare.'

While Sa'id went to search for the ink, Salma returned to her desk. There was little she could do without any writing implements. The more she thought of it, the more she was convinced that the inkwell had been full yesterday. Somebody had tipped it away, maybe accidentally or maybe not. She looked across at Marwen, who for once was working busily at his desk. He must have felt her eyes on him because he looked up and she caught the ghost of a smile on his lips. Surely that man wasn't so petty as to try to sabotage her work? Or perhaps he was. 'Nothing to do?' he asked. 'You don't seem very busy.'

'I'm planning the design,' she said, picking up a piece of chalk and sketching a plant on the smooth surface of her desk.

'Here, I've found you some ink,' said Sa'id, bustling across to her desk. 'One of the copyists had plenty to spare.' He poured some of the iron-gall ink into the inkwell. 'That should keep you going for at least a week.'

'Thank you, Sa'id. I really appreciate it,' she said, wiping the chalk off the desk and taking out her manuscript again. She could see Marwen glowering across the room at her.

'Ah, Salma. I'm glad you're here. I need you to come with me; the khalifa wants to meet you. He is very pleased with your work. More than pleased. He is enchanted,' said the chief librarian, in a loud voice, as he swept into the library and beamed at them all.

Everyone stopped work and looked at him in surprise. The khalifa had never sent for anybody before; this was most unusual. The only person who ever went to meet the khalifa was Yusuf himself.

Salma carefully placed the top on her inkwell and stood up, just in time to see Marwen's face, twisted into a mask of rage. Why did that man hate her so much?

'Sa'id, can you look after my ink, please,' she said, with a sideways glance at the assistant librarian.

'Of course, Salma.' The copyist took her inkwell and placed it on his own desk.

'Do I need to bring anything with me, sayyad?' she asked Yusuf.

'Yes, good idea. Bring that, the manuscript on your desk. I want him to see that the quality of your work is still as high as it was before. And hurry. The khalifa does not like to be kept waiting.'

Salma could feel a fluttering in her stomach, but it was excitement, not fear. She feared no man, certainly not a khalifa; she had seen enough of them come and go to know their fortune was never permanent. Carefully she picked up the unfinished manuscript; it was a book of love poems and she had woven a delicate design of plants and flowers around the borders. She hoped he would like it.

CHAPTER 9

Basma was bent over the cooking stove when he got home. Her long dark hair tied back from her face with a narrow scarf.

'Tagine, Mama?' he asked. 'With couscous?'

'Umar. What a surprise. I wasn't expecting you. Why are you home today? Has something happened?'

He smiled at his mother. She always expected the worst. 'No, Mama. Everything's fine. I've got extra duties this week, so the quaid said I could have a few hours' leave.'

'Only a few hours?' his mother looked disappointed.

'I hope there's enough for me,' he said, pointing to the earthenware pot that was bubbling away on the stove.

'Of course, my son. It will be ready soon, when your father and Ibrahim get home.'

'Umar. Come and meet your cousin, Layla,' said Abal. She was his father's first wife but treated him as though he were her own son. 'You remember her? She and her family arrived yesterday. They will be staying with us for a while, until they can find a place of their own. I've given them your room as you are rarely at home. Are you staying tonight?' She looked concerned.

'No, Umm Abal. I have to go back to the barracks.' He saw the curious look in her eyes but said no more. She knew something was going to happen and that he couldn't tell her about it. An entire corps was being deployed to the frontier with Morón but he was not allowed to share the information with anyone. In fact it was not even certain that he would be going with them. He'd been badly injured in the battle of Écija and only just returned to active duty. 'You know how it is,' he added with an affectionate smile.

'But you're staying to eat?' asked his mother, Basma.

'Of course. How could I resist that wonderful smell.'

His mother looked up, her face flushed from bending over the cooking pot and smiled at him. 'You remember them?' she said. 'Your cousins.'

He did remember them, but he'd had little to do with them when he was younger. In those days he hadn't had any interest in girls and that included his cousins.

A sound behind him made him turn around. It was Layla. His heart gave a skip. This was not how he remembered her; she was no longer the lanky girl who used to hang around him and his friends wanting to be included in their games. She had changed. Now she was... He felt lost for words. Beautiful. There was no other word to describe her. She was so beautiful. He felt a tightening in his loins and a flush of heat rising up his neck. He couldn't say a word. All he could do was stare at her. Her hair was as golden as a field of corn and her eyes as blue as the sea on a warm summer's evening. She was dressed simply, in a white robe, covered with a loose tunic that matched the colour of her eyes. How could this delightful creature be Layla? How could she even be related to him? He thought of his own swarthy skin and black, crinkly hair; he must look like a bear compared to her. All at once he became aware of the stink of his body and wished he'd had time to bathe and change his clothes before he met her. But it was too late. She came straight over to him and said, 'As-salama alaykum, dear cousin. It's so good to meet you again. My mother is always talking about her cousin Makoud and his family but I'd almost forgotten what you looked like.' She reached up and kissed him demurely on each cheek. He felt the colour rise in his face and stumbled back from her in embarrassment.

Out of the corner of his eye he saw Abal smiling at him. That woman never missed anything. 'She's grown into a pretty girl, that one,' she whispered to him. 'You could do a lot worse.'

Umar felt himself blushing and said, hurriedly, 'I'm going to have a wash. It will be time for prayers very soon.'

He went onto the outside patio and poured himself a large bowl of water, pulled off his uniform and began to wash himself vigorously. He was a man who liked women. His father was always complaining that it was time he got married and settled down, but soldiers rarely got married. They waited to see if they were going to survive and then when they were older, they maybe considered it. None of his comrades were married. But that didn't mean Umar went without women; there were always some women who liked a soldier, and he was happy to take advantage of what they had to offer him, especially when he was away on campaign. The truth was that he had never met anyone he wanted to marry, and he definitely wasn't ready to settle down, so what was the point of even thinking about it? His father had spoken of this girl and that, ones from good homes, who would give him many sons and look after him in his old age. What did that mean to him? He was a soldier. He'd be lucky if he had an old age. He rubbed himself dry and pulled his tunic back over his head and instead of tucking his sword into his belt, he laid it down on the table. He had no comb, so he ran his fingers through his hair, hoping to get it into shape, and tugged at his beard, smoothing it with cold water. Then, once he felt cleaner and more in control of his emotions, he went back to join the others.

Layla's parents were home now. Instantly he remembered where his cousin had inherited her blonde beauty; her father of course was from one of the northern countries. Nobody had discussed where Simon was from when Umar was a child, and it hadn't seemed anything strange to have such a fair skinned member of the family. Now he wondered if there was something about his background that they weren't mentioning. He knew they had all fled from Qurtubah during the civil war, but his father never wanted to talk about it. Were there secrets that his father was keeping from them? Maybe Salma would be more forthcoming.

'Is that you, Umar?' said a deep voice. It was his father, closely followed by Ibrahim. 'Good. Maybe you can tell us what all this activity is about?'

'Yes, there are soldiers everywhere you look. What's happening?' asked Ibrahim.

Umar sighed. 'Well, I suppose you'll find out soon enough. The khalifa is sending a corps of soldiers to Morón to defend the border. They say that Isbiliya is planning an attack.'

Everyone began to speak at once. Was Umar going? Did this mean war with Isbiliya? Was there going to be another coup? How well defended were they exactly? The questions came one after another. 'All right. Stop now. You know I can't tell you anything. I've already said too much,' he protested.

'But are you going?' asked his mother, her eyes beseeching him to say no.

'No, Mama, I don't think so. Not this time. Maybe if the fighting escalates my corps will be needed. At the moment it is only a rumour, but Hasan doesn't want to be taken unawares. He wants to make a show of force.'

'Leave the lad alone. Come and eat before it gets cold,' said Abal, as she bustled about setting out the table where they ate. 'Tell us about how you are getting on at the library, Salma.'

'It's different but I think we could be very happy there.'

Umar wasn't interested in hearing about Salma's day at the library; he was still mesmerised by her daughter. 'So what are you going to do now you are in Malaqah? Find a rich husband?' he asked her, and was dismayed to see the smile in her eyes fade. His words had been crass; this was no woman of the night. 'My apologies, cousin. I'm a rough soldier and at times I forget how to speak to a lady.'

Layla tossed her long hair back from her face and said, 'I'm not a lady, just the daughter of a humble family, and no I am not looking for a rich husband. If I marry, I will marry for love, not for money.'

'And what if your parents decide otherwise?'

Layla looked across at her parents, who were sitting side by side, their hands touching. 'I doubt they will do that. They married for love, so why shouldn't I?' She started to move away from him.

'Stay. Please accept my apology and let us start again. Tell me how you plan to spend your days in our lovely city.' He almost added 'but not as lovely as you' but thought better of it. She didn't seem a girl who would accept such a flippant complement.

'Very well, apology accepted,' she said sitting down beside him. 'Well, I may continue with my studies. Tomorrow I'll go to the university and see if they will accept me. What I'd really like to do is be a scribe like my mother,' she said, the smile returning to her face, 'but I have a lot to learn.'

'Layla, come and help me with the food,' Basma called, pointing to a large bowl of couscous. 'And bring those aubergines.'

He watched as the girl hurried outside to help her cousin. She wasn't just beautiful, she was feisty too. He liked that.

His thoughts turned to the impending campaign. He hoped he would be among the troops that were going to the border. He loved being a soldier: the excitement, the camaraderie, the adventure and that rush of adrenalin when the battle began. There was nothing quite like it. His father had told him that his uncle had been a brave soldier, and his grandfather and great-grandfather before him. It was in his blood.

His first real taste of active combat had been at Écija the previous year. He'd never experienced anything like that sweet taste of victory. He'd stood on the battlefield, his heart pounding, covered in blood and sweat and watched as the enemy had turned and fled. What a moment. It was all he could do not to break ranks, give his horse his head and chase after them. That's when it had happened, when he saw the khalifa lying on the ground, a dagger in his neck. He couldn't believe it. The Supreme Commander murdered. No victory for him. The assassin lay dead beside him, dispatched by one of the khalifa's guards.

What happened next was a bit hazy. He'd lost consciousness and slipped from his horse to the ground. When he woke up he was back in the camp, stripped of his armour and a blood-soaked bandage round his chest. At some point in the battle he must have let down his guard and an enemy soldier had taken advantage of it. He'd been so pumped up with adrenalin that he hadn't even noticed that he was wounded. Despite everything, it had been a great victory and it left him craving for more. Now his comrades would be defending the city once more, but it was unlikely he would be with them. He'd assured the quaid that he was fully recovered but he knew he wasn't as fit as he'd been before.

All of a sudden there was a loud, insistent knocking on the outer door. Who on earth was it? Nobody called at midday—

mealtimes were sacrosanct, along with the hours for prayer—
and they'd only just sat down at the table. Umar automatically
reached for his sword but he'd left it out on the patio.

'What the devil is going on? Who's out there making all that
racket when we're trying to eat?' asked Makoud, decidedly
annoyed at having his meal interrupted.

'I'll go, Baba,' said Umar. He crossed the patio, picked up
his sword, then pulled back the iron bolt that held the heavy
door fast. 'Bakr? What are you doing here? Has something
happened to Aisha?'

'No, your sister is fine. Let me in. I must speak to your
father,' he said and pushed his way past Umar as if the hounds
of hell were after him. 'I have to sit down. I've run all the way
from the shipyard.'

'What in the name of Allah is so important that you've done
that? Wife, bring your daughter's husband some sweet tea to
calm him down,' said Makoud. 'Come Bakr, sit down and eat
with us.'

Umar had never seen his brother-in-law so distraught before.
This huge, muscular man, with hands like shovels, was normally
unshakeable. A chill ran through him. What had happened to
upset him so? He realised he was still holding his sword and
tucked it into his belt; he felt naked without it.

'No, there's no time for tea. We must go down to the fishing
port right away. It's Dirar. He's been arrested.'

CHAPTER 10

Ben-Yahya couldn't sleep. His neighbour, that invisible phantom that was incarcerated in the cell next to him, had coughed and moaned all night long. He would have thought things couldn't get any worse, but the sound of someone else's pain aggravated his own.

'Here you are,' said the cheery voice of his gaoler as he opened the cell door and slid in his morning bowl of slops. Just the sight of it made Ben-Yahya feel sick. He had toyed with the idea of starving himself to death rather than eat another mouthful of the disgusting food, but in the end something inside of him wasn't ready to let go. He hobbled across and picked up the bowl.

The man in the adjacent cell let out an agonising groan. 'Not long now,' the gaoler said, with the same cheeriness. 'He won't last another night, that one. It gets them all in the end. The other prisoners call it gaol fever, but it's just the usual winter sickness.'

'It sounds worse than that,' said Ben-Yahya. 'Why haven't you sent for a doctor?'

The old man let out a hoot of laughter. 'A doctor? Well that's the funniest thing I've heard all year. Why would I pay for a doctor for him? He's going to die one way or another anyway. The sooner, the better for him. I'm surprised he's lived so long; most of them don't live out the year. That one's been here for five years.'

Five years. Where had Ben-Yahya been five years ago? In Sebta, eating well, living in luxury, surrounded by friends and without a care in the world. He tried to see in his imagination the clear blue sky of north Africa, the sea crashing on the harbour wall, the gardens where he would sit playing chess with his friends, but nothing would bring it back to him. Even his memory was clouded by this dingy, grey space that was now his whole world. He closed his eyes and imagined he was back in Sebta, his favourite hawk sitting on his glove, waiting for his signal, the dogs running behind his horse while he and his brother went hunting. His brother. Where was Hasan? What was he thinking about? Did he remember those happy days they spent together or had he erased Ben-Yahya completely from his mind? Five years. Had he been there five years or five months? He had no idea how long he'd been locked up, nor how much longer it would be until his release, if ever. All the days merged into one in this hell hole. It was difficult to even tell day from night, never mind keep a tally of the weeks and months. He prayed that Allah would take pity on him and let him die sooner than later. With that emptiness inside him that admitted complete resignation to his faith, he slumped back down on his sleeping pallet.

'Not hungry? If you won't eat it, I know plenty that will,' said the gaoler.

The prisoner in the next cell had ceased to moan. The only sound to come through the stone wall now was a strangled gurgling.

'I told you. Waste of money getting a doctor. He's had it. I know the signs. That's him on the way to meet his Maker. Won't be long now.'

Ben-Yahya put his head in his hands.

No sound came from the sick man's cell. Then Ben-Yahya heard the slow, heavy footsteps of the gaoler coming along the passage, followed by quicker firmer steps. Two men. Who were they? Were they coming to release him? For a moment a tiny hope kindled in his breast. He got up from his bed and try to stretch his legs. He groaned in pain; now he had the body of an old man, with stiff joints and aching limbs.

'As-salama alaykum,' he called. 'What's happening?'

'Nothing to concern yourself about,' the gaoler said. 'I told you your neighbour wouldn't last. He's dead. May Allah protect him. Best thing for him, in the end. He was a fighter all right, but even he couldn't survive in here. It takes them all eventually, young and old, healthy and sick; they all succumb in the end.'

'What are you going to do with him?' Ben-Yahya asked.

'What do you think? Sew him up in a burlap sack and throw him in the sea.'

'What about his family? Won't they want to bury his body?'

'His family probably think he's dead already. Why bother them? No it's us who'll send him to Paradise, if that's where he's going.' He laughed. 'But I doubt that very much.'

Ben-Yahya heard the neighbouring cell door open and the other men, grunting and groaning as they lifted the body and put it into the sack.

'Well you should get a good night's sleep, tonight,' said the gaoler. 'I'll be round later with your supper.'

So that was what his future looked like. Not even reunited with his mother at the end. Thrown into the sea like a dead dog for the fish to dine on. Surely that was no way to end his days. Ben-Yahya sat down on the sleeping pallet. He was too tired to even cry. There would be no one to remember him and no one to mourn him. He would have simply disappeared. Only Allah would know his fate.

CHAPTER 11

Makoud couldn't believe his youngest son had been so foolish. He'd listened to what his son-in-law had to tell him but none of it made any sense. What had Dirar to do with a runaway slave? How was he implicated? So many questions were running around in his head.

'Stop that noise,' he snapped at his wives, who were huddled together wailing in anguish. 'How can I think with all that racket?' He turned to Umar. 'Can you do anything for him, Umar? We have to do something before they throw him in the dungeon. You know as well as I do that once he's in there, it will be impossible to get him out.'

The women began to wail even louder at that.

'I'll do what I can, Baba. Stay here. I'll be back as soon as I have some news. If I can intercept them before they reach the alcázar, we may have a chance. Come on Bakr.' The two men rushed out into the street.

It wasn't far from Makoud's house to the entrance to the alcazaba; if they ran down the main street which led to the Boveda Gate, they would be there before the soldiers. Makoud groaned. He should have given Umar some money to give to the guards; they were always more agreeable if you slipped them a few silver dirhams. What was he thinking? He would give them gold. Was his son not worth more than a few dirhams? He went into his inner room and took a handful of gold dinars from the box in the corner. This was money he was saving for his old age, but his need for it today was of much greater importance.

'Abal, Basma, I'll be back shortly. Lock the outer door behind me,' he called to his weeping wives.

Umar could see no sign of the soldiers or the fishermen. His heart sank. Were they too late? He knew it was unlikely he could do anything to intervene in the arrest. That was how it was, but he had to try. If the khalifa had told them to arrest all the crew, then that's what they would do. Even if he knew one of the soldiers—and that was a long shot—how would he be able to persuade him to release Dirar? On what pretext could he go free?

'What's the plan, Umar?' asked Bakr. 'I have no sword with me, but I'm not afraid to fight.'

Umar laughed. 'I'm not planning to attack them; we'd have no chance against armed soldiers. How many did you say there were, four?'

'Yes, I think so. So what will we do?'

'If Allah is looking down on us, then one of the soldiers will be someone I know. If so, I hope to persuade them to release Dirar. After all, he was only doing what he'd been told by his captain. They're soldiers; they know about taking orders.'

'I think I see them,' whispered Bakr, drawing back into the shadows. 'Did you bring any money to bribe them? Surely you're not relying on friendship alone?'

His brother-in-law had a good point. Why hadn't he thought of that? He watched as the soldiers approached. There were six of them; surely he would recognise one of them. If not, what then? Maybe they'd have to fight after all.

'Thanks be to Allah, you're still here, my son,' said a breathless Makoud, stopping in front of them and doubling over with pain. 'I thought I'd be too late. Here take this. You will need it.' He thrust the cloth bag into his son's hand. 'Allah be with you.'

'Come, Bakr. Let's try to get to them before they are in view of the main gate,' said Umar.

As they approached the arrest party, he could see that the soldiers were escorting five fishermen. The captain of the fishing boat walked in front, his head down, followed by the rest of his crew. Dirar, instantly recognisable by his slight build and his youth, was the last. None of them were chained.

'As-salama alaykum, comrades,' said Umar, stopping in front of them. 'What's this then? Did the khalifa have some bad fish for his dinner? Arresting fishermen seems a bit extreme, don't you think?'

'Out of the way, soldier. This is the khalifa's business and it's nothing to do with fish,' said one of the soldiers, his hand moving instantly to his sword.

'Hang on a minute,' said one of the others, stepping in front of him. 'I know this man. You. You're Umar ibn Makoud. We fought together in Écija. I see you've been promoted. Well done,' he said. 'Don't you remember me? Al-Mubarak.'

Umar stared at the stocky soldier. Al-Mubarak? Of course. The fortunate one. The man smiled at him, his single eye twinkling in recognition. The other he'd lost in the battle when he'd been badly wounded and given up for dead. Now here he was. Allah was looking down on them today.

'Good to see you, brother. And good to see you're still alive.'

'Well I wouldn't be if it wasn't for you.' He turned to his companions and said, 'This young man saved my life. I was about done for, an arrow through my eye and a bloody great wound in my leg. Left for dead. Then up rides this young spark, first time in battle and never a care in the world. He hoists me up onto his horse and gallops back to the rear where he drops me off right by the army doctor. Saved my life, he did.'

Umar could see the others looking at him with respect. They all knew the fear of being left alone on the battlefield, badly wounded, unable to move, waiting for death, praying it would be swift. If the enemy didn't kill you, then infection or blood loss did— the enemy was preferable.

'So what have they done?' he asked, pointing at the fishermen.

'They took someone across to Sebta. Someone who was important to the khalifa. He's furious. He wants them to pay for helping the bastard to escape.'

Umar knew he'd have to move quickly. 'See that lad?' Umar said, pointing at Dirar. 'That's my stupid little brother. I doubt he has the wits to know what he was doing. He'd just have done whatever the captain told him. I wouldn't be surprised if he didn't jump overboard if he was told to. How about you let me take him home and his father can give him a good thrashing?'

He scowled at his brother, who was looking distinctly annoyed at having been accused of being stupid.

The soldiers looked at each other then al-Mubarak said, 'It's all right by me. They don't know how many we're bringing in anyway. What's one less?'

'It'll be our heads, if the khalifa finds out,' said the nazir. 'Can't risk it.'

Umar could see that the rest of his squad would be happy to do a favour for a fellow soldier, especially one who'd saved their comrade's life. 'I can make it worth the risk,' he said, taking the bag of gold his father had given him and weighing it in his hand. The men looked at the bag; he could see them trying to calculate how much it contained. He moved it to his other hand and then back again, watching their eyes follow it.

At last one of the soldiers spoke, 'Yes, let him take his brother. He's only a kid after all.'

'He couldn't have refused even if he knew what the captain was up to,' said the man next to him, his eyes firmly fixed on the bag of money as Umar continued to gently bounce it from one hand to the other.

'What do you say, sayyad? Shall we let the lad go?' The soldiers all looked at their nazir to see what he'd say.

'Let me see what you're prepared to pay for him,' the nazir said to Umar, holding out his hand. He pulled open the drawstring and looked inside, then he smiled. 'Very well. Take him, but do it quickly and keep quiet about it. If anyone gets to hear about this, you will have as much to lose as me.'

'Don't worry. I don't intend to blab to anybody about it. And as for him, when his father gets to him, he won't be going anywhere for a while.'

He grabbed Dirar roughly by the shoulder and said, 'Get home, you stupid bastard.' Now all he could hope was that the captain of the fishing boat kept his mouth shut about him.

The young fisherman ran as fast as he could in the direction of the apothecary's shop. As soon as he had disappeared from sight, Umar turned to the nazir and said, 'Thanks. May Allah be with you always.' He nodded to al-Mubarak and said, 'I'll see you in the Dar al-Jund, I expect.'

Makoud was waiting in the shop for Umar to return, hoping he would have his reckless son, Dirar, with him. What was it about the lad? He was always getting into scrapes. All right, he could understand that this time it wasn't his fault—he was only doing what his captain had told him to do—but then there was the time when Dirar made it his mission to rescue his brother-in-law from the pirates, and the time he fell off the mule and split his head open, and the time when Umar was accused of murdering the royal physician and he sneaked off with Talib to try to prove his brother's innocence. Dirar just couldn't keep away from trouble. Well Makoud had had enough of it. If the khalifa found out that Dirar was one of the crew of the fishing boat, he'd end up in prison. He was going to have to go into hiding whether he liked it or not.

'Baba, I'm back. Umar knew one of the soldiers. It's all right; they let me go,' said Dirar, grinning from ear to ear.

'Get inside and go to your room,' said Makoud, giving his son a slap across the back of his head. He didn't normally raise his hand to his children; it usually wasn't necessary, a word was enough.

Dirar stared at him in surprise and scampered up the stairs.

'It's not his fault, Baba,' said Umar.

'I know, but I have this feeling that his luck is running out. One day you won't be there to get him out of trouble. It's time he grew up.'

'Sorry, I had to give them the money. It was the nazir. The others were happy to let him go, but he didn't agree. It was for when you retire, wasn't it?'

'At this rate I don't think I'll live to retire. That boy will be the death of me,' said Makoud, with a rueful smile.

'But Allah is looking out for us, Baba. At least Dirar's not in gaol.'

'What if the captain says anything? He's always been a nasty piece of work.'

'Well, Dirar will have to lie low for a bit.'

'That's exactly what I was thinking. You go up and have a word with him. I need to go out. Ibrahim, keep an eye on the shop.'

'Yes, Baba.'

Without another word, Makoud picked up his djellaba and left the shop. As always when he had a problem he went to talk to his friend Avi. He looked at the sky; the sun was overhead. Good, that meant Avi would be home, having lunch.

As always, Avi was pleased to see his friend. Both had been very busy recently, and hadn't had time to meet for their usual evenings of late night chatter over numerous cups of mint tea.

'Aleichem shalom, my friend. It's good to see you. Too much business of late and not enough time to talk to friends,' said Avi, hugging Makoud.

'Indeed, my friend. I have missed our evenings together. We must make more effort to keep a little time for the important things in life,' Makoud said.

'So, lovely though it is to see you, I must ask what brings you here at this hour? I am just about to sit down with my family for lunch. Would you care to join us?'

'That is very kind of you. Yes, I would like to eat with you. But it is not for food that I have interrupted your midday meal, but because I need the advice of the one friend I know I can rely on to give me an honest opinion.'

'Come in. Come in, dear friend. You are always welcome here and I will do what I can to help you, because I can see that something is troubling you. Is it Umar?'

Makoud shook his head. 'No, no. Umar is fine. He has recovered well from his injuries and soon will be fit for combat duty again, although his mother would prefer that it were otherwise.'

'So?' Avi asked, leading the way into the dining room, where his wife and family were already seated.

'It's Dirar. Once again he has got himself mixed up in something that is none of his business. By a hair's breadth he is not languishing in the khalifa's dungeons at the moment.'

'That sounds serious,' said Rebekah, laying an extra plate for Makoud. 'What happened?'

As Makoud explained how Dirar had become involved in taking one of the khalifa's enemies to Sebta, Avi's wife filled his plate with a selection of vegetables and then handed him the basket of unleavened bread.

'So you see, this time it wasn't really his fault, but the consequences could be severe if the captain of the fishing boat mentions that he was there,' he concluded.

Avi nodded. 'So what advice can I give you? Young men get involved in things that we would prefer that they didn't. That's the way of the world. At least you were lucky enough to stop him being thrown into prison.'

'Yes, but I think it's time that he left Malaqah for a while. At least while we have this khalifa.'

'He could go and stay with Gideon,' said Rebekah. 'He needs some help at the moment.'

Makoud smiled at her. It was so like these friends; they always anticipated what he was going to ask so that he never had to ask them for anything.

'But Dirar is a fisherman. That's all he knows.'

'He's bright enough; he'll soon learn, and my wife is right, Gideon could do with some help at the moment,' said Avi, taking a piece of bread and chewing it slowly. 'He can go right away.'

'But…'

'Why the but? We need a man to work in the alcaiceria in Garnata, and Dirar needs somewhere to go for a while. You never know, he might enjoy the work.'

'Whether he enjoys it or not, that is what he has to do. I no longer think it's safe for him here. Anyway, it's time he took responsibility for his actions instead of always relying on Umar or me to sort things out.'

'I think that's a bit harsh, my friend, but I'm sure it will do him good to get away from home for a bit. I must say we have seen a great difference in Gideon since he left; he has grown into a man.'

'Well, once again, I thank you, dear friends. I hope that Gideon will be in agreement with our plan.'

'Of course he will. We all consider you and your family as our own. Come eat up, or you will offend my good wife,' said Avi, passing Makoud a plate of salted fish.

Dirar stared at his father in astonishment. Garnata? That was miles away and nowhere near the sea. What on earth was he supposed to do there?

'There's no point looking like that, Dirar. I don't like it anymore than you do, but it's for the best. It's only a matter of time before your name is mentioned and the guards will be knocking on our door. This way you will be safe,' his father said.

Dirar looked across the table at his mother; she continued to weep silently into a large white handkerchief.

'Basma, if you can't control yourself, please go to your room. Can't you all understand the danger that Dirar has put himself in? And maybe us too. If they find out that Umar bribed the soldiers to release him, he will be thrown into gaol as well,' said his father. Dirar couldn't make out if his father was angry or sad, but he certainly wasn't happy with the situation.

'Baba, what will I do in Garnata? I will be miles away from my family and friends. How will I live?'

'Don't be ridiculous, lad. I've told you. You will stay with Gideon and his family and he will give you work in his warehouse.'

'What sort of work? I don't know how to do anything else but fish.'

'How do I know what work he'll give you? But I'm sure it won't be beyond your capabilities. Stop making such a fuss and finish your food. Then go and pack. You're leaving tonight. Umar is going with you. He'll be here at sunset.'

When his father said that there was a renewed burst of weeping from his mother and Abal. Even Salma and Layla were subdued. There was no point complaining; it was obvious that Baba had made up his mind.

Dirar wiped the last of the fish tagine off the plate with the remnants of his bread.

'I don't suppose they eat fish in Garnata,' he said, sadly.

'Of course they do. They have rivers and lakes. There'll be lots of fish,' said Layla. 'You'll love it there. It'll be an adventure. I didn't want to come here, to Malaqah, but Mama insisted. Now I'm glad we came. I'm happy here. I have new friends.'

'That's not the same. You have your family here. I'm going alone. And besides that, I'll be staying in a Jewish family. How's that going to work? What if there's no mosque? What if I don't meet any Muslims? Maybe I won't be able to eat the food.'

'Then you'll have to starve,' snapped his father. 'I've had enough of this. Go and pack. I expect your mother will make up some food for you to take with you, if she stops crying long enough to do it.'

Basma leapt to her feet and hurried out onto the patio, but not before Dirar saw her glare at her husband. Poor Baba, he was trying to do the best for his family but this time he seemed to be on his own.

CHAPTER 12

Jamila had never been on a ship before; she had never left the city of her birth, Malaqah. Although she was nervous at the journey ahead of her, she was also excited, much more excited than she had ever imagined she could be. It was an adventure, the first adventure she had had in the fifteen years of her young life. As she stood in the prow of the ship, with the wind whipping her hair free of her scarf, she was exhilarated. The cold spray from the sea sharpened her senses: she became aware of the motion of the waves and felt her body sway and move with them; her ears were filled with the screeches of seagulls calling to each other; the glitter of the sun on the water dazzled her as she watched the dolphins racing ahead of them, as though leading them to their destination. As the ship continued to plough its way through the waves and out of the harbour, the haze on the horizon gradually gave way to the dark shapes of distant mountains. They turned south-west to follow the coast, the brown sails dipping and catching the wind. Never had she realised that she lived in such a beautiful and fertile country; it was as though she had been living in a golden prison, cut off from all that surrounded her. All she knew was a life inside the zenana, comfortable, luxurious and safe, but not exciting. She licked her lips and delighted in the saltiness of them. She wanted to stretch out her arms and let the wind fill her djellaba as though it were a sail, and take her up into its arms.

'Sayyida, you will get cold. Why don't you come and sit with us, out of the wind,' said her maid.

'Come and join me, Afra. It's wonderful up here,' she replied, turning to her and feeling the wind catch her off-balance. She laughed and clutched at the spar.

'Sayyida, please get down. You will have an accident.'

Her maid was almost in tears. Poor woman, it would be her who would be punished if Jamila hurt herself. Reluctantly, she backed down from the prow and joined the other women who were sitting huddled under a tarpaulin.

When Hasan had suggested she visit her brothers in al-Jazira she had been apprehensive, unsure of his motives, and remembering her mother's advice—*'Love and obey your husband, child, but never trust him completely. He is a man and men look at the world differently from us women'*—she had been concerned. Now those doubts were forgotten in her longing to see her brothers again.

Muhammad, the oldest one in the family, had been made the ruler of al-Jazira on the death of her uncle, Hasan's father. It had been a long time since she'd seen him. She had heard he was married now and had children of his own, her nieces and nephews; it would be wonderful to see his family, her family too. But most of all she longed to see her younger brother. She had been so happy when the grand vizier said Yahya was to become the next khalifa. She had never imagined that it would ever happen; their father always talked about honouring his brother's wishes and that meant giving the throne to Hasan, not Yahya. But then that old grand vizier stepped in and made him Khalifa. She'd been so excited, but before Yahya could be crowned, her cousin Hasan arrived and reminded them that he was the true heir to the throne. Her brother, who had always hated confrontation, simply backed down and agreed to everything Hasan demanded. She wanted to tell him he would regret his decision, that he should put up a fight, but she knew he wouldn't listen. For him this was a way of getting out of the responsibility of being his father's son; he'd never believed he could live up to Baba's expectations. She could understand that —Baba was a hard man to please—but why did Yahya have to give her to Hasan as a wife? She supposed she ought to feel grateful that her brother had thought of securing her future in that way, but she didn't. 'Wife of the khalifa of Malaqah, what more could any woman want?' she could hear her mother's voice saying. But she wasn't any woman; she had been brought up to be an independent thinker and she wanted to choose her own husband. Besides which she wasn't ready to marry; she hadn't even finished her education. If Baba had been alive he would have asked her for her opinion, and if she'd told him she didn't want to marry Hasan, then he would have offered him one of his other daughters. Baba always listened to her. Once he said that it was a shame that she wasn't a boy, that she had more courage than either of her brothers. She had never forgotten that.

'Are you cold, Sayyida?' asked her maid. 'We will be there soon.'

'No, not cold, just excited to be seeing al-Jazira for the first time,' she said, but nevertheless pulled her djellaba tighter around her.

When Jamila arrived at the alcázar, she was immediately ushered into the Sultan's private quarters, less luxurious than in Malaqah, but richly furnished nonetheless.

'As-salama alaykum, dear sister,' said Muhammad, folding her in his arms and hugging her. 'Welcome to my home. It is so lovely to see you.' Her older brother seemed very happy that she was there. 'And you've grown into a woman,' he said, smiling broadly at her. 'Our little Jamila is a married woman already.'

'Yes, dear sister, it is good to see you, although I am very surprised that your husband has allowed you to travel on your own,' said Yayha, taking her hands in his and kissing them. 'Are you well?'

'I'm fine, brother. And no, I'm not pregnant, if that is what you are really asking? Not yet,' said Jamila, bursting with happiness at seeing them again.

'Well I expect Hasan will soon see to that,' said Muhammad. 'I hear he wants to have many sons.'

'Insha'Allah,' Jamila said, blushing at her brother's boldness.

'You look a bit dishevelled, little sister. Did you have a good voyage?' asked Yahya.

'Wonderful. I have never experienced anything like it. Why didn't you tell me that the Middle Sea was such a beautiful place? And now I'm starving.'

Both brothers burst out laughing. 'You haven't changed, Jamila. Still a wild one at heart,' said Muhammad. 'Come, let me introduce you to my wife and children. And tonight, we will all eat together.'

Muhammad knew that Hasan had been angry when Idris had bypassed him and his brother, and had given al-Jazira to Muhammad, but he had never challenged it. So it had been a surprise when his cousin had come to negotiate with him over Malaqah which had passed to his brother Yahya on their father's death. Muhammad was not a greedy man, nor did he crave power; he was happy with what he had, a peaceful but prosperous taifa, so he had been happy to concede that Hasan was the legal heir to the throne in return for peace and quiet. It had been a relief when his brother Yahya had arrived in al-Jazira, unharmed and apparently content with the outcome. His brother was still very young and not a natural leader;

Muhammad had often thought that Jamila had more leadership skills than their young brother. And now she was here in al-Jazira as well. He should be feeling happy about that, but somehow it didn't feel quite right. His own wife was from Ronda, but he would never consider allowing her to travel back there to visit her family, certainly not without him. It was far too dangerous. The wife of the khalifa of Malaqah travelling without her husband; it was unheard of. So many things could happen. She could have been kidnapped. She could have been attacked and robbed. What was Hasan thinking of? His brother-in-law didn't seem to be a stupid man, nor a careless one; he would have known the dangers. So why had the khalifa sent his wife here, to the court in al-Jazira? What was he up to?

'Muhammad, where is your sister?' asked his wife, as he entered the zenana. 'I am longing to meet her.'

'She will meet us at dinner. The children may eat with us tonight, so make sure they are dressed and ready. I'm sure I saw little Muhammad chasing a dog around the courtyard. Tell him his aunt is here and wants to meet him.'

'What is she like, your sister?' asked his wife.

He shrugged.

'She's my sister. What can I tell you? It's a few years since I've seen her; she was still a child when I became Sultan. She's married now.'

'Has she changed much?'

He smiled, 'Not really. She was always a lively child and I don't think that has changed, not yet anyway. Mind you, now she's the wife of the khalifa she will have to settle down and behave in a more decorous manner. She will have standards to set and maintain. Like you, my dear.'

The evening meal was a happy affair; first they were entertained by a troop of musicians, who sang in unison while one played the oud and another a small tambor. Jamila tapped her feet to the music; how lovely it was to be there with her family again. They sat around a long, low table covered with green, embossed leather and once the servants entered with the food, Muhammad signalled for the musicians to stop.

Jamila sat opposite her brothers, and her nieces and nephew sat next to her. They were not usually allowed to join the adults for their dinner, as Muhammad always insisted they go to bed straight after the evening prayers, but tonight was an exception and they were making the most of it. The girls were wearing their best dresses and had jewelled combs in their hair and pearl necklaces around their necks. They tried to behave like young ladies, but the excitement was too much for them and soon they were giggling and joking with their young brother, who could barely sit still for more than two minutes at a time.

'Your children are delightful,' Jamila said to her sister-in-law. 'I hope I have such lovely children one day.'

'I'm sure you will. You haven't been married long, have you? A few months? Too soon to be having a child.'

'I agree. Beside which, I'm not ready to have children yet, although I know my husband is anxious for an heir as soon as possible.'

The servants removed the soup bowls and then brought in a platter of fresh tuna and served each one in turn. This was followed by a mixture of spicy vegetables sprinkled with sautéd almonds and, lastly, a rich, creamy sauce.

'My favourite,' said Yahya, helping himself to a large portion of the sauce. 'I haven't had this since I was in Malaqah.'

'The Sayyida's servant said you liked this sauce. The head cook hopes you enjoy it,' said the servant.

'How thoughtful. Well, isn't this nice, having all the family together again.' He put another spoonful of sauce on his plate and handed the jug back to the servant.

'It is, brother. I feel like a child again, with my two big brothers to look after me,' said Jamila, with a giggle. 'I do miss you both, now that you too are living in al-Jazira.'

'You have Sara and Fazila to keep you company,' said Yahya.

'They are just children and spend all their time in the zenana. I might as well not have any sisters for all the company they are.'

'Well, you can stay here as long as you want,' said her sister-in-law, squeezing her arm, affectionately.

'If your husband permits it,' said Muhammad. 'But I doubt that he will.'

'Sauce, Your Majesty?' asked the servant.

Muhammad took the jug and peered in it.

'It's excellent,' said Yahya. 'You should try it, brother.'

Muhammad wrinkled his nose and said, 'It smells a bit odd to me.' He handed the jug back to the servant.

'I'm not keen on it, either,' said Jamila. 'Hasan loves it. Especially with roast kid.'

'Excuse me, I'm not feeling very well,' said Yayha, struggling to his feet. 'I'll …' He groaned and slid to the floor, clutching his throat.

'Yayha, what is it?' Jamila cried. 'What's the matter?'

Her sister-in-law began to scream. Jamila stared at the body of her brother writhing on the floor. She couldn't move; fear had taken all her strength. Her brother was struggling to breathe and she could do nothing.

Instantly Muhammad was by his side, lifting him up, trying to help him. 'Get the physician and hurry,' he shouted to Uday, who was standing in the doorway. 'Jamila, open the windows; give him some air. He can't breathe.'

Together they tried to help their brother to the open window, but Yahya was unable to stand.

'He can't move his legs. What's wrong with him? Why can't he move? Is he paralysed? Muhammad, what can we do?' Jamila cried.

Her sister-in-law had taken the crying children out of the room, and now she and Muhammad were alone, watching their brother lying on the floor, gasping for air.

'I can't understand what's happened,' she whimpered. 'He was fine just a moment ago. Why is he like this? Why can't he move? Has he been ill?' she asked, looking accusingly at her other brother.

He continued to stare at Yahya. 'No, he was very healthy.'

She could see from the resignation on Muhammad's face that Yahya was going to die. Then the tears began to flow. She couldn't control them; they ran down her cheeks soaking her djubbah. She could hear a howling sound and realised it was coming from her; she couldn't stop herself. Her dear, kind, gentle brother was dying and they could do nothing to help him.

'Where is that bloody physician?' Muhammad shouted. 'Where is he?'

'Your Majesty, I'm here. Please step back so I can see the patient,' said a rather out of breath man, his djubbah dishevelled as though he'd just got out of bed. He carefully pulled Yahya's mouth open and examined his throat.

Yahya was lying quietly now. The gasping had stopped. He no longer writhed in agony; he lay still.

The physician laid his hand on Yahya's face and closed his eyes. 'I'm sorry, Your Majesty, but your brother is dead. There was no hope. There was nothing I could have done for him. The poison was too strong.'

'Poison?' Jamila screamed. 'They have poisoned our brother?'

'Yes, and by the musty smell, I'd say it was hemlock.'

Muhammad knelt beside Yahya and held his body in his arms. 'Who has done this to you, dear brother? Who has taken away your life, your future, your dreams?' He rocked him back and forth, like a baby and all the time, the tears flowed down his face.

CHAPTER 13

Simon watched his wife bending over the tiny robe she was sewing for their grandchild; Zara had given birth to a baby boy, just two weeks after they arrived in Malaqah. It was their first grandchild and Salma had been beside herself with joy. To his surprise, he too had fallen in love with the tiny child from the first moment he held him in his arms. Salma had been sewing and crocheting tiny clothes for him for months. She bit her lip in concentration, just as she did when she was decorating one of the books, as she embroidered tiny yellow flowers around the neckline, each one a minuscule gem of golden thread. She was so absorbed in her work she didn't see the sadness in his smile as he gazed at her bowed head; she was so talented. Talented and lovely, despite the grey hairs that were appearing in her long, black hair. How lucky he was to have her as his wife. He didn't know what he'd do if he lost her. A sudden chill ran through him as he thought about the risk he was taking; he could lose everything if anyone found out about his visits to the Christian church. He stifled a sigh; they would never understand how hard it had been to reconcile his deep-seated faith with his love for a Muslim woman. He had tried to turn his back on the Church, but in the end it had pulled him back into its fold. When they had escaped from Qurtubah he had planned to follow his abbot's orders and return to England, but he couldn't leave her. His conscience didn't trouble him when he told them he would go with them to Ardales; he knew God would not condemn him for choosing between the celibate life of the cloisters and the life of an ordinary man, the chance to be a father and a husband. But what he hadn't realised was that God was a jealous god; he would not forgive him for abandoning the Church and turning to Islam. For years he had struggled with trying to meld his love of God with his love for Salma.

At first she didn't know about the visits. She knew he prayed to a Christian God in secret, but not the rest. When she'd found out she was angry with him; as much because he'd kept it hidden from her, as the fact that his actions were putting them all in danger.

'What is it, husband?' she asked, looking up from her sewing and squinting at him in the flickering light.

'Nothing. I was wondering what the khalifa said when you went to see him this morning. You have spoken very little about it.'

'Well, there's not much to say. He liked my work. He said he would like me to copy some poems for him.'

'You're too modest, my dear. You do realise what an honour it is to have the khalifa himself make a request for your work?'

She nodded. 'I would feel happier about all this attention, if it weren't for Marwen. He watches me all day long. I know he's just waiting for me to make a mistake.'

'You're imagining it. Why would he be interested in you? Or me for that matter? You heard what Yusuf said; they need more scribes. And they are lucky to have one as talented and experienced as you. Come, put away that sewing; you can hardly see in this light. You should save your eyes for your work.'

'You're right, as usual, dear husband. Tomorrow I am to start work on a poem by the Jewish poet, Solomon ibn Gabirol. He is a very accomplished young man. He was only sixteen when he wrote his first poem, "I am the Master and Song is my Slave."

That's the one the khalifa wants me to inscribe. I have a wonderful idea for illustrating it.'

Salma's face shone with enthusiasm; her doubts and fears seemed to have faded into the growing shadows, banished by her excitement over this new task.

'I have heard of his name, and his reputation, but I have to admit, I don't know his poems,' said Simon.

'But you might know of his great work of philosophy, "The Fountain of Life." It is a profound work for someone so young.'

Simon shook his head. Sometimes his wife's knowledge made him feel inadequate. He would seek out this young poet, and see for himself how good he was. 'A Jew, you say?' he asked. 'From Garnata?'

'A Jew, yes, but born here in Malaqah. That's why the khalifa wants to be his patron.'

'You had a long chat with the khalifa, then?'

'I listened. One doesn't chat with the Supreme Commander,' she said, laughing. 'One listens and nods their agreement.'

'Do you really think Marwen is watching you?' Simon asked. The man was no friend to either of them. What if he was watching Simon as well?

'It's probably my imagination. It's just that he's so unfriendly. Everyone else here has welcomed us, but not him.' She explained her suspicions over the missing ink.

'He's probably like that with everyone,' said Simon.

Suddenly Salma took his hand and whispered, 'You will be careful, won't you Simon.'

He stared at her. So she knew. He felt the heat rising up his neck and knew she had caught him out. 'What do you mean?' he blustered. 'I'm always careful.'

'I think it would be better if you didn't make any more visits for a while,' she whispered. 'Just for a while, until Marwen has lost interest in us. This isn't sleepy Ardales, you know: it will be much harder to keep your secret.'

He forced himself to smile and said, 'Don't worry, Salma. Nothing will happen. Now, let's get some sleep. We need to be up early, tomorrow.'

But Simon couldn't sleep. He lay on his mat, beside his wife and listened to the gentle rumblings of her tiny snores. He hadn't meant to deceive her; he hadn't meant to deceive anyone but he had no choice. He had been trying to keep her safe. The only way they could be together as man and wife was if he became a Muslim and married her. So that was what he had done; she'd been so happy when he told her. And Makoud, he'd been delighted with the news. All the family rejoiced that Salma would at last become a married woman and the gossips in Ardales would be silenced. But it wasn't as easy as he had thought; he had felt such a hypocrite when he went to the mosque every Friday with the other men in the family, and he knew that the only way he could cleanse his soul of this sin was to pray for God's forgiveness. So he started to slip away to join the Christians for their Sunday mass. They lived in the ruins of Babastro, outside the walls of the town, where they had their own church, so nobody was aware of his duplicity. Simon went in disguise and at first he told nobody, not even Salma. The Christians were breaking no laws; they were free to worship in their own way and had been for years. It was only Simon who was breaking both God's law and the law of men.

But it became hard to hide his actions from Salma, and although she wasn't happy about it, she didn't try to stop him; she knew how much his faith meant to him. It was only when they decided to move to Malaqah that she made him promise that he would no longer go to a Christian church. She said it was too dangerous, for him and the rest of the family. He had given her his word and now he'd broken it.

By chance the poet that Salma had spoken about came into the library to see Yusuf, the chief librarian, the next day. He was a tall, young man with a very serious demeanour for one who had not completed his twentieth birthday. Yusuf was obviously delighted to see him and introduced him to all the scribes and copyists; his family as he referred to them.

'And this is our new scribe, Salma,' he said, stopping by Salma's desk. 'She used to work in one of the great libraries of Qurtubah. And her husband, Simon. He is our new translator.'

'Indeed. Aleichem shalom, my friends.'

'As-salama alaykum,' said Simon, grasping his hands in his own. 'My wife has been telling me about your poetry; she is a great admirer of your work.'

'And I have heard good things about hers. I am looking forward to seeing how she will illustrate the book for the khalifa.'

Simon thought he saw a blush of pleasure creep up Salma's cheeks.

'Well I will leave you to talk; I have a fresh manuscript to translate into Latin. Not poetry I'm afraid, a treatise on the workings of the blood. I am not familiar with much poetry, other than the works of Homer.'

'Ah, the Greeks? What could be better? Who will write an Iliad these days?'

'Is that your ambition? To write an epic poem?' asked Simon.

'I think it probably is. How wonderful to write something that will be remembered for centuries to come. Who would not want to do that?'

Simon smiled at him. He was so young and enthusiastic.

'Maybe later, when you have finished your work, we could drink some tea together,' the poet suggested. 'We can talk about Homer and how easy it is to translate into Arabic.'

'I like the idea of the tea. And maybe you can kindle a love of poetry in me at the same time; my wife considers me a Philistine when it comes to verse.'

'I'm sure that's not true. I'll meet you in the tea house, just before sunset. I find that a most relaxing way to end the day.'

'Very well. Now, I must do some work,' said Simon. He could feel Marwen's eyes burning into his back. He bowed slightly and moved across to his own corner of the library; he needed somewhere quiet to concentrate,

No sooner had Simon and Salma arrived at Makoud's house that evening when Zara rushed out to greet them.

'As-salama alaykum, Mama, Baba. I have some news to tell you,' she said. 'Iqbal has found an alfarería to buy.'

'Good news indeed. Come inside and tell us all about it,' said Simon, kissing his daughter and her tiny son.

'Yes he's there now. The alfarero has died and he had no sons to take it over, so his widow has sold it. Iqbal is very happy about it,' Zara said, relinquishing the baby to Salma's open arms.

'And you? Are you happy? Salma asked.

'Of course. It's what my husband wants. As he is always telling me, he didn't walk all the way to Malaqah to sit about in Makoud's house doing nothing all day.'

'Well I'm very happy for you, said Salma, burying her face in the soft belly of her grandson to make him laugh.

'Yes a man needs to work,' added Simon.

'There's another thing,' Zara said. 'We are going to live there; there are two rooms adjacent to the alfarería, and room to build more when we need them.'

'That's wonderful. Your own home. Iqbal has done well,' said Simon.

Salma hoisted the baby onto her shoulder. Her daughter didn't seem as happy as she should at the prospect of having her own place. 'What is it Zara? It is wonderful news isn't it?' Iqbal and Zara had lived with Iqbal's family during the first year of their marriage, in a tiny room and sharing the house with his five brothers and their wives. Her daughter ought to be happy to have a home of her own at last, but she didn't look it.

'Of course it is Mama, but I will miss you and Baba and Layla.'

'Don't be silly. You'll be too busy running the house to have time to miss us. And we'll come and see you. You don't think I'd stay away for very long from this little charmer.' The baby had caught hold of her scarf and was chewing it happily.

'Yes, there's nothing to worry about, dear child,' said Simon. 'You'll soon get used to running your own home, although I'm not sure how Iqbal will enjoy your cooking.' He smiled at her; like her mother, Zara's cooking had never been her strong point.

Salma knew he was only joking with their daughter but Zara burst into tears and ran from the room. 'Oh dear, what have I done now?' said Simon.

'You've upset her, that's what you've done. Don't worry; she's probably just anxious about how she'll cope on her own. Once she's got used to the idea, she'll feel better.'

'Maybe you should go and stay with her for a few weeks, until she settles in,' suggested Simon.

'How can I do that? I'll be at the library every day.'

'Well send Layla. She's not started at the university yet. She can go.'

'Yes, I'll talk to them. That sounds an excellent solution.'

Salma found Zara in the bedroom with Layla, the two sisters curled up on their sleeping mats together, just like they used to when they were small.

'Zara, I know you're anxious about running a house on your own, and I know Iqbal can be quite demanding, but every young bride has these fears. In a year's time you'll look back and wonder why you were so worried.'

Zara sat up and wiped the tears from her face. 'Yes, Mama.'

'I thought it might help you if Layla stayed with you for a while. She could help you with the baby and,' she hesitated, 'and she could give you some advice on which meals to make for Iqbal, you know, simple dishes that are unlikely to go wrong.'

'Me?' said Layla, sitting up and glaring at her mother. 'Why me? I'm going to university. Why not you?'

'It's only for a short time; it won't make any difference to you and you could be a real help to your sister.' She ignored the suggestion that it should be her helping her daughter.

'Well, if you had taught her to cook properly in the first place, Mama, she wouldn't be so worried,' snapped Layla.

At this Salma laughed. She had no illusions about her own standard of cooking, and it had been a family joke for many years. There was no denying it; she was a terrible cook.

'It doesn't matter, Mama. Iqbal wouldn't allow it anyway. He keeps telling me how wonderful it will be when there are just the three of us.'

'But it would only be for a few weeks, just until you are settled. He can't object to that. I'll tell him when he gets home.'

'No. No Mama, please don't mention it. He's in a good mood at the moment, please don't upset him. Please Mama.' She turned to her sister and added, 'You don't have to come Layla; I'll be fine. Please don't worry about me. I was just being silly. I'm overtired. Honestly, I'll be fine on my own.'

Salma stared at her daughter. Was she imagining it or was Zara frightened? 'Very well, if you're sure you'll manage we will leave you to it, but you won't object to me calling in to see how you are getting on, I hope?'

'Of course not, Mama. You will always be welcome in my home. Always. Now I should wash my face and see to the baby before Iqbal gets back.'

'I'll see to the little one. You get yourself cleaned up. And Layla, go and help Basma with the evening meal. At least she will be pleased to have two less to cook for. I don't know how she does it, cooking for such a big family,' said Salma, with just a hint of envy in her voice. She watched her daughter as she filled a bowl with water and began to soap her face and hands. Something was not right. She would need to keep an eye on her.

CHAPTER 14

Fatima walked outside onto the terrace that overlooked the harbour. The rising sun had turned the distant mountains of al-Andalus a dozen shades of pink and the morning air was so clear it seemed as though all she had to do was reach out her hand and touch them. Al-Andalus, so close and yet so far. She wiped the tears from her eyes. This longing to see her youngest son was so strong she felt it would devour her; even her earlier bitterness about her own treatment had waned in the light of what had happened to Ben-Yahya.

When Naja had brought her the news that the young prince had been arrested, she had been so angry that it was all he could do to stop her from rushing down to the port and getting on the first ship to Malaqah. As usual he was right; such an action would serve no purpose and would probably mean that she too would end up in gaol. The only way to rescue Ben-Yahya was by outwitting her older son. They needed a plan and they needed to approach it carefully, and without alerting the khalifa or his ministers. In her heart she didn't think Hasan was capable of making his brother 'disappear' as Naja had euphemistically put it, but she was not going to risk it. Naja had promised to do all he could to rescue Ben-Yahya and at the moment, her only alternative was to trust him. She prayed to Allah that her trust was not misplaced.

It was months since Naja had fled from Malaqah, leaving his young master languishing in gaol. He knew he had to do something soon; every day the boy's mother sent for him and each time he had nothing to tell her. While Hasan was the khalifa it was impossible to rescue Ben-Yahya. The dungeons of the alcazaba were impregnable; he would need to mount a full-scale attack on the alcazaba and how could he do that with no army? He had to find some other way of reaching Ben-Yahya. Or some way of persuading the khalifa to release him.

'Sayyad, there is someone to see you,' said Qusay. 'Shall I show him in?'

'Who is it?'

'He didn't give his name, but he said you would want to see him.'

'What does he look like?'

The servant shrugged. 'Like most people here. A Berber. But an old man with a white beard. I don't think I've ever seen him before.'

'Oh, very well. Show him in, but tell the guards to remain stationed at the door.'

'Yes, sayyad.'

The young slave bowed and hurried out of the room. Moments later he returned, followed by a man shrouded in a long djellaba, its hood covering his head. He waited until Qusay had left and then removed the hood.

'As-salama alaykum, Naja. It's been a while since we last met.'

'Ibn Baqanna. May Allah defend me. I never expected to see you again. I thought you were going as far away from al-Andalus as was humanly possible?'

'That was my intention, but in the end my heart got the better of me. I am an old man. Why would I want to end my days in exile? I decided to retire to Ronda and have been living there incognito, peacefully tutoring the local boys in mathematics.'

Naja stared at him. In his wildest dreams he never thought he would see his old ally again. When Hasan had asked him to get rid of the grand vizier, he had warned the old man that he should disappear or he would be forced to kill him. Ibn Baqanna hadn't needed to be told twice. He'd thanked him and promised Naja would never see him again. Now here he was. If Hasan learned that his former grand vizier was still alive and that Naja had disobeyed him, he would be in even more danger.

He looked around the room; as requested two guards stood at the doorway. He walked across to them and said, 'You do not need to stay. Go back to your posts.'

Once they had left, he closed the heavy wooden door and turned to ibn Baqanna. 'Come, sit down and tell me why you have come here to Sebta. You must realise that you could be recognised. There are many people here who know you, and who know that you're supposed to be dead.'

'If they think I'm dead then they won't be looking for me. If anyone asks, I'm an old man on my way to Mecca.'

'You're doing the Hajj?' Naja asked, rather surprised, as he had never found ibn Baqanna a very religious man.

'Is that so surprising? Every man wants to make the Hajj before they die, don't they?'

'But not you?'

'Maybe you're right. But it is a good disguise, don't you agree?' He smiled.

'So why are you really here?'

'I have some news that I think you will find interesting.' He paused and when Naja remained silent, he continued, 'The khalifa's brother-in-law is dead. Murdered.'

'Yahya? Jamila's brother?' Naja stopped; for once he didn't know what to say. 'Dead?' He was stunned. Who would kill that boy? He'd given up his throne peacefully and asked for nothing in return. Was Hasan insane enough to be behind it? Did the khalifa see threats from every quarter now? 'Murdered?'

'Yes. What's the matter with you? Has your brain turned to soap since you returned to Sebta?'

Naja scowled at him and snapped, 'How do you know? You've been stuck up in that backwater, Ronda.'

'We get plenty of news up there; it's not the backwater you think it is. There's a continuous stream of merchants and travellers passing through the town. Poisoned in his own home, they said.'

'So? What's it got to do with me?'

Ibn Baqanna sighed and said slowly, as though he were speaking to one of his mathematics pupils, 'He died while his sister was visiting him. Hasan had sent her and his old servant, Uday—the one who never leaves his side—to visit Yahya. A strange thing to do, don't you think? Send your wife to al-Jazira to visit her brother, without you? I can't think of any man who would do such a thing, never mind a khalifa.'

'You think Hasan had him murdered? But why would he? If he was going to kill Yahya he would have done it when he took over the throne.'

'Because he's paranoid. I hear that he has locked up Ben-Yahya. He obviously believes his brother wants the throne, and maybe he also fears his brother-in-law wants to take it back.'

'It's a shame. Yahya was a nice young man, and harmless, but I still don't understand why you think I would be interested.'

'Well before I answer that, tell me one thing. Do you have a plan to rescue Prince Ben-Yahya?'

Naja glared at him again. It had always been like this; ibn Baqanna enjoyed treating him like an idiot. Well, one of these days he'd show him that he couldn't dismiss him quite so easily. But for now, he'd play along with the old man.

'No, I don't have a plan, but I'm working on it.'

'I think you'd agree that the only way to get Ben-Yahya out of gaol is for Hasan to give the order to release him?'

'That's obvious.'

'What's also obvious, is that he's never going to do that. It's likely that Ben-Yahya didn't have any intention of taking the throne from Hasan, but after even a few days in that hell hole, it's also likely that he's changed his mind. I know I'd be wanting revenge, if I were him. So the chances of Hasan releasing him are nil.'

'I'd already worked that out,' said Naja, irritably.

'But, if he were dead, then Ben-Yahya would automatically inherit the throne.'

'If who were dead? Hasan?'

'Which is what will happen when his wife learns that it was him who murdered her brother.'

Naja stared at him in astonishment. It was brilliant. He'd heard that Jamila was a passionate woman, with a fiery temper, but was she capable of murdering her own husband in revenge? She would have the opportunity and the motive. But could she do it? 'So why do you need me?' he asked.

'I can hardly go to Malaqah, can I? As you so astutely pointed out, I'm supposed to be dead. Someone needs to be close enough to make sure that Ben-Yahya is released and crowned Khalifa,' explained ibn Baqanna. 'That is you. As soon as you hear of Hasan's death, then you must make your move.'

'It is an excellent plan, my friend. Even if Jamila doesn't murder her husband in a passionate rage, we can make it look as though she did. There is only one question in my mind.'

'Yes, and what is that?' asked ibn Baqanna.

'Why are you doing this? What is in it for you? You're supposed to be dead.'

'And I can tell you, that being dead is very boring. And so is teaching mathematics to boys who would sooner be galloping around the countryside looking for wives, but I have to make a living. I miss the mental stimulus of being at court, the challenges, the intrigues. I hope that Ben-Yahya will realise that I have always had his interests at heart and will reinstate me as grand vizier. A small price to pay for securing his release.'

'But it was you who stopped him and his brother from inheriting the throne in the first place. It was you who insisted that their uncle Idris should be Khalifa. I don't think Ben-Yahya will have forgotten that, even though he was a young boy at the time. His mother will have made sure of it.'

'Maybe. But I think he will be so pleased to be free that he will realise that he needs someone like me who can manipulate the wheels of power and make things happen.'

'By that I suppose you mean, lie, murder and betray?'

'You are not so lily-white yourself, Naja. Don't forget that. So, are you in agreement? All you have to do is be in Malaqah at the right time. I will make sure that Jamila gets to know the truth. Then we will see what happens next.'

'I have another idea. It's very likely that Jamila is still in al-Jazira. You're not known there. You could call and see her on your way back to Ronda and tell her how her husband has betrayed her.'

'As long as she doesn't decide to take it out on the messenger.'

'She won't do that. Her rage will be stored up for her husband. It will give her time to plan her revenge.'

'Very well. But you need to be close by when it happens. You will be the one to remind the people that Ben-Yahya is in prison. That he is the heir to the throne. Once men go through those gates they are soon forgotten. It will be up to you to remind them.'

'Why so solicitous about our prince?'

Ibn Baqanna shrugged his shoulders and said, 'A change of heart, perhaps.'

CHAPTER 15

Salma could still feel the warmth of the praise that Yusuf had bestowed on her. He was delighted with her work, and even more so because of the khalifa's pleasure. She had an exciting new project, copying and illustrating the poems of Solomon ibn Gabril, although she had been embarrassed to admit to Yusuf that she had never heard of him before; not unsurprisingly as he was very young and news of such people never reached Ardales. That was one of the reasons for leaving the small town; she had felt stifled there and longed to live somewhere more vibrant and cultural.

It was only a little after daybreak as she walked through the deserted Jewish quarter but she wanted to call in to her daughter's new home, to see how she and the baby were getting on; she was still worried about her. After that she was going to the university where she would meet Solomon.

'Mama. As-Salama alaykum. What a surprise. Are you not working in the library today?' Her daughter asked, opening the door to let her in. She was wearing a black shawl over her head and across her shoulders, like one of the old widow women in the souk, and had the baby strapped to her chest. 'Can I make you some tea?'

'Here, give me the baby,' Salma said, taking him from her daughter, while Zara began bustling about the kitchen. 'What is it child? Why are you wearing your shawl indoors? Are you unwell?'

Zara put down the jarrah and turned to her mother, tears streaming down her face.

'Come here my dearest child. What is the matter? Come, sit here and tell me.' Salma put her arms around her oldest daughter and hugged her. 'I will make the tea and you nurse the little one while you tell me all about it.' She'd been right; something was making Zara unhappy. Or someone. She filled the jarrah with water from the tap and put it to heat on the stove, then said, 'Now tell me Zara, what is wrong?'

Her daughter blew her nose and taking a deep breath said, 'It's Iqbal. He's impossible to live with. He treats me like a slave, and…' she sobbed, 'I'm sure he doesn't love me.'

'Well my dear, not everyone can have love. He's a hardworking husband and he cares for you and your children.' She sighed. Zara was just like Layla, always looking for love in a marriage. It was her own fault; she had brought them up to believe that because she and Simon had, that it was normal to marry for love. In fact it was just the opposite. If you were lucky, love grew gradually over the years, but most women were happy to have a husband who treated them and their children well. To have love was a bonus.

'You don't understand Mama.' Zara pulled off her shawl and lifted her arms; they were covered in bruises.

'He beats you?' Salma asked, astonished at this revelation. 'But why?'

'He's so jealous. He questions me about everyone I speak to.'

'I'm sure he's just concerned about you, my dear.'

'Concerned? Is this a sign of concern?' She stuck her arm in front of Salma's face. The bruise was a livid purple. 'I'm not allowed to leave the house except to go to the souk, and then he insists I cover my hair. He wanted me to cover my face as well, but I said people would stare at me so he relented. I can't even go to the mosque to pray. He's convinced I only want to go out to meet other men. He's even taken to coming home at strange times to check I'm still in the house. It's all so humiliating; he treats me like a slave. I really can't stand much more.'

'Oh my poor girl,' Salma couldn't believe what she was hearing. Surely Iqbal hadn't been like this in Ardales; she never would have taking him for a violent man. Then suddenly she remembered how quick he'd been to defend them when they were attacked, how he struck at the men without any hesitation, and would have left that poor soldier to bleed to death on the ground if she hadn't intervened. The look on his face afterwards was one of satisfaction; whereas the rest of them were in a state of shock because it had all happened so fast. He on the other hand had seemed to thrive on the excitement.

'And now he tells me he's taking a second wife. I know it is just so he will have someone to spy on me. Mama, what can I do?' She began to cry again. 'And I'm pregnant as well.'

'What, so soon?'

'He says we will have so many children that I won't have time to wander; I will be too busy caring for my family.'

'What? He said that?'

'He wants to control me completely. That's why he was in such a hurry to move out of Makoud's house.'

'He can't be jealous of me and your father, that's ridiculous,' Salma said. She was becoming very worried now. This didn't sound like a normal marital spat; Zara could be in real danger. She had seen marriages like this before where the wife was no more than a child-bearing slave to her husband. They never ended well for the woman.

Zara laughed. 'Oh he is. I think sometimes he's even jealous of his own son.'

'My poor child, we must speak to your father about this. In the meantime you must try not to upset him, so he doesn't beat you again.'

Zara looked at her in horror. 'Can't I go home with you and Baba?'

Salma shook her head sadly. 'Not at the moment my dear. Remember we are still living with Makoud; I can't expect him to take you and the baby as well, not when you now have your own home.' At this Zara began to cry again. 'Now there's no need to cry. We will help you I promise. But first I speak to Baba. You know you can't just leave Iqbal; he is your husband and his word is final. But he's a greedy man by nature, so maybe we can return the bride price to him, and he will divorce you.'

'No no, he's already used my dowry to set up the alfarería. I don't have any money left. And even if he divorced me, I know he would keep my son. Oh what am I going to do?'

'Calm down Zara. I will speak to Baba this evening, I promise. You are not alone. We will help you. I promise, my child.'

Simon was furious when Salma told him about Iqbal. Not normally a man of quick temper, this time he grabbed the cudgel that Makoud kept in case of intruders, and headed for the door.

'Simon, wait. We have to think about this. You can't just confront him like that. He's her husband,' his wife said, trying to hold him back. 'He has the law on his side.'

He barely heard her words. The thought of that man, any man, mistreating his lovely daughter made him see red. This was not a time for talking, but action.

By the time he arrived in the northern part of the city, where the smoke from the alfarería's kilns curled into the still air like ghostly spirits, his temper had cooled but his anger still burned inside him.

The smell of burning pinewood filled the air, as Iqbal stacked the next lot of pots next to the kiln, ready to be fired.

'Father-in-law, as-salama alaykum. What brings you here so early in the day?'

'I must speak to you Iqbal, about my daughter,' Simon said, brandishing the cudgel rather menacingly in his face.

'I'm busy now; I have to get these pots fired, today,' Iqbal said, turning his back on him. Simon looked at his son-in-law, and for a split second he was tempted to strike him a heavy blow across his head. It shocked him that he could even think such a thing and he dropped the cudgel on the floor.

'It can't wait Iqbal. My daughter is unhappy. She wants to come home. We want her to come home.'

At these words Iqbal spun round and glared at Simon. 'My wife is already in her home. She is under my protection now,' he spat.

'What protection is that, that leaves her covered in bruises?' asked Simon, his anger rising again.

'What did you say? Are you accusing me of mistreating my wife?' Iqbal's face had grown pale with anger. 'Get out of here and mind your own business.' He stood close to Simon and stared at him.

'It is my business; she is my daughter. I won't stand for you treating her in this way,' said Simon.

His son-in-law was quite a bit shorter than him but muscular and strong. Attack was the only way. Take him by surprise. He closed his fist and punched Iqbal in the face. 'That's for hurting Zara,' he said, gritting his teeth against the pain of the impact. 'And that's for treating her like your slave,' he said, punching him again.

Within seconds they were grappling on the ground, punching and kicking each other. Each time Iqbal got to his feet Simon pulled him down again.

'What is the name of Allah is going on?' shouted one of Iqbal's alfareros. He was a big man, stronger than Iqbal and Simon together. He grabbed Simon and pulled him off his battered son-in-law. 'You'd better have a good explanation for attacking my boss,' the alfarero said, 'or I'm calling the muhtasib.'

Simon pulled himself away from the alfarero and said, 'Ask your boss; he'll explain.' Then he turned to his son-in-law, who is still lying on the ground, and spat at him. 'This isn't over, Iqbal. This isn't over.'

'Should I send for the muhtasib, sayyad?' asked the alfarero.

'No, leave it. Help me up and then clear up this mess. That bastard's cost us a day's work.' He kicked the broken pots and glared after Simon. 'I'll make him pay for this.' He limped over to the fountain and washed his bloody face and hands. 'I'll get rid of you, father-in-law, one way or another. Just you see.'

CHAPTER 16

Pablo sipped slowly at his tepid glass of mint tea, trying to make his stay in the cool tavern last longer before the tavern owner took it upon himself to throw him out. He longed for a pitcher of wine, but to ask for one would draw too much attention to himself. He tugged at his robe, adjusting it across his shoulders with his one remaining arm. How strange that there were days when he could still feel it there, itching and throbbing, heavy against his side. But one look at its ragged stump soon dispelled that idea. The bitterness welled up in his throat; he was no longer a man. The army didn't want him now; they had no use for cripples. Nobody did. He wasn't even any good at thieving, not with his left hand. He chuckled. Today he'd been lucky. An old man had got into an argument with one of the stall holders in the market. He was so busy complaining about the weevils in the rice, that he hadn't noticed when One-arm cut the purse from his belt. One-arm, that's what they called him now. No respect for an old soldier. He'd told everyone he'd lost his arm fighting at Écija but those that had known him before knew it was a lie and the others didn't care. Pablo took another sip of the tea; it was good but not as good as a strong flagon of wine.

'Are you going to sit there all day, One-arm? You're scaring away my customers with your ugly mug. And that smell. Where do you sleep? In with the goats? Come on with you. Drink up and be on your way,' said the owner of the tavern, adding as he turned away, 'May Allah preserve me from filthy wretches such as you.'

Pablo ignored him and took another sip of his tea. Two men came into the tavern and sat down at the next table. One of them looked very familiar. The other was a Jew; he had no time for the Jews. But who was the other man? Maybe he'd take pity on him and give him a few coins.

'If you don't drink up, I'll throw you out on your ear, you wretched cripple,' shouted the barman.

The new arrivals looked up, their gaze falling on One-arm for the first time. 'Give the poor man another glass of tea,' the Jew told the owner. 'He's doing no harm.'

'He's a disreputable wretch; that's what he is,' muttered the owner, but poured some hot mint tea into a glass jar and took it across to One-arm. 'Here. Drink it up and don't be all day about it.'

One-arm didn't bother to reply. He had recognised the man sitting opposite to him. It was one of the group he and Juan had ambushed on that fateful day when he'd lost his arm. He was certain it was the husband of the woman who had saved him from being killed. He was sure of it. If the man recognised One-arm he'd probably call the muhtasib and have him arrested. He gulped down the scalding tea and pulled the hood of his djellaba over his head, then without a word, he left.

'Typical of that one. Not a word of thanks for the tea,' grumbled the owner of the tavern.

'Who is he?' Simon asked.

'Nobody worth bothering your head about.'

The next day was Sunday, so One-arm decided to leave the city and walk over to the church of the dhimmis. There were always a lot of the Christian dhimmis there on a Sunday; it was their special day or something. He'd seen them before, coming out of the heavy church doors, wearing their blue turbans and surreptitiously hiding their crosses under their djellabas before they returned to the city. Some of them were quite generous and if he sat by the entrance, with his djellaba pulled back to expose his missing arm, he'd collect a lot of money. They thought their charity would get them through the gates of Heaven. Just like the Muslims. Didn't they realise that there was nothing beyond this world? Certainly not for him. No amount of charity and good works, no prayers and psalms would get a murderer into heaven.

He settled down and waited. It was strange. They didn't call the faithful to prayer like the Muslims did. There was no imam reminding them where they should be. Well, what did he care as long as some of them came along and took pity on him.

He didn't have long to wait; even without the imam to remind them these dhimmis seemed to know what time they were expected to arrive. Within a short time the small church was overflowing and his begging bowl was full. Suddenly his heart gave a lurch; there was that man again. The woman's husband. What on earth was he doing here? They were Muslims; he was sure of it. He remembered her words to him; she had asked Allah to forgive and protect him. So what was happening here? He bent over his bowl, hiding his face.

'May God bless and keep you,' the man said and dropped a couple of dirhams into the bowl.

As he walked away, One-arm lifted his head and watched him. Yes he was going into the church. He waited a moment until he saw the man cross himself and sit with the others. So he was a Christian. A Christian married to a Muslim woman. Even he knew that was against the law. Interesting. His mind began to race; there was some money to be made here, without a doubt.

One-arm had had a good morning; his begging bowl was full. He would go to a tavern and order a good meal and maybe a flagon of wine to celebrate; and he knew just the place. The food was always hot and spicy there, and he was unlikely to run into the woman's husband again; he didn't want to see him until he had decided what to do. He was still wondering how he could turn this new information to his benefit. There had to be something in it for him; such a secret was worth a few gold dinars, surely. There was one drawback; he didn't know his name or where to find him. All he could do was lie in wait for him next Sunday and accost him as he approached the church. But would that work? One-arm was not exactly a menacing figure these days. If he threatened to expose the man, he might kill him. But was he capable of doing that? He looked more of a scholar than a fighter. It had been the other one, the little dark one who had whipped out his sword and killed poor Juan. He was the one who had turned One-arm into a cripple.

The tavern was full by the time he arrived, so he squeezed onto the end of a long table next to a man with ink-stained fingers. Who was he, he wondered, some sort of scribe. He'd seen him in there before. Solitary type he was, like him, didn't talk much. Well, whoever he was, he looked in a foul mood today and, by the look of the empty jug beside him, had been busy drowning his sorrows with copious glasses of wine.

'Ready for another?' One-arm asked.

The man looked up and scowled. 'What?'

'Another jug of wine?'

'Why not.' He managed what was probably a smile but looked more like a grimace.

One-arm signalled to the tavern owner to bring him some wine and a plate of food. He was known in there, but not for splashing his money about.

'Not looking for scraps today, One-arm? Had some good fortune have you? Find yourself a rich wife to marry?' The tavern owner said laughing.

'Wouldn't you be surprised if I did now,' said One-arm, grabbing the jug of wine and pouring it into two glasses. 'Good health my friend. May I introduce myself, my name is Pablo, but they usually call me One-arm, on account of this.' He thrust his truncated arm out for him to see.

'Peace be upon you, Pablo. I am Marwen.'

'I've seen you in here before,' said Pablo.

'Possibly. I like it here because I can sit and drink without anyone pestering me,' said Marwen taking a swallow of the wine. He seemed disinclined to talk but at last he said, 'So how did you come to lose your arm? A soldier were you?'

'I was once. Until this happened. One evening I was minding my own business when I was attacked by a bunch of foreigners. Didn't stand a chance. They were on me in an instant. Killed my companion out right and left me for dead.' One-arm had told this version of events so often he almost believed it.

'Mmmn,' grunted Marwen. He didn't seem very interested in knowing more, just continued to drink his wine in silence.

One-arm rarely had money to spend on wine and he soon begin to feel it going to his head. He took a mouthful of his supper; it was some spicy concoction of beans and fish.

'That looks disgusting,' spat Marwen, suddenly glaring at the plate. 'I don't know how you can eat that muck.'

'It's tasty and I'm hungry. What other reasons do I need? I suppose you dine on roast kid and the best fish from the sea every night?' He was becoming irritated with this man. He was happy enough to drink his wine—the jug was almost empty already—but he couldn't be bothered to make pleasant conversation. That was what One-arm was in the mood for tonight, some pleasant company, but it looked as though he chosen the wrong man to sit next to.

'I hope you can pay for this One-arm?' said the tavern owner, as he replaced the empty jug with a full one.

'I told you I would surprise you one day,' One-arm said, but the owner has heard it all before and walked away. 'I'll be eating roast kid next time you see me,' he called after him.

'So what is the source of this good fortune, then?' asked Marwen, looking up from his flagon.

'Allah is looking after me,' he replied. 'He has led me to my attackers.'

'What, the men who took your arm?'

He had his attention now. What's more the wine was loosening his tongue. 'Yes.'

'What were they like? Foreigners you said.'

'Well one was a foreigner, a tall man with hair the colour of corn. The others were Berbers, but not from north Africa, from the countryside somewhere.'

Marwen poured himself more wine and stared at One-arm. 'Tell me about him, this foreigner. What did he look like?'

'Like I said, tall and blond. What more can I say? In the name of Allah, do you think I had time to examine him? He was coming at me with a bloody great sword. I only just escaped with my life.' Marwen had a strange expression on his face. 'Why so many questions? Do you know this man? Do you know where he lives?'

Marwen smiled his strange smile; it sent shivers down One-arm's spine. 'I might do. Tell me more about how finding your attackers will bring you great fortune,' said Marwen, pouring some more wine into One-arm's glass.

'I can't tell you, but I do know it's going to make me rich.'

I bet you say that every time you've had a drink,' Marwen said, looking as if he was getting up to leave.

'No, it's true. I know something about him that he will pay handsomely for me to keep quiet.'

'You're planning on blackmailing him? You must be mad. The man almost killed you the first time, how is he going to react to that? You'll end up losing your other arm.'

'So do you know this foreigner or not?' One-arm was getting irritated with him, and besides which he was beginning to feel very drunk.

'He may be someone I know, but before I tell you, I want to understand how you plan to get money from him. What is it that you have found out?'

'He's a Christian. I've seen him make the sign of the cross,' One-arm blurted out.

'A Christian? So what's wrong with that? It's not illegal.'

'Worse than that, he has a Muslim wife. I've seen her.' He stopped suddenly; the vision of the woman bending over him and bandaging his arm came back to him. She had such a sweet smile and she spoke to him softly as though he were a child. The woman had saved him and here he was betraying her. She had asked Allah to protect him.

'I've said enough,' One-arm said standing up and knocking over his half empty flagon. 'Here, barman. This is for you.' He put a handful of small coins on the table and staggered out.

'Don't you want to know where to find him?' called Marwen. 'I know him. I can lead you straight to him.'

One-arm stopped and turned to the man. This was his chance. The husband would pay him without doubt, but now his conscience wouldn't let him do it. He had already said too much. 'Don't listen to me. I'm drunk. Tisbah ala-kheir.' He lifted the curtain and went out into the night.

The moon was waxing; in a few more days it would be full. It followed him as he made his way through the narrow streets to his humble lodgings, and before he went inside, he lifted his face to it and thought he saw her smiling down at him.

Marwen sat staring at the doorway. He was decidedly drunk, but exhilarated. So, Simon was a Christian, a practising Christian. That was very useful information—if he could trust that vagabond to be telling the truth. All he had to do was expose him to the chief librarian and that would be that. Then his life in the library could return to normal. He didn't have anything against Simon in person; he was a good translator and worked well. It was the damned wife he couldn't stand. It wasn't right that she worked alongside the men. Women were supposed to be at home, caring for the family, not giving themselves airs and graces, and behaving as if they were equal to men. Marwen saw it everywhere. It was time the imam spoke out about it. Women lawyers, poets and teachers, they had invaded society; he couldn't understand how their fathers and husbands allowed it. His own daughters, Allah bless and keep them, had never shown any interest in going beyond a basic education. They were all happily married now and were exemplary wives and mothers; he was very proud of them. They were not like the female students at the university, who came into the library showing their ankles and flaunting their beauty as if it were a weapon. None of them wore veils, and some even painted their faces; it was unseemly. All the other scribes in the library were men; that had always been the case until that woman arrived. Now suddenly the chief librarian couldn't praise her enough. Imagine, he'd even taken her to meet the khalifa. What an insult to the rest of them and to him in particular. He had worked as a scribe all his life, but never, never had the chief librarian singled him out for praise, and never invited him to meet the khalifa. The chief librarian was bewitched by her. Well he'd change his mind when he heard that she had broken the law. That's what came of having no father to bring her up, although surely someone in her family could have stopped her marrying an infidel.

He drained the last of the wine from the jug, put his djellaba around his shoulders and slipped out into the night. Tomorrow he would decide what to do; he didn't want to be too precipitous in case it was just a pack of lies. He walked slowly towards his home, head down, lost in his thoughts. Simon had never denied that he was once a Christian monk; that was how he came to be in al-Andalus in the first place. He had converted to Islam, so he said, and now he was a true Muwallad. The question was, was this the truth or was he continuing to worship the Christian God in secret? Had he abandoned Allah? Had he even embraced him in the first place, or was his marriage a sham? But how could Marwen find out? He couldn't go to the head librarian without proof. Maybe that son-in-law of Simon's could tell him more. Only this morning he had heard Salma telling her husband that he must try to make it up with him, for the sake of their daughter. There had obviously been some sort of quarrel between them; Simon's hands had been covered in bruises and there was a nasty cut on his lip when he arrived at work that morning. He knew whom they'd been talking about; he'd seen him with Simon before and recognised him from the tea shop, where he was a regular customer. He seemed a surly man, with his boots always covered in clay. Maybe he'd be in there tonight.

CHAPTER 17

The shop had been quiet all morning, so Makoud decided to make up a new batch of a perfumed cream that his female customers bought in great quantities. He put on his overall and had just started to gather the ingredients together when Ibrahim came in and said, 'Baba. I've been thinking it's time I got married.' Makoud was so surprised he almost dropped the stone mortar on the floor. 'What's that? Am I hearing right? You want to get married?'

'Why so surprised? You've been saying it's about time one of your sons found a wife.'

'And have you? Found a wife?' He couldn't believe that at long last, after all the efforts he'd made to make suitable matches for them, one of them actually wanted to get married.

'Not exactly. I just think it's time I settled down. You will be retiring one day, and I will need someone to help me with the business.'

'So, you haven't met someone you want to marry? Would you like me to speak to the wasit alzaway, to see if she has anyone suitable?' Makoud said, slightly disappointed.

'Not yet. I was wondering, do you think Layla would make a good wife?'

'Layla? Your second cousin?' He knew he was repeating everything Ibrahim was saying, but he was too astonished to think clearly.

'Yes, she's a clever girl and she's very pretty.'

'Well, I really don't know, Ibrahim; she's still very young. I will have to speak to her parents.'

'Do you know if she can cook?' his son asked.

Makoud laughed. 'Well, if she's anything like her mother, then probably not very well.' His son's face dropped. 'But as I said she is still young; she will have lots to learn if she is to be married.' He knew it was too good to be true. Nothing was going to come of this. Layla did nothing but talk about when she was going to the university; he was sure that marriage was the furthest thing from her mind. 'So, son, do you want me to speak to Simon?'

'Yes, Baba. I think Layla will make a good wife. She is intelligent enough to learn all she needs to know.'

'Have you spoken to her yourself? Do you think it would be a good idea to do so, first?'

'No. let's keep it formal, Baba.'

'Very well. I'll speak to them tonight.'

That evening when they had finished their meal and Abal and Basma were busy washing the dishes on the patio, Makoud said to Simon, 'I would like to speak to you. Will you come upstairs and drink some tea with me, where we will be undisturbed?'

Simon looked at him. 'What's this about?'

'I would prefer to talk about it when we're alone.'

'We have no secrets from each other,' said Salma, getting up.

Makoud looked at them in silence for a moment, and then said, 'Well, in that case I might as well tell you that my son, Ibrahim, has asked to marry your daughter.'

Salma couldn't believe her ears. A husband for Layla, this was wonderful news; Ibrahim was a delightful man, with good prospects. He would make an excellent husband for their daughter. She beamed at her husband, 'You hear that Simon? She will be married.'

'Has he spoken to Layla yet?' Simon asked, glancing at Salma. 'You know how she is over such things.' She knew what he was thinking; Layla swore she would only marry for love. How would she react to this news?

'No. But they get on well enough. They'll make a lovely couple.'

'I agree. We would both be very happy if Layla and Ibrahim married. When do we tell them?' asked Simon.

'Let me prepare my wives first and then we will announce it tomorrow, ' said Makoud, a smile as wide as the bridge across the Guadalmedina on his face.

Salma knew they were making a mistake. Her daughter was as stubborn as she was beautiful. She would not be told whom to marry, and she said so, loudly and firmly when a beaming Makoud announced the news to the family.

'How could you agree to this without asking me first, Baba?' she said, flushed with anger, her blue eyes flashing sparks at him.

'Calm down, Layla; have you no consideration for Ibrahim's feelings?' Salma said.

Layla stopped and looked at the embarrassed Ibrahim. 'What about my feelings?' she asked, her rage giving away to tears.

For a moment nobody knew what to say, then Ibrahim moved across to her and said softly, 'Layla, let us talk privately for a moment. Come, put on your djellaba and we'll go for a walk.'

She meekly picked up her cloak and followed him outside.

Once they had gone, Salma turned to her husband and said, 'I told you it was too soon. These things have to be handled carefully, slowly.'

'I agree but this is a wonderful opportunity for her, and I want her to take it.' He smiled sadly at Makoud and added, 'I'm sorry for her outburst, cousin. Please forgive her.'

'Don't worry. Salma is right; we should have spoken to them both before announcing it. My son will not be pleased with me either. Now he will always think she has been forced to marry him.'

'I think it's time we sat down to eat,' said Basma, interrupting them She looked completely baffled by the news. 'The food will be spoiled if we leave it much longer.'

Salma went out to the patio to help her bring in the plates of fried aubergines and a large bowl of rice and mixed vegetables. It smelled delicious, but she had no appetite. What was she going to do about Layla? She understood perfectly how she felt; her independence would be gone once she married. All the dreams she had would come to nothing.

Layla and Ibrahim walked in silence through the deserted streets; this was the hour when everyone was inside their homes eating the evening meal. A cool breeze sprang up from the sea, making her pull her djellaba closer about her.

At last she could stand it no longer and said, 'Well, it was your idea to come out. What do you want to talk about?' Her voice sounded harsh, and instantly she regretted using that tone with her second cousin. She liked Ibrahim, but she had never considered marrying him. She looked at him sideways as they passed under the street lamp; he was a good looking man, a bit serious, but always nice to her.

'Nothing really. I just thought we should get away from them for a bit and let things cool down. You were very forceful in there.'

'I was angry.'

'Are you not angry now?'

'No. I understand my parents are concerned about me. They want me married so that they don't have to worry about me anymore. I suppose that's natural.'

'So why are you so against marrying me? It's normal for our parents to choose whom we marry. Are you in love with someone else?' Ibrahim looked downcast at the idea he was the reason she didn't want to marry.

She hesitated before replying; the image of Umar smiling at her in confusion after asking her if she was looking for a rich husband came back to her. Although she didn't show it, she had been pleased to see him again and to notice the effect she had on him; the tables had turned from when they were children. But Umar was a soldier; everybody said soldiers made poor husbands. 'It's not because it's you,' she said. 'I don't want to marry anyone. I don't feel ready to be married. To be honest with you, I wanted to do something else with my life. That's why we came to Malaqah. I've only just started at the university and now I'm expected to give it all up and get married. It's not fair.' She could hear the whine in her voice. 'They didn't even discuss it with me,' she continued. 'I would have liked to know what they were planning before they announced it to the whole world.'

'Is that the only reason?' he asked.

'Isn't it enough?'

'Well, getting married doesn't mean you have to give up all your dreams,' Ibrahim said. 'It really depends on whom you decide to marry.' She stole another quick glance at him. He seemed perfectly serious. 'I overheard you talking to my brother that day you arrived in Malaqah,' he said. 'You told him you would only marry for love.'

She felt herself blushing. 'I remember.'

'Few people marry for love, Layla. I'm sure my father didn't, but he's happy and so are his wives. The best that most people can hope for is that love grows once they are married.'

'It didn't happen for Zara,' she snapped.

'No, I was sorry to hear that her husband had been ill-treating her. She was very unlucky.'

'Unlucky? Or unwise? She should never have married him. He was always a bully, even long before he asked to marry her.'

'So why did she agree to marry him?'

'She just wanted to be a wife and mother; that was her dream. She wanted children and a home of her own, but I don't expect she realised that she was giving up her freedom to become his slave.'

They had arrived close to the shipyard where Ibrahim's sister lived with her husband. If they walked any further they would be expected to call in and say hello to them. Beyond the shipyard were the city walls and the West Gate; leaving the city would not be a wise move so late in the evening.

'I think we should head back home; your parents will be worrying about you,' said Ibrahim. Layla shivered. A sea mist was drifting across the harbour wall, and winding its way around them.

'Here, take my djellaba,' Ibrahim said, removing his cloak and putting it over her shoulders. 'The air has turned very damp.'

'Thank you,' she murmured, smiling at him. Maybe Ibrahim wouldn't be such a bad choice after all; he was dependable and kind. She could do worse. Layla was a dreamer, but she also had a practical side to her nature, and she knew she would have to marry one day. In her heart it was unlikely she would ever meet the prince of her dreams; all girls dreamed of the ideal husband but most of them were content with someone kind, who would care for them and their children. Perhaps it was better to marry someone like Ibrahim, gentle and loving, and hope that she would grow to love him. But why did it have to be so soon? Why were her parents suddenly so keen for her to find a husband?

CHAPTER 18

Jamila sat in the garden of her brother's palace, listening to one of the royal musicians playing a love song. The plaintive music matched her feelings exactly and seemed to soothe her aching heart. As he sang of his lost love, she thought of her murdered brother; images of him in his death throes still passed before her eyes. Now he was in Paradise; she had no doubt of that. He was a good man, kind and loving. She tried to remember happier times they'd spent together but no sooner had she thought of them when they slipped from her grasp. All that was left for her was his pain and his death. She watched the doves sitting in a pomegranate tree close by, cooing to each other. Everything was about love and loss. A tear trickled down her cheek. One day she must return to Malaqah. Hasan had sent word as soon as he heard the news about Yahya; she was to stay with Muhammad until the period of iddah was over. Maybe by then her anger would have subsided and she could think more clearly. At the moment all she knew was that she didn't want to be with her husband. Not yet.

'Sayyida, there is someone here to see you. He says his name is ibn Baqanna. Do you know him? Or shall I send him away?'

'What does he want?' she asked, signalling for the musician to stop.

'He wouldn't say, but he did suggest that you would be very interested to hear what he had to tell you. He said it was a family matter.'

'Oh, very well. I'll see him inside.'

She stood up and smoothed her white djubbah into place, and pulled the white veil across her face. Who could it be? The name seemed familiar, but she couldn't place it. Someone her husband had sent, perhaps?

An old man with a white beard came into the room; he bowed and came towards her, slowly. His staff tapped rhythmically on the marble floor.

'As-salama alaykum, hajj,' she said. 'You wanted to speak to me?'

A palace guard stood at a discreet distance behind her.

'Wa alaykum e-salam, Sayyida. Yes, I have some news for you, but you may find it distressing. May we speak in private?'

'Has something happened to my husband?' she asked, immediately.

'No, but it does concern your husband. I wouldn't want anyone to overhear our conversation,' he added, looking towards the guards.

Jamila was intrigued. Who was this man and what information did he have about Hasan?

'Very well. Please come and sit with me in the garden.'

She led him outside, away from the guards and out of earshot, and invited him to sit beside her.

'Now, tell me what this is all about.'

'First of all, Sayyida, I was very sorry to hear of the untimely death of your brother.' He waited while she nodded an acknowledgment of his commiseration, then continued, 'I believe the khalifa sent his personal servant with you on this visit?'

'Uday? Yes. My husband didn't want me to travel unprotected.'

'Of course, Sayyida. But he didn't come with you himself?'

'No, he is much too busy preparing for the campaign.'

'And you didn't find it strange that the servant who never leaves his side, should suddenly travel with you to al-Jazira to visit your brothers?'

'My thoughts on the matter are private. What are you trying to tell me? Why so many questions?'

'Sayyida, I believe that Uday was the man who murdered your brother. And he did so on the orders of your husband.'

The words fell like stones between them.

'What are you saying? If we were in Malaqah now, I'd have you thrown into the dungeons for such treason,' Jamila cried, leaping to her feet. Who was this man to come to her and make such an allegation? 'How can you suggest such a thing? Why would my husband want to murder my brother? It doesn't make sense.'

But in her heart she knew that it made perfect sense. She had heard how Hasan had locked up his own brother; she knew he was making sure that no-one could threaten his throne, not even poor Yahya.

'I don't know who you are, but I would like you to leave now,' she continued, struggling to remain calm.

'Very well, Sayyida, but please take care. I suggest you don't return to Malaqah with Uday. I would hate to hear that something had happened to you on the journey; the roads are very dangerous between here and Malaqah.' He stood up and bowed. 'Ma'a salama, Sayyida. May Allah keep you safe.'

As soon as the old man had left, the tears she'd been struggling to control began to flow down her cheeks, tears of sorrow and tears of rage. If this were true what did it mean for her? Was she in danger too? She smiled bitterly at the idea. No, she was too insignificant; she hadn't even given Hasan an heir yet. This was all about removing anyone who could have a claim on the throne.

How could he do it? To murder her brother? And in such an underhand way, sending his servant to poison him. Again the images of Yahya writhing on the ground and then the stillness of him once the poison had done its work. She couldn't bear it. This would not go unavenged.

'Jamila, what is wrong, dear sister?' asked Muhammad. 'And what was that man doing here? I thought he was dead.'

Jamila wiped her face with her veil. 'You know him?'

'It looked like ibn Baqanna to me, despite the grubby djellaba and the untidy beard.'

'That was his name. Who is he?'

'He used to be the grand vizier of Malaqah before your husband got rid of him. As I say, I thought he'd been killed. Anyway what did he want and why is my lovely sister in tears again?'

'He says Uday murdered Yahya,' she said, between sobs. 'Hasan told him to.'

At first Muhammad didn't speak. He sat down beside her and put his arm around her. 'That is quite an accusation. Did he have any proof?' She shook her head. 'There is not much we can do about it without some proof,' he said. 'But I won't have that man in my house a moment longer.'

She looked at him, 'Uday? You're not going to let him go back to Malaqah? He has to be punished.'

'You really think he did it?'

'That evening it was him who brought in the sauce, Yahya's favourite. All the other dishes were carried by your own servants. And he gave it straight to Yahya, to make sure he took some first.'

'I was going to try it.' said Muhammad. 'We all could have been poisoned.'

'Not me. I don't like it. And Hasan knew that. But the rest of you, yes. Fortunately no-one other than poor Yahya got the chance to eat any.'

The horror of what she was saying began to come home to her; her husband didn't care who got murdered as long as his throne was safe. She could have lost both brothers that night. And the children, her little nieces and nephews. She couldn't bear to think about it. The rage was building inside her again, only now it had a clear direction, towards her husband.

'You have to do something, Muhammad. We can't let him get away with it.'

'I'll speak to the kitchen staff and see what they can tell me, and in the meantime I will have Uday arrested before he can send a message to Hasan. But more than that I cannot do. I can't risk a direct conflict with Hasan even over this. I have too much to lose.'

She scowled at her brother. He was just like Yahya; he hated confrontation. Baba was right; she was more man than either of them.

'I'm going back to Malaqah,' she said. 'Can you spare some guards to go with me; I don't trust the ones Hasan gave me. Not now.'

'Of course, that is not a problem. But are you sure that you want to leave. The period of iddah is not finished yet. Won't your husband find it strange if you go home now?'

'I don't care what he thinks,' she snapped, her anger with her husband giving her courage. 'I'm leaving tomorrow.'

Muhammad went straight to the palace kitchens. He had to know if ibn Baqanna had told the truth or if he was taking advantage of poor Yahya's murder to blame it on Hasan. The khalifa had banished ibn Baqanna from the court—in fact the story he had heard was that Hasan had had him killed yet here he was, alive and accusing the khalifa of murder. What was true and what was false? So much intrigue. That was why he had encouraged his brother to give up the throne peacefully, to avoid all this subterfuge, but in the end it had made no difference. It seemed that Hasan could not rest until all the pretenders to the throne were dead. Ben-Yahya would be next, already he was languishing in the dungeons. How long before Hasan sent someone to murder his own brother?

'Your Majesty, what can we do for you?' asked the head cook, looking distinctly flustered to have the sultan visiting the kitchens.

'I want to know how it was possible for poison to be introduced into my brother's food? Was there anyone in the kitchens who shouldn't have been there?' The cook shook his head. 'Any strangers?'

'No, Your Majesty.'

'Well, Your Majesty, there was that servant who arrived with your sister. He came in here pushing his weight about. Said the Sayyida wanted him to make a special sauce for her brother. We told him we don't serve those kind of sauces with tuna, but he insisted. Said it was her brother's favourite,' said one of the kitchen hands. 'He wouldn't go until we did what he wanted.'

'That's right and then he insisted on tasting it and putting it in a jug and sending it through, as though we'd made it for him.'

'What happened to the rest of the sauce?' asked Muhammad.

The head cook looked at his staff. 'Well?'

'We threw it out. We threw all the food out. Didn't even give any to the cats. We didn't know what else to do with it.'

'Just as well.'

'Was it hemlock, Your Majesty?' asked one of the staff, a young lad with a huge burn on his arm.

'I believe so. Why do you ask?'

'Your sister wanted me to show her what it looked like. I took her down to the stream where it grows,' the lad said, nervously.

'I see. Well, no matter.'

So ibn Baqanna was telling the truth. What should he do now? If he told his sister what they had told him she would want him to march against Hasan and demand retribution. His army was weak; he had a few ships but nowhere near enough to fight against Hasan's navy. There was nothing he could do to avenge his brother's death, but would Jamila understand that? Or was she planning to take matters into her own hands?

CHAPTER 19

Marwen still hadn't discovered anything to prove that Simon was breaking the law, and he knew he couldn't expose him without proof. It could so easily turn against him and then the chief librarian might get rid of him instead. He couldn't risk that. He needed to find One-arm again. He'd go to the tavern; he felt in need of some convivial company anyway.

The tavern was almost empty. Marwen ordered a jarrah of wine and sat in the corner with a good view of the door so he would be able to see One-arm if he came in. After a while the door opened and a rather battered looking individual limped up to the tavern owner. It was Simon's son-in-law.

'Wine,' he said banging his money on the table. Marwen watched him for a while. The man looked around the deserted tavern, trying to decide where to sit.

'As-salama alaykum, friend. Come and join me,' Marwen called. 'Nobody drinks alone in the tavern.'

'There's plenty of room, I see,' the man replied, rather ungraciously.

'I've seen you before,' Marwen said. 'In the teahouse. I didn't think you drank wine. Had a bad day?'

'I've had better.'

'What happened to your face? You seem to have taken quite a beating.'

'The other fool looks worse. Great soft bastard. Never been in a proper fight in his life, too busy with all those books.' He glanced at Marwen's ink-stained fingers. 'No disrespect to you friend.'

'Want to tell me about it?' asked Marwen, pouring some wine into Iqbal's glass. I'm Marwen, by the way; I work in the university library.'

'As-salama alaykum. Iqbal,' the newcomer said. 'You're a librarian then, Marwen?'

'A scribe.'

'Me, I'm an alfarero. Just opened my own business,' he drank thirstily from his glass then continued, 'Well I expect you know my mother-in-law if you work at the library. Stuck up bitch. Thinks she's someone special just because the khalifa liked one of her books. Her fingers are always stained with ink too.' He nodded at Marwen's hands.

'Yes, I think I do know her; she's not worked there long,' said Marwen, feigning disinterest. 'Salma is it?'

'Yes that's her. We've only just arrived in Malaqah. To make our fortunes, they said. Well we'll see about that. Damn hard work at the moment. New business you know,' he repeated. 'Not helped by that soft bastard breaking all my pots this morning. Do you know how long it's going to take me to replace them? Weeks.'

'That why you were fighting?

Iqbal looked at him suspiciously. 'No it wasn't. Just a family misunderstanding.'

'So who gave you that black eye, your mother-in-law?' Marwen laughed.

'No, it was her bastard husband. He went too far this time. Doesn't understand that he has no control over his daughter anymore? She's my wife and she'll do what I tell her to. But don't worry I know how to get him out of my hair. He's not as pure as he likes to pretend. I know things about him that could blow our family apart.'

'But you wouldn't want that to happen, would you?'

'Maybe. If it stopped him from meddling in my business.'

Must be something pretty bad,' said Marwen, calling for more wine.

'Enough to get him sent back to his own country, or even worse.' Iqbal drank some wine. 'You married?' he asked.

Marwen nodded. 'Yes but my wife can't bear any more children, so I'm thinking of taking a second wife.'

'Good idea, but make sure you choose the right sort of wife, one who knows her place in life. Don't pick one of those educated types like my mother-in-law; they think they know better than you. You need one who will respect and obey her husband.'

'I'll remember that advice, my friend. I take it your wife is not like that.'

'She is when her parents aren't around. I know how to control my family; I don't need advice from them but they always want to interfere. Well I'm not putting up with it anymore.'

'I'm intrigued. What has he done that was so awful?' asked Marwen, as casually as he could.

'Well, he's a Christian you know,' said Iqbal.

'Yes, I believe he used to be a monk but converted to Islam and is now a Muwallad.

'So he says.'

'What do you mean by that?'

'Oh he was always slipping away to the Christian church before we came to Malaqah. They didn't know I knew about that, but he wasn't as careful as he thought he was. I bet he's still doing it here in Malaqah.'

'Really. If what you say is true, that's a big risk he's taking.'

'Well he thinks he can do as he wants. Those dhimmis are like that.'

'You're not a fan of the dhimmis then?'

'Well the Jews are all right, but you never know where you are with the Christians, crafty bastards. They say their churches are full of gold and precious jewels but they go around looking as poor as the mice in the church.'

Marwen stood up. 'I'm sorry for your troubles, friend but now I must get home to my dear wife. Maybe we'll meet again and you can tell me if you've wreaked your revenge. Ma'a salama.'

'Alla ysalmak,' said Iqbal, helping himself to the wine left in Marwen's jug.

Marwen was exhilarated both from the wine and the fact that now he could see a clear way of getting rid of that conceited woman. The khalifa wouldn't think so highly of her when he found out she was a whore and her children were bastards; her marriage was illegal, null and void.

CHAPTER 20

Jamila set sail at dawn; she was eager to get home, buoyed up by the anger that raged inside her. This time when she looked at the waves breaking over the prow of the ship all she could think about was her brother lying in his shallow grave. The beautiful coastline that had captivated her when she left Malaqah, now held no attraction. She saw everything through a mist of her own tears. Even the dolphins escorting the ship raised no more than a cursory glance.

Jamila had no doubt that ibn Baqanna had spoken the truth. It all made sense now: Hasan suggesting she visit her brother without him, and sending Uday to protect her when the palace guards that accompanied her were more than adequate. Her husband had planned it all. Betraying his own brother wasn't enough, he had to get rid of hers as well. Well he wasn't going to get away with it. She knew which poison Uday had used; she had heard the doctor say it was hemlock. It had been finely chopped and mixed with a rich sauce made of eggs, goat's milk and heavily flavoured with spices. Poor Yahya would never have known it was there.

She clutched a small bag to her body; it contained the deadly plant. Before she'd left al-Jazira she had asked one of the young lads in the kitchen to show her where it grew. He'd looked puzzled by her request, but did as he was asked and took Jamila to a narrow stream that ran close to the alcazaba. There she saw the innocuous looking plant that had taken her brother's life, and while the lad was gathering some edible herbs for lunch, she had slipped some hemlock into her bag.

'Sayyida, we are almost there. Shall I get someone to bring your luggage up on deck?' asked the young maid that Muhammad had sent to accompany her.

He had arranged everything, the ship, a captain and crew whom he said he could trust with his life, and a guard of twenty hand-picked soldiers.

'Yes, Inma. I want to waste no time in getting home.' Home. The word was bitter in her mouth. 'Tell Afra to come here. I want to speak to her.' Her personal maid was lying down, overcome with sea-sickness, but she needed to speak to her before they landed.

As they approached the harbour the gulls became more numerous and whirled overhead in black and white clouds, shrieking and screaming in anticipation of the fish they would steal.

'You wanted to see me, Sayyida?' asked Afra. Her skin had a greenish tinge to its normal blackness.

'Yes, I want you to speak to the captain and tell him he must wait for me tonight. I plan to sail for al-Jazira before daybreak. But he mustn't tell anyone. No-one at all. All our lives could be in danger, his included.'

'But, Sayyida, we've only just arrived in Malaqah. Why do we have to go back so soon?'

Jamila could see that more days at sea were not what her poor slave had in mind. She was probably hoping to spend some time in the zenana to recover from her sickness, or at least on dry land.

'Don't worry, the journey back will be much calmer. You can see that already the waves are not so high. Hurry, do as I say, we are about to disembark.'

She had barely entered the alcázar when Hasan came striding towards her, his djellaba billowing behind him. She forced herself to smile as he enfolded her in his arms.

'My dearest wife, what a delightful surprise. I was so sorry to hear about your brother, my dear, but what are you doing here so soon? The period of iddah is not finished yet.'

'I was so unhappy, Hasan. I wanted to be home with you,' she said, burrowing her face in his robes and sobbing. 'I couldn't stay there any longer.' The tears came easily.

'My precious girl, I am very happy to see you,' Hasan said, holding her away from him and looking at her carefully. 'You are sure you're all right?'

'Yes, husband. Apart from my sorrow, I am well.' She dabbed at her eyes and gave him a watery smile.

Hasan looked around him. 'Uday? Did he return with you?' he asked.

'No, I came by sea. Uday didn't feel well; he said the sea makes him ill, so he decided to ride back. My brother lent him some horses and he and the guards are on their way. I expect they will arrive tomorrow.' She smiled sweetly at him, but Hasan turned away, a dark scowl on his face.

'He was supposed to keep you safe,' he muttered. 'I told him not to let you out of his sight.'

'But my brother gave me some of his own guards for protection. He said it was too dangerous for the khalifa's wife to travel overland and organised a ship to take me home. Wasn't that kind of him?'

'Most thoughtful,' Hasan said, through clenched teeth. 'And if you'd been attacked by pirates?'

She could see he was not happy with this turn of events. 'But we weren't, husband. Here I am, safe and sound. How are the plans for the campaign progressing?' she asked.

'We leave very soon,' he said. 'I have high hopes about our success. Soon you'll be married to the man who defeated Abbad I. My name will be written in the history books. In fact I am taking an eminent historian with me on the campaign to make sure an accurate account is made of all that happens.'

'What an excellent idea, husband.'

'Now, I must leave you, dear wife. I will come to you tonight, after dinner.'

'So long to wait. Those dinners go on forever. Why don't we eat in the zenana tonight? Just you and I?' She reached out and stroked his cheek.

'Indeed, why not? I ought to spend time with my wife before I go into battle. Yes. We will do that. I will leave it to you to speak to the cook. And we will have music and wine.' He smiled at her, his annoyance over Uday forgotten. 'Now run along, dearest one.'

Jamila bowed and headed back to the zenana, where Afra was already waiting for her.

'Did you speak to him?'

'Yes, Sayyida. He will be waiting.'

'Good, I don't want anyone to know what I'm planning. You understand?'

'Of course, Sayyida, but won't your husband think it strange that you leave again so soon, and in the middle of the night?'

'No. He will understand. Now come and help me bathe. I want to look particularly desirable tonight.'

Jamila lay back on the cushions and carefully arranged the folds of her flimsy dress. It was her favourite, made from a blue silk so fine that the whole garment could pass though one of her toe rings. Unlike the rest of her siblings, Jamila's hair was blonde, shot with a reddish hue, an inheritance from her grandfather whose mother had been a Christian slave from the north. Her maid had dressed her hair with ribbons and precious jewels, and it cascaded over her shoulders like a golden shawl. She had painted Jamila's eyes with kohl, rubbed carmine on her lips and applied a perfumed cream to her skin, and as she did all this, the young queen sat quietly, while inside her hatred bubbled like a poison. The hemlock had been chopped finely, then ground to a powder and added to one of the two flasks of wine that stood on the table. Two glasses and a plate of olives had been placed beside the wine, along with dishes of fruit and cold meats, nuts and flat bread. The musicians played softly behind an embroidered screen, the oil lamps were turned low and everything was ready. Only Hasan was missing.

She closed her eyes and tried to relax but her mind was churning. Images of her dead brother plagued her thoughts and fuelled her anger against her husband. She breathed deeply. If this failed, if he saw what she was trying to do, if he guessed her intentions for one moment, he would have her killed immediately. She was afraid, but her mind was clear. She knew what to do and she would not hesitate. He had taken her brother's life and put the rest of her family in danger; now she would get her revenge.

The door to her room opened and Afra came in. 'Sayyida, there is a servant who wishes to speak to you. He has a message from your husband.'

'Send him in.'

Hasan should be here by now. What had happened? She picked up a velvet djellaba and threw it over her shoulders.

'Sayyida, forgive the intrusion,' said a slight man, whom she vaguely recognised. 'I have a message from the khalifa.'

'Well what is it?'

'His Majesty is very sorry but he cannot dine with you tonight. He will come to you, later.'

'Very well.' She was about to turn away and then stopped and added, 'Tell my husband I am very disappointed but I will be waiting for him when he has finished whatever it is that keeps him from his loving wife.' She smiled at him as sweetly as she could.

'Yes, Sayyida,' said the servant, bowing and leaving.

Jamila sat down, her head in her hands. She could feel herself trembling with fear. Did he know of her plan? Had he heard about Uday's arrest? If he did then he would know she wanted revenge. She tried to breathe calmly.

'Sayyida, are you all right?' asked Afra. 'Shall I get you some water? Or maybe a glass of wine?'

She picked up one of the glasses and was about to pour some wine into it, when Jamila snapped, 'Nothing. Just leave me alone.'

'Yes, Sayyida.'

'And get rid of that food. All of it.'

'Yes, Sayyida.'

She must remain composed. Nothing had changed. She would have less opportunity but she could still get him to drink a glass of wine with her. He might even be more amenable, given that he had disappointed her and dined elsewhere.

Three servants came in and began to clear the table. They moved silently, like ghosts, not daring to look at her. She lifted her head just in time to see them removing the wine.

'Leave the wine,' she called. 'And the glasses.'

'Yes Sayyida,' said one of the servants and put the flask of wine on the table.

She stared at it. Which one was it? The one with the poison in it or the other? Her heart began to race. She had had a clear picture of which was which, but now?

'Is that where the wine was before?' she snapped. 'Put it back exactly where you found it. Do you hear me?'

'Yes, Sayyida.' The servant, a boy no older than her nephew, looked dismayed. Jamila never shouted at the servants; she always treated them kindly and even asked about their families.

'Thank you,' she said after he had replaced it. They would all have heard about her brother by now, maybe they would put her bad temper down to grief.

At last she was alone. She removed the heavy djellaba and lay down on the couch; she would sleep for a while. The musicians continued to play, this time a soft lament about a lost love. Jamila closed her eyes and slept.

When she woke there was not a sound; the wicks in the lamps were low and the room was in semi-darkness. Jamila sat up and removed the blanket that Afra had obviously placed over her. She knew the musicians would still be there behind the screen, but they too had fallen asleep. Suddenly the doors were flung open and Hasan strode into her room.

'Dearest one, I'm here.' He flung his djellaba on the floor and sat down beside her. 'I had to talk to my new commander. A fine fellow. They call him Jabalah. He commands fifty thousand men. They will make all the difference to the success of our campaign. Yes, we will be invincible. He is not your usual soldier; he's a Christian.'

'A Christian?' she asked, feigning interest.

'Yes, that doesn't bother me; now he fights for the Muslims. As long as he and his army help me defeat Abbad, I will pay his price.'

She felt irritated. Her carefully worked out plan was not going well. He didn't seem very interested in her; all he wanted to do was talk about his bloody campaign and this man, Jabalah. She had to do something or he would leave, complaining that he was tired.

'Would you like me to dance for you, dear husband?'

'Yes, my dear. That would be nice.'

He reached over and took an olive.

Jamila clapped her hands for the musicians to resume playing, then picked up her veil and began to dance. Like a snake, her body swayed first one way and then the other, the veil half-covering her. The tune, which started slowly, gradually became faster and faster; her feet flew over the floor, the ankle bracelets jangling and clinking. She raised her arms letting her gold bangles slide down her arms as she turned and twirled, her silk dress billowing, the veil no longer covering her splendid hair which fanned out behind her, until the music stopped and she fell at her husband's feet. She lifted her head and smiled at him.

'Wonderful,' he cried, clapping his hands. 'You are the most delightful wife.'

'Shall I pour you some wine, husband?'

'I don't think so, my dear. I must keep a clear head. Tomorrow Jabalah and I must talk about the details of the campaign. I have to be sure that he follows my orders and doesn't just go on the rampage, looting and killing wherever he feels like it. We have to have some boundaries and I'm not sure he understands that.'

'I see,' said Jamila. She was beginning to feel desperate. 'I will take a little wine, if you don't mind. The dance has made me thirsty.'

She poured a little wine into a glass and replaced the untainted flask on a table further from the couch.

'I didn't know you liked wine,' said Hasan.

'I just thought I'd try it. What is it after all but squashed grapes? I like grapes.'

Hasan laughed, 'You're such an innocent. Well, see what you think.'

She sipped the wine. It tasted sweet and warming. She liked it. 'Yes, it's very nice, but it makes me feel a bit funny,' she said, sitting next to him.

'Here, let me have a taste,' he said, kissing her lips. 'Hmmn, not bad.' He took the glass from her and drank it down in one gulp. 'Well you didn't leave much.'

'I'll pour you some more,' Jamila said, taking the glass from him and getting up.

'No, I really must keep a clear head,' he said.

'Will one glass make all that difference?' she asked, leaning down and kissing him on the lips. 'It might make everything clearer.'

'Very well, but just a small glass. You know we shouldn't be drinking wine at all.'

'Everyone at court drinks it. They just don't tell the imam,' she said pouring him a full glass from the second flask. 'Here, let's drink to a successful campaign.'

'To victory,' he said, drinking deeply from the glass.

'What about you? Where's yours?'

'I'll get some in a minute. I'm just going to tell the musicians they can go to bed,' she said, picking up the clean glass and walking over to the screen. The musicians did not need to be told twice; they collected their instruments and left.

She sauntered over to the first flask and poured some wine in her glass. 'At last we're alone, my dear husband,' she said, sipping from her wine.

Hasan seemed unaffected by the poison. He emptied his glass and said, 'Not the best wine I've tasted. I thought it was a bit bitter, but then I don't often drink wine, so I'm no expert.'

'It will help you to relax, that's what they say,' said Jamila. 'Would you like some more?'

'I'll try some from that other flask. Maybe it will be less bitter.'

'It's the same.'

'Give me a glass anyway.'

She brought the first flask over to him. Had she got it wrong? She had had no idea how much hemlock to use. The doctor had said it was very poisonous but not in what quantities, and she could hardly ask him. As she poured the wine into Hasan's glass she looked at him carefully but there were no signs that anything was wrong. It hadn't worked. And the ship's captain was waiting for her in the harbour. What was she going to do? Hasan had taken off his sword belt and placed it and his dagger by the couch. Maybe she should stab him. But he was much stronger than her; she would never succeed.

'Careful, you're spilling it. I can see that the wine has gone to your head already, my little pumpkin. Come and sit down here and let me remove your lovely dress,' Hasan said. His voice sounded a little strange.

She replaced the flask on the table and sat closer to him. He leaned towards her but instead of caressing her, he said, 'I'm feeling a little drowsy. Just sit by me, my dear, while I rest my eyes for a moment. That wine was stronger than I thought.' He leant his head against her shoulder and closed his eyes.

What was she going to do? The poison had obviously not worked. Should she try to creep away? No, that wouldn't work either. Even if he didn't wake when she tried to move, how could she run away while he still lived? He would find her. He would kill her and probably her brother too. She would have to be patient. She lay beside him, trying to remain calm but the thought of her brother dying in agony, made her so angry that she was on the point of grabbing his dagger and slicing his throat, when suddenly Hasan awoke and clutched at his neck.

'I can't breathe. Help me. My throat. It's burning. Arghh.' He tried to sit up, but fell back on the cushions, croaking, 'Doctor. Send for the doctor. Quick. My chest is on fire.' His eyes were beginning to bulge and he clawed at his throat in desperation. 'Jamila, help me...'

He said no more. It was over. His body slumped forward, pinning her beneath him. She could smell the vile odour of the hemlock on his breath. For a moment she lay there, hardly daring to believe that he was dead. Then she wriggled out from beneath him. She pulled him up onto the couch and covered him with the blanket. He lay there staring up at her with dead, unseeing eyes. She forced herself to close them and then called for Afra.

'We are leaving now,' she said. 'I hope you have everything ready?'

'Yes, Sayyida. Here are your travelling clothes; I borrowed them from one of the servant women. No-one will recognise you dressed like this. I took the rest of your things to the ship earlier. But what about the khalifa?' Afra looked towards the prostrate figure on the couch.

'My husband is sleeping. He drank too much wine. By the time he wakes we will be at sea.'

Jamila quickly dressed in the servant's clothes; they smelled of stale food, but she was not going to complain. She would change once she was on the ship. She picked up Hasan's dagger and tucked it into her pocket, then took one last look around the room and left.

They walked past the guards, who barely gaze them a glance, and out into the alcazaba. Jamila sighed with relief, but now they had to get past the sentry on the main gate; that was going to be more difficult.

The guard was lounging against the wall; he looked as though he'd been dozing, but he sprang to attention when they reached him. 'Where are you two off to?' he asked.

Jamila let her maid answer. 'We're taking some food to my husband,' Afra said, smiling sweetly at the guard. 'He's down in the harbour. Poor man has had nothing to eat all day.'

'And her?' he stared at Jamila.

'She's my sister. I don't like going down there alone, so she said she would come with me.'

'Doesn't say much, does she?' he said, staring even harder at her. 'Don't I know you?'

'You wouldn't know her; she's only just arrived in Malaqah. She's from Ronda. All my family are from there. She's come to keep me company; my husband is always away working, you see.' The maid was beginning to ramble and that was making the guard suspicious, so Jamila said, 'Maybe you're hungry too? There's plenty of food.' She lifted the lid of the cooking pot and the smell of cooked rice and meat escaped.

The guard was not tempted, instead he barred their way with his lance, and said, 'Stay where you are. You're not going anywhere, neither of you.'

CHAPTER 21

One-arm sat in a shady corner near the apothecary's shop. It was right by the Boveda Gate, the main entrance to the alcazaba. All day long there were people coming and going from the fortress, on their way to the market or tending to their daily business: afareros, fish sellers, merchants hoping to sell their wares to the Royal Buyer, butchers hauling meat to the Royal kitchens, victuallers, spice merchants, and soldiers of course and domestic staff. All acknowledged him, and some stopped and dropped a coin in his bowl. He was doing well today; it was almost full. Mostly it was the soldiers who gave him something; more than anyone else they recognised the uselessness of a man with only one arm. To increase their sympathy, he wore an old military cloak over his shoulders; it hadn't been his but who was to know that. In fact he'd never been a soldier, not really. He'd enlisted once as a volunteer when he was younger, but soon decided it wasn't for him and deserted. But he never mentioned that part of his history; he liked to refer to himself as a soldier who was down on his luck. People took pity on him then.

'As-salama alaykum,' he said to an old woman who, having no money to spare, handed him some unleavened bread, still warm from the oven.

He took a bite of the bread just as she came out of a house opposite; that kindly face was smiling at the apothecary who accompanied her. One-arm would recognise that sweet smile anywhere. Then before he knew it, she was standing in front of him.

'As-salama alaykum. I am happy to see you survived,' she said. She had recognised him. But then, how could she forget him after what happened? When he didn't reply, she said, 'Here take this,' and she dropped two dirhams in his bowl.

He was speechless. He had tried to rob her and her family, threatening their lives, and she still had it in her heart to forgive him. At last he said, 'Thank you, sayeda. May Allah bless and protect you.' He looked away; he didn't want her to know that he'd recognised her. He wanted her to go away before her husband arrived; he might not be quite so magnanimous, and One-arm didn't fancy spending the rest of his life in gaol.

As soon as she moved away, a look of disappointment on her face at his coldness, he stuffed the money, begging bowl and bread into his bag and left. This wasn't such a good place after all; he hadn't realised that was where they lived. He'd look for somewhere else.

However he didn't get far before something made him hesitate. Where was she going? The man in the tavern had been very interested to know more about her husband, and not in a good way. Was she in danger? He pulled his tattered cloak around him, and set off down the alleyway to follow her. She wound her way through the tangled streets of the Jewish quarter and then carried straight on until she came to the university library. At the entrance stood that man from the tavern, Marwen, his arms folded as if he were waiting for her. The man scowled at her and began to berate her about something. One-arm inched forward, hoping to hear what he was saying, but it was impossible without being seen. However what was obvious was that he didn't like her, not one bit. One-arm thought back to that night in the tavern. That Marwen had asked a lot of questions. What was he up to? Why so interested in her husband? He now regretted telling him so much, but that was what always happened to him when he taken some drink; his tongue ran away with him. Nothing he could do about it now, but he needed to find out a bit more about Marwen and why he was so antagonistic towards her. It looked as though he worked in the library in a position of authority, from the way he was ordering her about. But what else? Why such interest in two people who'd only just arrived in Malaqah?

Later, as the sun was setting over the mountains to the west, One-arm decided to make another visit to the tavern. Marwen had told him he often went there; perhaps the tavern owner could tell him more about the man.

The tavern was busy, so he'd drunk at least two glasses of wine before he had a chance to talk to the owner.

'You're becoming a regular customer, One-arm,' he said, pocketing the coins that One-arm placed on the table.

'I wanted to ask you about another of your regulars, a man called Marwen.'

'I know who you mean, miserable geezer. Why do you want to know about him?'

'Curiosity.'

'Well, I can't tell you much. As I say, a miserable geezer. Nothing's ever right. In fact I'd say he was a thoroughly bitter and unpleasant man. Always complaining about the dhimmis, saying we are too tolerant and if we don't watch out they will be taking over. Madness. The Jews are too busy with their own community, and anyway they bring prosperity to the city. As for the Christians, well they aren't bothered with things like that. They just want to get on with their lives, not make a bid for power, but he's always complaining about them. And if it's not the dhimmis then it's women. Thinks they have too much freedom these days and too much power. At the moment he has it in for some new scribe who started working at the library. You should hear him going on about her, especially when he's had a few jugs of wine. And he knows he shouldn't be drinking wine, a man in his position, but does he care? No. Too busy looking at the faults of others, he is.'

'I take it you don't like him much? said One-arm.

'Like, dislike, all I'm interested in is the colour of his money. But I wish he'd be a bit more cheerful. People come to the tavern to have a good time, not to listen to him complaining all the while.' He wiped the table with a wet cloth and asked, 'Now do you want another jug of wine or are you planning on sitting there all night pestering me with questions?'

'No, I must be off. Ma'a salama.'

One arm felt warm and mellow as he wandered out into a night that was lit by a thousand stars. He stopped and looked over the harbour wall for a minute; there were at least half a dozen ships moored in the port, their oil lamps bobbing in the dark and casting their light on the calm water. He'd never been on a ship. One day, perhaps. He pulled his dirty red cloak around his shoulders and headed towards the tiny room he called home. As he walked under the flickering light of the street lamps, he thought about what the tavern owner had told him. It was obvious now that Marwen had a grudge against the woman who had saved One-arm's life. Was it just because she was a woman? Or was it something deeper? And what was he planning to do? Blackmail the couple just as One-arm had originally planned? For a moment he thought about the money he could ask them for, enough to pay for his passage on the ship. But where would he go? North Africa maybe. His great grandfather had come from Sebta, and he'd always had a longing to go there. Well whatever Marwen was planning, the only way to find out more was to follow him, and to keep an eye on the foreigner. He'd wait outside the apothecary's house the next morning and see where he went.

He found a spot where he couldn't be easily seen and sat waiting until he saw the foreigner and his wife emerge. They headed in the direction of the library, with One-arm a discreet distance behind, keeping close to the shadows in case either of them decided to turn around. When they entered the library, he watched them embrace and go their separate ways. So he settled down and waited. At mid-afternoon first the woman emerged, blinking in the sunlight and then, a few minutes later, her husband. Neither of them remarked on the dusty figure sitting outside the tea shop watching them. He waited until they had passed and followed them until he was sure they were going home. There was nothing suspicious in either of their behaviours. Nor was there any sign of Marwen. Then on the fourth day he noticed someone else was also following the foreigner; it was his son-in-law, the one who had killed Juan. But he wasn't as good at trailing people as One-arm, and while his wife carried on walking, the foreigner stopped to speak to him. It wasn't a friendly encounter; he could hear them arguing. What was that about? One-arm crept forward until he could hear what they were saying.

'I don't care. She's my wife,' the son-in-law was shouting. 'She's none of your concern anymore.'

'I know that, but I won't stand by and watch you ill-treating her.'

'Well I suggest you and your whore leave Malaqah before I tell the muhtasib about you. And what would that do to your beloved daughter when she discovers her parents aren't legally married?'

'You wouldn't dare. To your own wife?'

'You think so?'

'Is something wrong, Simon? Marwen called, coming down the library steps to see what the commotion was about.

'No, nothing. Just a disagreement with my son-in-law. Nothing to worry about. A family matter,' he said.

'Well come along; there's a new book that the chief librarian is particularly interested in having translated into Arabic. You'll have to sort out your family differences later.'

One-arm watched as the man, whose name he now knew was Simon, turned his back on his son-in-law and went into the library. What was going on? Of course, he was family; he would know if Simon was still a Christian or not, and now he was using that information to threaten him. But could he prove it? After all he was a newcomer in the city; who would listen to him? He decided to watch the son-in-law and see what he did next

Iqbal was angry. He'd tried to reason with his father-in-law, but he was too stubborn. He didn't seem to understand that Zara was not his concern anymore; it was unheard of for a father to interfere in a daughter's relationship with her husband. He was tempted to divorce her and send her back to him, but he wouldn't give Simon the satisfaction of thinking he'd won. No. First he'd find out if it was true that his father-in-law was still worshiping at one of those village churches, then he'd make a decision.

'Where are you going?' Zara asked. 'Your food is ready. Are you not hungry?'

She stood there, her pale skin and blue eyes a constant reminder of her father. The ugly bruise on her cheek had turned purple, and although she was attempting a smile, her eyes were sad. This was Simon's doing, him and his wife; they had never instructed their daughter properly. They had brought her up to believe she was as good as a man and had the right to do and say what she wanted. With that attitude, she was lucky she'd even found a husband.

'Later. I'll eat later. I'm going for a walk,' he said.

She opened her mouth to say something, then changed her mind and removed the tagine from the table.

Iqbal knew where the Christians met; the church was just on the outskirts of the city and it didn't take long for him to get there. A couple of people were gossiping outside the small stone building which even though it displayed nothing to indicate it was a place of worship, was obviously the right place, as more and more people arrived, each wearing the regulation blue turbans. Finally he saw him, Simon, so much taller than those around him, with no turban and his pale complexion and blond hair illuminated by the rising moon. It was impossible to miss him. What was he thinking of? Didn't he realise he was putting all the family in danger by his reckless behaviour? He was putting his faith before his family. How could he do that? Iqbal felt his anger rising as he considered the ramifications of his father-in-law's actions; if Simon and Salma weren't legally married then Zara was illegitimate. That made her a whore. He'd married a whore. Their children would be illegitimate. He couldn't let anybody know about that. It could affect him and his business. However he could be arrested for not reporting Simon. What was he to do? Iqbal couldn't suppress a loud groan as he considered his predicament.

One of the Christians looked across to where he was hiding in the sugarcane, and started to move towards him, but before he could investigate, the priest arrived and one by one they all filed into the church.

There was only one solution. Simon was putting them all in danger and he had to be stopped. Iqbal had tried to reason with him, but Simon had denied he was still worshiping Christ. Told Iqbal to mind his own business. How infuriating. Mind his own business? He was the one who was meddling in other people's business. He was meddling in their marriage, and Iqbal was not going to stand for that; it was intolerable. There was no alternative. He had to stop him. An accident, that was what should happen. Nowhere near the church of course, so that his secret was never uncovered; it would be just as devastating if it was revealed after his death. The more he thought about it, the more he convinced himself that it was the right thing to do, for everyone's sake, especially his own family.

CHAPTER 22

Afra couldn't stop trembling; Jamila could swear she could hear the poor girl's teeth chattering. 'Don't worry,' she whispered to her. 'Just don't say anything else. Let me speak to him.'

The sentry was talking to his companion and they were both watching them; now she was sure that he had recognised her. What would they going to do?

The first sentry walked across to them. 'Well, ladies, I think you'd better come with us.'

'But the food will go cold,' said the maid, her eyes filling with tears.

'Don't worry about that,' said the other guard and took the pot from her. He lifted the lid and added, 'Very tasty, this will do us for tonight, thank you very much.'

'But, my husband…' Afra began to say.

'You can't stop us from leaving,' said Jamila, her voice taking on a more authoritative tone. 'Her husband is a sea captain. He is expecting his supper.'

'Oh, can't I?' The sentry grabbed Jamila by the arm. 'Come with me. It's time we found out exactly who you are.'

Jamila felt sick. Once they discovered Hasan was dead and she'd tried to leave the city, they would know that she was to blame. They would execute her and her poor maid. She had to get away before it was too late.

They had barely gone a few steps when a young soldier ran up to them. 'Guards, the quaid wants to speak to you right away; the khalifa's been murdered. He wants to know who has come into the alcazaba in the last few hours. You've been on duty all night, haven't you?'

'We have.'

'Hurry. He's in a foul mood. I'm to stay here, on guard.'

The sentries looked at each. The one holding the cooking pot, put it on the ground and said to the soldier, 'Here's some supper for you, then.' The other sentry released his hold on Jamila's arm, and said, 'Think yourself lucky, ladies; we've more important things to do now. But the next time I see you trying to slip out at this time of night without a good reason, I'll lock you both up.'

Jamila could hear Afra's sigh of relief. They waited until the sentries had disappeared into the dark night, and walked through the gate. 'Tisbah ala-kheir,' she called to the young soldier, as they made their way down the cobbled path and into the city.

As soon as they were out of sight, she said, 'Come Afra, we must hurry. Let's pray to Allah that the captain is still waiting for us.' She took her maid's hand and they both began to run as though the soldiers were already chasing them.

As they ran down the path to the harbour they could see the ship, moored in the same spot they had left it. The harbour was eerily quiet without its usual bustle of merchants and seamen. A pale moon slid from behind the clouds and lit up the sea. The captain already had the ship's sails set, ready to leave.

'My apologies, Captain,' she said, as they clambered aboard. 'We were delayed.'

The captain stared at her grubby djellaba , but all he said was, 'You are lucky, Sayyida, a strong breeze has sprung up; we will make good headway tonight. We will set sail immediately.'

Jamila sat in the prow of the ship, heedless of her humble clothes and her dishevelled appearance; she was just glad to be there. She watched the captain give orders to his crew, and the oarsmen, who'd been dozing in their places while they waited for her, now sprang to life and, as the drum began to beat out its rhythm, they pulled away from the harbour and headed for the open sea. With the help of the following wind, they would be in al-Jazira by the next day. But what would Muhammad say when she told him what she had done?

First her brother was delighted to see her again so soon, then he was horrified when he knew that Hasan was dead, and by her hand.

'Are you sure that no-one saw you?' he asked. 'Jamila. Why couldn't you have waited. You could have got your revenge some other way. And now that you have run away, the finger of guilt will point at you. Foolish girl. What are we going to do?' She knew her brother was angry with her, but she was heartened to hear him say, 'What are *we* going to do? Not *you*.' He would help her. She had no doubt of his love for her. 'You will have to stay inside the zenana for now, where nobody can find you. If anyone comes from Malaqah looking for you, I will deny that I have seen you.' He thought for a moment, then asked, 'Who do you think will be the next khalifa?'

'It's hard to say. Hasan's brother is still in prison. If he's released and becomes Khalifa, I don't think he will care who killed his brother.'

Muhammad looked at her. 'Why not? He was his brother after all.'

'Don't you know? Hasan had his brother arrested two years ago. He's been rotting in gaol ever since.'

He looked surprised, 'In that case you may be right, but in the meantime, you will stay here with me. It won't take long for everyone to forget about Hasan. Loyalties change with the wind in the court at Malaqah.'

'I will deny it anyway,' she said, with a sudden surge of bravado. 'Just because I ran away, it doesn't mean I killed him. Maybe I was frightened for my own life.'

'Maybe, but for the next few months you are going to live a quiet life in the zenana. No more bursts of rage or passion, my girl. Time to settle down, and then, when I am sure it is safe, we will find a new husband for you.'

She smiled at him sadly; her life was about to change, but not necessarily for the worst.

CHAPTER 23

Naja al-Siqlabi had just finished his early morning prayers when a slave entered his quarters and said, 'Forgive me for disturbing you, sayyad, but there is someone here to see you and he says it is urgent.'

'What is the name of this man whose business is so urgent that he disturbs me when I'm at prayer?'

Before the slave could say anything more, ibn Baqanna burst into the room, closely followed by another, rather distressed slave.

'I'm sorry, sayyad. I couldn't stop him,' the slave said, nervously flapping his arms.

Naja waved away both slaves and turned to ibn Baqanna. 'What on earth are you doing here? I thought we agreed not to meet openly?' he said.

'She did it,' he cried. 'His wife. She did it; she murdered Hasan.'

'Hasan is dead? When did this happen?'

'Two days ago. The court is in chaos. That fool Labib doesn't know what to do. We have to get to Malaqah as quickly as possible.'

'This is good news. Now they can release Ben-Yahya,' said Naja.

'Hold on a minute. You must stop and think about this. Do not do anything hasty. People will have forgotten about Ben-Yahya by now, that is if they ever knew he was in prison in the first place.'

'Are you suggesting we should leave him there to rot? His mother would never stand for it.'

'There won't be much she'll able to do about it when you are Khalifa, now will there?' ibn Baqanna said, with a sly smile. 'Don't tell me you haven't thought about becoming the khalifa of Malaqah. You wouldn't be the first slave to have risen to those heights.'

Naja looked at him. He was right. Mujahid al-Amiri, the emir of Denia, was once a slave. And they say that the taifa of Badajoz was founded by the slave Sabor, a man of Slavic stock. It was not unheard of.

'Are you suggesting that I go to Malaqah and claim the throne?'

'I am. Ben-Yahya would never be able to rule. He's been incarcerated for too long; his mind will have gone. It happens to them all. They pin all their hopes on being released or escaping from that terrible place and then one day they realise that it will never happen and that's when they give up and go mad. You don't need to worry about him.'

'What's in this for you?' asked Naja. He knew ibn Baqanna of old, and although he didn't like him he recognised his usefulness.

Ibn Baqanna smiled. 'My old job. I will be your grand vizier. A small price to pay, wouldn't you say?'

'Maybe I don't need you. What is to stop me having you locked up now and going to Malaqah without you?'

'Nothing. But I know you won't do that. You need my support.'

The wily bastard was right. They wouldn't listen to him if he went alone. He hated to admit it but he did need ibn Baqanna by his side.

'Very well. But I must speak to Queen Fatima first.'

'If you must. But we have to hurry. We should leave on the first tide. And in the fastest ship you can find.'

Fatima sat in the gardens overlooking the harbour. The last echoes of the muezzin had died away and everything was still. An orange sun hung in the sky just above the horizon, casting a warm glow over the walls of the alcazaba. She looked up, surprised to see Naja approaching, and in a hurry. He bowed before her and took her hand.

'Sayyida, I have sad news for you. Your son Hasan has been murdered.'

'Hasan? Dead?' She felt herself go cold. One son in prison and the other dead. She stared at the man kneeling at her feet. 'How so?'

'They say his wife poisoned him. She was mad with grief after the death of her brother.'

'His wife murdered him? Her own husband,' she murmured, barely able to say the words. 'She murdered the khalifa?' How was this possible? Where were the guards who were supposed to protect him?

She thought back to when they first came to Sebta, Hasan was still a child then but he was so brave. He had promised to take care of her and his young brother. She remembered his little face, so serious when he announced that he was head of the family now; she had wanted to hug him to her and remind him that she was still there and she would care for them both, but his grave expression demanded he be taken seriously.

Unlike his younger brother he'd always had his eyes on the throne. He declared he was meant to rule and one day he would take back what was his. And he had. But now he was dead. Less than two years later. How could that be? What had driven his wife to do such a thing? Why avenge her brother's death by killing Hasan? What had Hasan to do with it?

She began to wail and sob, and would not be comforted, even though Naja was waiting by her side.

'Sayyida. I must leave today. I promise I will release your son from gaol and make sure he inherits the throne. It is rightly his now,' he said. 'Everyone will see that.'

'Ben-Yahya,' she moaned. 'My poor son is still imprisoned? So they haven't released him yet?'

'I don't believe so, Sayyida. That is why I must go and help him.'

'I will go with you,' she said, standing up and wiping the tears from her face. 'I want to see my sons. I have to see them. Hasan must have a proper burial. I am his mother; I need to be there.'

'Of course, Sayyida, but I can't let you walk into danger. I must go first and make sure it is safe for you. I am leaving within the hour. But I will send word when all is well. Then you will be reunited with Ben-Yahya.'

She looked at him; he had been with her sons since they were tiny. He had cared for them and educated them. Surely he would never do them harm. But could she really believe him? She was beginning to feel that she couldn't trust anyone, anymore. Hasan had imprisoned his brother for no good reason. Now he had been murdered by his own wife. The world was in turmoil. Whom could she trust? Naja? An ex-slave? She felt a pain grip her heart. What choice did she have? Her grief overwhelmed her again and she collapsed on the ground. Within seconds her maid was by her side.

'Come with me, Sayyida. Let me take you inside,' she said, putting her arm around her and helping her into the zenana.

She could hear Naja's voice, talking to her, on and on but she couldn't make sense of his words. Nothing made sense anymore.

Ibn Baqanna had commissioned a small ship, but a fast one. They were already on their way, the rocky outcrop of Sebta fast disappearing behind them. Naja's head was spinning with thoughts about what he should do. Ibn Baqanna was right when he said this was an opportunity not to be missed, but could Naja really go through with it? Could he leave Ben-Yahya to rot in that cell? And Queen Fatima, what would she say? He knew if he proclaimed himself Khalifa, she would not let it go unchallenged. He had given her his word that he would rescue Ben-Yahya and put him on the throne, and yet even as he said those words he had no intention of keeping them. This was his chance. They called him a free man but he didn't feel free. He was born a prince and, if he didn't do something to change his life, he would die a servant. In his opinion neither Hasan nor Ben-Yaha were capable of governing Malaqah; at heart they were children still. The taifa needed a strong ruler, someone aware of the political manoeuvring that went on at court, someone who had listened to the intrigues and duplicity of men like ibn Baqanna and knew how to get the better of them. Before they had been exiled to Sebta there was little that went on in court that Naja was not aware of. Yes, the more he considered his situation, the more he was convinced that this was his moment and it wouldn't come again.

'We'll be arriving soon,' ibn Baqanna said, moving over to stand behind him. He stood so close that Naja could smell his sour breath.

'Good. There are still a couple of hours of daylight left. We will go straight to the alcázar and find Labib. I want this done straight away before any of Idris's relatives come crawling out of the cracks to claim the throne as their own.'

'What are your plans for Ben-Yahya?'

'I haven't decided. We'll leave him where he is for now. If, as you suggested, imprisonment has consumed his reason, then maybe I will have him released and returned to Sebta to live with his mother.'

'I do not think that would be wise, sayyad.'

Naja spun round and stared at the ex-vizier. 'I said I haven't decided. Did you not hear me?' he snapped. Did ibn Baqanna think he could manipulate him as he had manipulated Idris I? Well, he would soon find out that Naja was no fool. While the man was of use to him he could have his coveted role as grand vizier, but when he no longer needed him it would be a different story. If there was one thing he could guarantee, it was that ibn Baqanna could not be trusted.

They were pulling into the harbour. Even from the deck of the ship he could smell the spices in the nearby market and the aroma of slow cooking food. It was good to be in Malaqah again, the jewel of the coast, the city of so many dreams, and now he would be its ruler, Khalifa of Malaqah and all its lands. He whispered the words to himself, savouring them in his mouth, yet frightened to bring a curse down on his head if anyone heard him.

CHAPTER 24

Umar's mother was busy preparing the dough to take to the baker's; something she did every morning. As a boy he'd loved the smell of the freshly baked bread when it came out of the baker's wood oven, and would trail behind her hoping for a piece while it was still warm.

'Umar? Is that you again? I'm beginning to get worried about you; this is the third time this week that you've been to see us. We normally don't see you from one full moon to the next. What's wrong, son?' his mother asked, giving the dough a final thump before shaping it into a flat round and putting it in her basket with the others.

'Nothing. Just thought I'd visit my mother. We're waiting for orders about the campaign, and everyone is getting restless.'

'Well, I must go out or we won't have any bread for lunch. Here, give me a kiss.' She let him embrace her and then added, 'Your father will be pleased to see you. He's upstairs on the terrace.'

He watched as his mother hoisted the basket on her shoulder and headed for the market. Why was he hesitating? Why didn't he just go up and tell Baba how he'd been feeling? The truth was that he couldn't understand it himself. He couldn't stop thinking about her; she haunted his dreams and filled all his waking moments. It couldn't go on like this. But, his mother was right; this was the third time he'd come to speak to his father and each time he couldn't bring himself to say anything. What if she rejected him? He couldn't stand that, but it was a possibility: she'd made it perfectly plain that she would only marry for love. But surely she could grow to love him? He would make her a good husband and give her many fine sons. His pay was good; she would never want for anything.

He climbed the stone steps to the roof terrace where his father liked to sit in the early morning, sipping his mint tea and watching the seagulls following the fishing boats.

'Umar. What are you doing here? Come sit down and have some of this delicious tea.'

'Baba. How are you?' Umar leaned down and kissed his father on the cheeks.

'Look there's a school of dolphins in the harbour. Over there. See?' his father continued.

It was now or never. Umar took a deep breath and said, 'Baba, I'm thinking of getting married.'

His father put down the jarrah and looked at his son; his face was wreathed in smiles. 'Married? Well, I thought you were never going to say those words. That's wonderful, my son. I can't tell you how happy it makes me to think that you will have a wife and a family of your own. There is nothing like a family to make a man feel complete. Now, tell me, who is the woman who has managed to worm her way into your heart? I will have to speak to her father as soon as possible. Is it someone I know? Yes, I'm sure it must be. Come, lad, who is she?'

'Yes, Baba, you do know her. It's the daughter of your cousin; it's Layla. I decided I wanted her for my wife from the first moment I saw her. She has stolen my heart.' He felt himself blushing, as he spoke his feelings aloud.

His father said nothing, just stared at him, the smile gradually fading from his face.

'What is it, Baba? Why so serious? A moment ago you were happy at the news. Why this gloom? It is permitted to marry a second cousin, isn't it?'

'Of course, son. The law does not forbid it.'

'Then what? Is it because her father is a Christian?'

'Simon is not a Christian. Don't ever say that; you put all the family in danger with such talk,' he snapped.

'Well you should tell him to be a bit more careful then; I have seen the cross he has around his neck, even though he tries to hide it,' said Umar. This was not the reaction he had hoped for from his father. 'So if it's not about Simon, then what is it?'

'If you wanted her for your bride the first time you saw her, then why did you hesitate? Why didn't you tell me straight away? Now it is too late.'

'What do you mean, Baba? How can it be too late?'

'Listen, my son. You are not the only man in this household who has fallen under the spell of Layla's beauty. Your brother Ibrahim spoke to me about it last week; I have already talked with Salma and Simon and they are very happy with the match, as long as Layla agrees. We are still waiting for the girl to make up her mind.'

'Ibrahim?' Umar felt as though he'd been punched in the gut. Never for one moment had it occurred to him that Ibrahim would want to marry Layla. 'But I'm the eldest son; I should marry first,' he said petulantly, rather as a small boy would do.

'To be honest, your mother and I thought you would never marry. Many soldiers don't.'

Suddenly he couldn't bear to be there a moment longer. Without a word, he turned and sprinted down the stairs. His dream had been shattered. Why had he been so foolish? An intelligent, beautiful girl like Layla could have her pick of any man, why would she choose an uncouth soldier, who was away from home more than he was there, and who lived with the shadow of violent death hanging over him? No, he'd been an idiot to even consider it.

'Umar, I didn't know you were here,' Ibrahim said, as he brushed passed him and strode out into the street. 'Is everything all right? Umar? What's wrong?'

He could hear his brother calling his name but he didn't turn round; he headed straight for the stables. He would saddle up his mare and ride and ride until the pain that was tearing at his guts had left him.

Makoud sat for a while longer, watching the seagulls wheeling overhead, trying to decide what to do. Who would be a father? For years he'd prayed to Allah that his sons would ask him to find them a wife and now they both wanted to marry the same one. And unless Layla made up her mind soon, neither one of them would get her. Well one thing was certain; it was good that Salma and Simon were moving out. If Layla refused to marry Ibrahim then it would be impossible for them all to live under the same roof.

Suddenly he remembered what Umar had said about the cross Simon wore. Could that be true? Maybe Umar was mistaken. After all these years had Simon abandoned the Muslim faith and returned to Christianity? Or had he been deceiving them all this time? Maybe he had never given up his faith at all; but in that case why had he married Salma? Makoud groaned; he knew the answer. Cold fear gripped his throat. Maybe that was why his cousins were planning to leave the city. It was too dangerous to stay here; people were in and out of the shop all day long. Sooner or later someone would start to talk. He couldn't risk his family's safety, not even for Salma. If Simon was discovered to be a practising Christian, nobody would believe that Makoud wasn't complicit in the deceit; he'd be ruined. Helping someone to break one of the strict rules of the Hadith was a crime which could not go unpunished. And Salma would be disgraced. Layla would never find a husband; her reputation would be tarnished beyond redemption by her father's actions. What a mess. Why, oh why had he urged them to leave Ardales, where they were safe, and come to Malaqah? He should have guessed that Simon was not the sort of man to turn his back on his religion, regardless of the danger.

CHAPTER 25

Ben-Yahya lifted his head from his hard bed; someone was coming. He knew those footsteps as though he'd heard them all his life; it was his gaoler. His empty bowl lay beside him, scraped clean of the evil mixture they called his breakfast. Why was the old man coming back so soon? Had something happened? He sat up in anticipation. Maybe today was the day when he'd be released. The familiar sound of the iron bolt being drawn back, and the glow from the gaoler's lamp as the heavy door creaked open, made his heart beat wildly. The old man rarely altered his routine. What had he come to tell him?

His ancient gaoler shuffled into the cell. 'Well young prince, I've got some news for you,' he said. 'The khalifa is dead. Murdered by his own wife. Can you believe that? His own wife. Of course she's disappeared; not a trace of her or her maid.'

'My brother, Hasan? He's dead? Ben-Yahya asked. It was hard to comprehend. 'But why would she do that?'

'Don't know. Never could understand women; strange creatures,' he said.

'So you're going to release me? Ben-Yahya said, finding new energy and pulling himself up from his bed.

'Release you? No, I just thought it would cheer you up to know there was someone worse off than you,' the gaoler said, with a cackle of laughter.

'But if he had me arrested then surely I can go free now he's dead?'

'You're not thinking straight, my lad. If every time a khalifa died, we released all of the prisoners he'd sent us, the dungeons would be empty. Now I don't know why you were arrested, and I don't want to, but I do know that nothing has changed. In fact, and don't think I'm trying to upset you, because I can see you are a nice young fellow, the truth is that it's made things worse for you. The only person who could pardon you was the last khalifa and now he's dead. But at least you now know where you stand. You're never going to get out of here.'

Ben-Yahya stared at the gaoler, his pasty face and white beard illuminated only by the light of the oil lamp, although he knew from the crack of light coming through his cell window that it was sometime near midday. The man looked neither sad nor happy. He was indifferent to Ben-Yahya's fate. 'Get out of here, you filthy old bastard. May you rot in hell,' Ben-Yahya shouted in rage and threw himself on the ground in despair.

'I wondered how long you could hold out; it gets to them all in the end,' the gaoler said, not the least perturbed by Ben-Yahya's outburst.

The door clanged shut behind him, leaving Ben-Yahya in almost total darkness. So this was how it would end. Like his dead neighbour he would slowly go out of his mind until one day he caught some disease and died. No escape. No pardon from the khalifa. No rescue attempt by Naja. He was never leaving this place.

How many weeks passed Ben-Yahya had no idea. But one morning, when the gaoler brought him his food, he said, 'There is a new khalifa. Foreign chap. Naja he's called. They say he was once a slave.'

'What?' Ben-Yahya was instantly awake. 'Naja al-Siqlabi?'

'Yes that's him. He's taken over, him and one of the old viziers. I remember him, sneaky bastard, ibn-Baqanna. He's been appointed grand vizier.'

'But he's supposed to be my friend. You must get word to him that I'm still alive. He'll get me out of here.'

The gaoler stared at him and Ben-Yahya could swear that for once he saw pity in the man's expression. 'I don't know what you did to upset so many important people, but the guards say the khalifa has given them orders to kill you and throw your body in the sea.'

'What? But they can't do that.' He slumped down on his pallet and put his head in his hands. Betrayed by his brother and betrayed by Naja, a man he'd known for years, a man he counted as a friend, someone he could trust.

'Now don't take on so. I have an idea,' said the gaoler. Ben-Yahya looked up. 'I don't want to see you killed. You're the only prisoner in here that I can have a sensible conversation with.' Ben-Yahya waited. What was the old fool going to suggest? 'Why don't I move you into your neighbour's empty cell, and we tell them that you're already dead. It won't bother them. They were told to kill you, but well they can't kill you if you're already dead, can they?' He cackled at his own cleverness.

It wasn't much of a plan, but Ben-Yahya was prepared to try anything. He stood up and picked up his food bowl. There was only his bed to take with him; he had nothing else, only the rags on his back and what was left of his gold coins, still hidden in the straw pallet.

'Come on,' the gaoler said. 'They're coming when they've finished their breakfast.' He shuffled out of the cell and taking a large key from the belt around his waist, he pushed Ben-Yahya inside the empty cell and locked the door behind him. 'Now, lie down there, and keep quiet,' he said.

Ben-Yahya did as instructed. He had little hope that the gaoler's plan would work, but it was better than just waiting for the guards to slaughter him.

After an interminable wait he heard the old man return with two soldiers.

'I told you, he's dead. Died of the sickness a week ago since.'

'But we've been ordered to kill him and take his head to the khalifa as proof,' one of them protested.

'Well that will be difficult because he's at the bottom of the sea; I doubt if there's much of him left after the fish have been at him.'

'You're sure it was him?'

'Look, you young pup, I know my prisoners. This is his cell. Look for yourself. It's empty. Mind you, I wouldn't go poking about in there; he died of a pretty nasty disease.'

'Well that's that then,' said the second soldier. 'We'll just have to tell that jumped-up slave we were too late. He's already dead.'

'Come on, let's get out of this filthy hole. Gives me the creeps,' said his companion.

Ben-Yahya heard the cell door slam shut and the footsteps recede. The gaoler had gained him some time, but he knew how meticulous Naja was. He wouldn't be satisfied with that; he would want to make sure that Ben-Yahya was really dead.

CHAPTER 26

One-arm couldn't stop thinking about Salma and her husband. Something was going on but he couldn't quite get to the bottom of it. Once again he left his humble lodgings at sunrise and set off for the apothecary's house. He needed to protect her, but from whom? Patience, that was what he needed. He'd keep his distance and follow them. But how? And who? Salma? Simon? Marwen or the son-in-law? He couldn't follow them all. It had to be Simon. He would follow the husband and see if anyone was trying to do him harm.

He sighed. What if they were? What could he do about it? He wasn't much of a fighter, not much of a man even; nobody wanted a one-armed man. Sometimes he wished she hadn't saved him, just left him there to die. It had been an act of kindness on her part. Nowadays that was all he had; he lived on the kindness of others. Each day the feeling that he should repay it grew stronger. He had to help her; he couldn't let anyone destroy her life. After all it was the other one who'd struck the blow that had changed his life, and now it looked as though he had a grudge against his own father-in-law. What kind of a man was he, that he would want to hurt his wife's father?

One arm had never married. He had never had anything to offer a wife; no self-respecting father would let his daughter marry a man like him, a deserter, a thief and now a cripple. A wave of self-pity almost suffocated him when he thought of what he had missed. He imagined going home each evening to an angel like Salma, having sons and a place to call his own. But it was not to be.

The door to the apothecary's house opened and there she was, radiant with happiness. He couldn't let anyone take that away from her.

One-arm's patience was almost stretched to breaking point; every day he followed Simon, always keeping well back so that he wouldn't be seen, often finding a good spot to set out his begging bowl while he waited, and on the constant look out for Marwen or the son-in-law. And every day Salma and Simon headed straight home. He was beginning to think that it was all in his imagination; nobody seemed interested in the couple and he never saw anyone else following them. Then one evening Simon came out of the library on his own and headed in the direction of the river. One-arm knew where he was going, to the church. He waited until Simon was almost out of sight, then gathered up his belongings and followed him.

It wasn't long before he noticed another man ahead of him; he too was keeping to the shadows. Darkness fell quickly and even the moon was hidden by thick cloud, but One-arm could just make out the dark figure ahead as he passed beneath the pools of yellow light cast by the street lamps. It was the son-in-law. Then he stopped for a moment, and One-arm saw a glint of metal as he pulled a sword from his scabbard. So this was what he had planned. The man's rage had led him to consider murder. One-arm didn't hesitate. He wasn't going to fail her. With no thought of how he would be able to overpower him with only his dagger and one good arm, he threw himself on Iqbal and plunged the dagger into his side. Iqbal spun around, completely taken by surprise at this vicious assault. Blood was pouring from the wound in his side, but he managed to push One-arm off him, and raising his sword thrust it through his chest.

A gasp of agony escaped from One-arm and he fell to the ground. So this was it? No, he wasn't going to fail her. The dagger was still clutched tightly in his hand and as Simon's son-in-law bent over to look at his attacker, One-arm took a deep breath and plunged the dagger into Iqbal's chest. He fell back, feeling his life slipping away from him. Now he could die in peace; he had repaid her kindness.

A loud knocking at the door woke him. Who on earth could it be at this hour? Simon could hear Makoud grumbling and the sound of the iron bolts being pulled back and then the creaking of the heavy door as it swung open.

'Who is it? whispered Salma, rubbing the sleep from her eyes.

'I don't know. Stay here while I find out,' said Simon. Had his secret come out? He felt an icy chill at what that could mean. He pulled a robe around him and went out onto the patio, astonished to find his own daughter sitting there in tears, and the baby yelling its head off.

'It's Iqbal,' Makoud said. 'He's been attacked and killed.'

'Iqbal?' Dead? But when? How?' They both looked at Zara, hoping she could enlighten them.

'She can't tell us any more, Simon. Leave her for a bit. As far as I can make out, she ran straight here as soon as she saw his body.'

'Oh my poor child,' Simon said, taking her into his arms.

The baby began to cry louder than ever and soon all the household had assembled on the patio to see what the commotion was about.

'They say he was attacked near the Antequera Gate,' sobbed Zara. 'Just after sunset.'

'What was he doing there? asked Makoud. 'That's nowhere near the alfarería.' He looked at Salma and then at Simon.

Simon looked away; that was the route he always took to the church. Could it be the Iqbal had been following him? He'd been very angry the last time he'd seen him, very angry indeed.

'Did they say anything else?' he asked his daughter. 'Had he been robbed?'

Zara wiped her eyes and whispered, 'They said there was another man. He had been killed with Iqbal's sword. They gave it to me.' At the memory of the blood stained sword she burst out crying again.

'Another man, a thief you mean?'

She nodded, 'I suppose so.'

'Did they say anymore about him?' Simon asked.

'No. Just that they were both dead,' she sobbed. 'Oh what will I do now?'

'Hush child, you have your family here to help you,' said Salma, still blinking in the candlelight. 'Now I suggest we leave any more questions until tomorrow. Simon, in the morning, you should go and talk to the muhtasib and find out all you can.'

'I'll go with him,' said Makoud. 'I know the chief of police well.'

'Now let's get these two to bed,' said Basma, beginning to bustle around with extra sleeping mats and blankets.

'She can sleep in our room,' said Salma.

Simon took his daughter's hand and said as gently as he could, 'Where is he now?'

'At home, Baba. He's at home.'

He looked at the women gathered around her. 'Don't worry Simon; we will see to that. We'll go around there now and clean his body.'

'Yes and we'll let the imam know,' added Abal. 'We'll take care of everything. You look after your daughter.'

How easily the women took it in their stride. Births and deaths, they handled them both in the same calm and practiced manner, with the minimum of fuss and yet ensuring that these most important events in one's life went as smoothly as possible. How glad he was that they were there.

The next morning Makoud and Simon sat listening to the muhtasib explaining how the night watchman had come across the two men just before sunrise. He'd recognised Iqbal straightaway because he'd had occasion to buy some large pots from him only the week before. He knew the other man as well, a local beggar who normally sat outside the main gate to the alcazaba. Some said he was a disabled soldier, down on his luck, others that he was a petty thief. Whichever he was, he was dead now. It was up to Allah to judge him.

'Anyway,' the muhtasib continued, 'The night watchman came straight here and we sent someone to collect the bodies.'

'So do you know what happened?' asked Makoud.

'Simple case of a robbery that went wrong, that's what it looks like; except, he paused. 'If it was a robbery, why didn't they take his money bag? And a couple of other things puzzle me.' The police chief looked straight at Simon, who could feel a flush of heat creeping up his neck.

'What's that?' asked Makoud.

'Why was a law-abiding alfarero carrying a sword? And where was he going at that time of night? His wife said he wouldn't eat dinner and stormed out of the house straight after evening prayers.'

'Did he tell her where he was going?'

The policeman shook his head, 'No, but it's strange isn't it? We don't know if he was about to leave the city, or if he was returning. Either way he encountered his assailant, and it was lucky he had his sword with him.'

'I can't see anything lucky about it. My son-in-law has been murdered and my daughter is now a widow,' said Simon, his fear of discovery making him bold, despite the man's fixed gaze.

'Quite so. You don't know if he had any enemies in the city?'

'Not that I know of; I wouldn't have thought he'd lived here long enough to make enemies,' said Simon.

'So where was he before that?' asked the muhtasib.

'Ronda,' Simon lied. 'We only arrived here a few months ago.'

'And the reason for coming to Malaqah?' He seemed interested in this new information.

'I invited them,' said Makoud. 'Simon's wife is my cousin. She's a scribe. I wrote to tell her that they were looking for more scribes at the university.'

'And that's where she works now?' he asked.

'Yes. We both work there,' said Simon.

'What about you? Did you get along well with your son-in-law?' he asked, turning his attention back to Simon.

'Naturally. He wouldn't have come with us if there was bad feeling between us. He and his wife would have stayed in Ronda.' Simon was getting angry now. 'I don't know why you're asking me all these questions.'

'Well, I have a witness who says he saw him arguing with a tall man, the day before he died. A foreigner, he said. Would that have been you?'

'No, it wasn't. Maybe he'd had an encounter with that beggar.'

'I've often seen beggars outside the gate; I suppose he was one of them. Surprising though, because they always seem so harmless,' said Makoud.

'Yes and they certainly don't look strong enough to take on someone like my son-in-law,' said Simon.

'I expect that's why he's dead as well,' said the muhtasib. 'Well, I'm afraid there's no more I can tell you, at the moment. It's a very unfortunate situation. I will contact you again if I find out anything more.'

'Ma'a salama, and thank you,' said Makoud.

The police chief was obviously puzzled by Iqbal's death, despite the fact that his killer was lying dead beside him. And why was he focussing his attention on Simon? 'Do you think he suspects me?' he asked Makoud.

'No, why would he? He's just trying to find out why a respectable afarero was found dead, with a sword in his hand. I think you might be reading too much into it. Don't worry, Simon. I doubt if we'll ever find out what happened that night.'

'But if he finds out I went to the alfareria and had a fight with Iqbal, he may think I had something to do with his death.'

'What and then you killed an innocent beggar? No.'

They walked back towards the apothecary's shop in silence until Makoud said, 'It is strange though that Iqbal should be out at night on his own, with a sword. Is that like him, do you think?'

'Well I don't know. We haven't seen that much of him since they moved out,' Simon replied, hoping this lie wouldn't reveal itself in his customary flush of colour. 'But after we were attacked on the way to Malaqah that time, I think he felt it was necessary to be armed whenever he went anywhere.'

'And where do you think he was going?'

Simon shook his head. 'Zara said he was thinking of taking a second wife; maybe he was going to meet her father. Who knows, he could have had a dozen reasons.'

Makoud stared at him. 'Taking another wife? What did Zara feel about that? They've not been married long.'

'She keeps these things to herself.' Simon didn't want to discuss his son-in-law any further; Makoud had a way of getting information out of people, and he didn't want him to know his fears. Makoud, like everyone else in the family believed he was a converted Muslim. He would not be happy to know he had a criminal living in his house. He looked over his shoulder, suddenly worried that he was being followed, but the cobbled street was empty. Perhaps Makoud was right, perhaps he was seeing trouble where there was none.

That night when prayers were over, the family meal eaten and everything closed up for the night, Simon and Salma spread out their sleeping mats and lay down. Salma was desperate to find out what had happened, but Zara and the baby were there, curled up together beside them. She could see something was worrying Simon, but it was impossible to ask him without Zara overhearing.

'Tisbah ala-kheir, husband,' she whispered in his ear. 'Sleep well. We'll leave for work early tomorrow, so we can talk.'

He took her hand and squeezed it gently. 'Sleep well, my love,' he whispered.

But Salma couldn't sleep. Her head began to spin with thoughts of what they should do, and each time the wheel came back to one solution; they had to leave Malaqah. Tears fell silently onto her pillow. Her dream had been short-lived, and although it broke her heart to admit it, that was the only solution.

She brushed away her tears and turned away from Simon, who, by then, was sleeping as peacefully as if he hadn't a care in the world. What had he said to her a few days ago, the day after his fight with Iqbal? Yes, Marwen had seen them arguing outside the library. She wouldn't put it past the assistant librarian to try to find out more about their history. What if Iqbal had told him about Simon visiting the church in Ardales. She shivered and pulled the blanket closer around her.

In Ardales had nobody really cared what Simon did. So much tragedy had hit the town in recent times that people minded their own business. If they suspected Simon was not what he claimed, then they kept it to themselves, but here it was different. Marwen hated her; she knew he would do anything to get rid of her. And if, by chance, he had found out about Simon, then it wouldn't be long before he told someone. She couldn't let that happen.

CHAPTER 27

Fatima stood by the ramparts watching her maid scamper up the path towards her. As usual her hair was loose and a mess, and she was sure she could see a tear in the hem of her dress. When would that girl learn to dress herself properly? Did she have no respect for her role as maidservant to a queen? Such things had never happened in Malaqah. She would have to speak to her again.

'Sayyida, Sayyida, the leader of the Barghawatas wants to speak to you,' the girl began to say before she even reached her.

'Calm down. Now come here and speak to me properly.'

The maid approached and bobbed down in something between a curtsey and a bow. She flicked her untidy hair back from her face and began again, 'Sayyida, Abu Mansur Isa, the ruler of the Barghawata, would like to speak to you about a matter of the utmost urgency.'

'Where is he?'

'Below, Sayyida, in the throne room.' She bobbed again.

'I won't see him there. Take him to the gardens and I will talk with him by the fish pond. But before you do that, run and tidy yourself up, child. You look like a ragamuffin.'

'Yes, Sayyida.'

Fatima watched as her maid hurried back into the zenana, desperate to run but aware of her mistress's eyes on her. What did that old man want that was so urgent? He had never been to visit her before; in fact he completely ignored her presence in Sebta, preferring to talk with Naja. Maybe he was going to treat her with more respect now that Ben-Yaha would soon be khalifa.

She smoothed her dress into place and pulled her scarf over her head so that it partially covered her face. The Barghawata women didn't wear the veil; they wore embroidered caps and brightly coloured scarves similar to those that women wore in Malaqah. Today, however, she was meeting Abu Mansur Isa, and he was an old man who had reigned for many years. She did not know what to expect. The Barghawatas were Muslim, but they did not worship all the same things that she did. It was said that their religion was a mixture of many things, including Judaism and even astrology. Would he expect her to have her head covered? She didn't want to show him any disrespect, after all she lived in Sebta at his assent.

By the time she had wandered down to the gardens, the king of the Barghawatas was already waiting for her. He rose and gave her a brief, but courteous bow.

'Sayyida Fatima,' he said. 'As-salama alaykum.'

'Wa alaykum e-salam, Your Majesty,' she replied. 'Welcome.'

She motioned for him to sit, and sat opposite him on a low bench, close to the fountain. Listening to the water tumbling into the pool helped her to relax. Why was he here? And what did he want with her?

'I was very sorry to hear of the death of your son. Young Hasan was a capable young man; he would have made a strong ruler, given time. Sadly, time is not always available. But that is not why I have come here today, Sayyida, in such haste. It is because what I have to tell you could not wait until your period of iddah had passed.'

Fatima stared at his grizzled face, as brown and wrinkled as a walnut. Her heart began to race. What was so bad that he had come to give her the news in person?

'It is about your second son,' he continued. 'He languishes in prison still. And your servant, Naja al-Siqlabi has declared himself khalifa. Worse still, he has appointed as his grand vizier, a man of whom you may have heard, ibn Baqanna.'

Fatima thought she would faint. Naja, whom she'd trusted with her sons when they were tiny, who had promised faithfully to release Ben-Yahya, who had gone to Malaqah with her blessing, had betrayed her.

'I can see it is a shock for you, Sayyida. But I must urge you to be strong. We must act at once.'

'We?' she managed to whisper.

'Yes, we. I will provide you with a ship and one hundred armed soldiers. You must go to Malaqah and confront Naja al-Siqlabi. You must release your son from prison before it is too late. If you delay they will undoubtedly kill him. They will throw his body into the sea and nobody will ever be any the wiser.'

'But…' she began.

'There is no time for hesitation, Sayyida. Your ship sails tonight. In two days you will be in Malaqah and you will take them by surprise.'

'But, I am not a soldier, Your Majesty.'

'No, but you are a mother and a queen. The people will listen to you. They will throw out the imposter and release your son.' He took her hand and squeezed it gently. 'Have courage, Sayyida. I will send my most experienced quaid with you. He will be by your side all the time.'

'Thank you, Your Majesty. But why are you doing this for me? Why does it matter to you if my sons are both killed and another man has taken what was rightfully theirs?'

'Many years ago, I promised your husband that if ever the time should come when you and your sons were in danger, I would protect you. I am an old man now, and I don't want to go to Paradise with that promise broken.' He stood up. 'Now I must go. There is a lot for you to do. Be at the harbour at sunset and bring all your household with you. If we are victorious you won't be coming back to Sebta.'

'Ma'a salama, Your Majesty, and thank you,' Fatima said, her head whirling with thoughts, not least of which was whether she could trust this old man.

'Alla ysalmak, Sayyida. May Allah keep you safe.'

Fatima was woken from her troubled sleep by her maid shaking her arm.

'Sayyida, the captain says we will be landing very soon.'

Fatima rubbed the sleep from her eyes and took the djellaba from the maid and wrapped it around herself. The sun was creeping over the horizon, staining the harbour walls pink. Soon it would be daylight. She shivered, more from fear about what would happen, than from the cold. All around her the soldiers were gathering their belongings and preparing to land. It was like a dream, dark figures silhouetted against the pale sky, moving soundlessly, the captain giving orders in hushed whispers, the ship gliding silently into the harbour, its oars cutting through the still water. But it was no dream. Behind the towering walls of the alcazaba her son was waiting to be released. Had he heard about his brother? Did he know that Naja was in Malaqah? She doubted it. Was he even still alive? Her heart gave a jump as she considered that she might already be too late.

'Quaid, what is the plan? Tell me what I have to do,' she asked the officer that Abu Mansur had sent with her.

'Don't worry, Sayyida. As soon as we land we will march up to the alcazaba and demand entry. Then we will go straight to the dungeons and release your son. We can deal with the traitor later.'

'And me?'

'You will walk at the head of the army, with me by your side. People will recognise you. They will welcome you back to Malaqah.'

It seemed a simple enough plan but why was he so sure that people would welcome them? And would they indeed recognise her? She had been gone seven long years. It had seemed a lifetime on that barbaric rock. Had Abu Mansur sent her here to be killed? Was this a trap or did the quaid actually believe that she would be welcome in Malaqah?

'Come Inma, dress my hair. I must look like a queen, not a weary traveller. Get out my royal djellaba and bring me my bag of jewels. Win or lose I want everyone to know who I am, Sayyida al-Malika, the mother of the khalifa.'

Suddenly they had arrived and the soldiers were disembarking. One of them took her hand and helped her climb out of the boat. Fatima could feel herself shaking as her feet touched the soil of Malaqah once more. She was home. No longer nervous, no longer hesitant, now she was angry. Abu Mansur was right; she was a queen and her son had been wrongfully imprisoned. She would set him free or die in the attempt. She would call on her people to help her honour their shared past. The reign of the Hammudids was not yet over.

She pulled her djellaba open so that everyone could see the jewels sparkling around her neck and touched the gold crown that sat upon her greying hair.

'Sayyida, walk here, between us,' said the Barghawat quaid, positioning her so that there were soldiers on both sides of her and behind.

They set off up the path towards the alcazaba, the soldiers' boots drumming on the cobbles. As they passed the fishermen unloading the night's catch, the women collecting fish to take to the market, the merchants making their way down to their ships in the harbour, she could see people beginning to stare at her and then a murmur began and gradually it grew louder and louder.

'Sayyida al-Malika, Sayyida al-Malika, Sayyida al-Malika,' the people began to chant. They had recognised her and they were pleased to see her. Fatima felt her heart swell with pride. The people of Malaqah remembered her. She was not forgotten. Someone in the crowd began to sing a traditional song, and she felt her eyes fill with tears.

When they arrived at the gates to the alcazaba, the guards stood aside without a word and let them pass. One young soldier bowed as she passed and then they were all bowing to her. The people followed; there were more than a hundred of them now and they continued to chant her name as they all marched towards the alcázar.

She and the Barghawata soldiers crossed the parade ground to the Garnata Gate and stopped. A soldier dressed in the uniform of an officer came up to them.

'As-salama alaykum, Sayyida. Welcome home. How may we help you?' he asked.

'I will tell you all what you can do to help me,' she said, turning round and opening her arms to the people following her.

Instantly they were silent and each one bowed before her. 'I have come here today to release my son Prince Idris ibn Yahya ibn Ali from the dreadful dungeon where he has been incarcerated these last two years.' A gasp went up when the people heard these words. It was just as she had thought; nobody knew he was there.

'We thought he was dead,' shouted one man. 'Who did this to the prince?'

'He must be released,' shouted another.

'At once.'

'Release him. Release him.'

'He's only a lad.'

'How can this have happened?'

'Release him.

'We thought he was still in Sebta.'

The crowd began to chant his name, 'Idris, Idris, Idris. Idris.'

She raised her hands again and the crowd went quiet. 'My son is the rightful heir to the throne,' she said, her voice no longer weak and trembling. Her words echoed around the parade ground like a carrion call. 'The man he thought was his friend, his former tutor who had served him since he was a boy, has betrayed him and my family. The man to whom we gave his freedom, a man we welcomed into our home, has double-crossed us, taken us for fools. This traitor, the saqaliba, promised me that he would release my son and place him on the throne. Instead he has declared himself your new khalifa. He thinks I am a weak, helpless woman. He thinks no-one will stand against him. He thinks no-one cares that my son still languishes in the prison.'

'We care, Sayyida al-Malika,' shouted a man. 'We care.'

'Free the prince,' the crowd began to shout.

'Guards, open the gate and let us get to the dungeons.'

'The khalifa's son. It's a disgrace.'

Everyone was shouting now and pushing forward.

'Where's the traitor? Where's Naja al-Siqlabi? Bring him out.'

'Let's string him up,' shouted someone and was immediately greeted with cheers of assent.

'Come with me, Sayyida,' said the officer. 'I will send someone to release your son. I think we can leave the people to deal with Naja.' He waved the Barghawata soldiers forward and led Fatima into the inner courtyard. 'You and your maids can stay here in the zenana. I will have them bring your son to you there.'

Fatima looked behind her. Already Naja and his guards had come out of the palace to see what all the commotion was about. For the first time that she could remember her old slave looked frightened, but she knew he was not one to run and hide, and she watched him walk forward trying to remonstrate with the crowd.

'Best you go now, Sayyida,' said the Barghawata quaid. 'You won't want to see this.'

He was wrong. She did want to see the crowd turn on the traitor; she wanted to see his blood flow on the cobble stones. She wanted her revenge. But the officer had her arm and was pulling her gently away. He was right; she had to concentrate on the release of her son. The people were still chanting his name but she knew how easily swayed a crowd could be and how silver-tongued Naja was when he wanted to be. She turned again to look for the old tutor but he had disappeared amid the sea of angry faces.

Naja couldn't believe it when he saw Fatima talking to the people. How had that been allowed to happen? Why had the guards let her into the alcázar? And where was ibn Baqanna? He signalled to his personal guard to follow him and marched out to the parade ground. He would speak to them in person. He'd explain to the people that their prince was no longer capable of ruling, that it was nothing to do with him that he was in prison; Idris's own brother had locked him up and would have incarcerated Naja as well if he'd had the chance. They would soon realise that he was doing the right thing. He'd show that stupid woman that she was too late; he was in charge now. He knew the people; they wouldn't listen to a woman, even if she was the widow of a khalifa.

But the crowd didn't part before him as he expected; they took no notice of his soldiers and rushed forward, not giving him time to speak. He was surrounded. He felt his blood run cold as he realised that the people were not interested in his words; they wanted his blood. He lifted his hand and called for order but it was too late; no-one was listening. This was not the time to reason with them; he had to get back to safety. He turned in panic, calling for his guards, but they were nowhere to be seen. He realised he was alone, with only his sword to defend himself, and the angry mob was cutting off his retreat. He tried to push his way through, but the people began to jostle him, pushing him one way and then the other.

'Did you want to speak to us, traitor?'

'What lies do you have for us, now?'

A stone caught him on the forehead and he felt blood run down into his eyes, blinding him. He pulled out his sword and brandished it at the mob, but they laughed in his face.

'What do you think you can do with that pinprick?' jeered one of the women, as the man next to her wrested it from his hand.

'Let me explain,' Naja said, but his voice was nothing more than a croak. Fear was paralysing him.

'String him up,' someone shouted.

'Yes, a traitor's death for him.'

The call went out, 'String him up. String him up.'

'We'll put his head on the gates. Let everyone see what happens to traitors.'

Naja felt his legs go weak and would have fallen to the ground but the force of the crowd crushing him from all sides kept him upright. Then a savage blow to the back of his head knocked him sideways and suddenly he was lifted up and carried on the shoulders of the protestors. Not to the victory parade as he had expected; this was to his execution. For a few moments he was aware of the blinding pain in his head then he lost consciousness.

CHAPTER 28

Although Umar had seemed surprised to see the changes in her, Layla remembered him very well from their days as children. As an impressionable seven-year old she had been in love with her older second cousin. He was handsome, brave and very funny. But, much to her disappointment, he barely noticed her, and it wasn't for want of trying on her part; she followed him at a discreet distance when he exercised her uncle's horses, she tagged along with the older children when they went swimming in the lake and she always tried to get his attention when the whole family got together for celebrations. She even suggested to her parents that she should go and live with her mother's cousin, Makoud, so that she could be near him. None of her schemes worked, and Umar remained oblivious of her presence; to him she was as annoying as a summer fly, and as dispensable. By the time she was ten, Umar was working on his uncle's stud farm and she had lost interest in him. Her attention was now firmly fixed on one of her classmates, a boy who lived next door to her.

She thought back to their recent encounter. He was as handsome as ever, but broader and more muscular. He had coarsened a bit, but that was to be expected; he was a soldier, after all. She smiled to herself. She could swear that he was nervous when he spoke to her; his remark about finding a rich husband had been a bit rude, but he had apologised.

'Layla, what are you doing, child?' her father called. 'Stop daydreaming; your mother wants your help with the washing.'

'Coming Baba.'

They had come to an agreement. They would leave, and in the meantime Simon would stay away from the church. She wasn't happy about it but what else could they do? Zara and the baby would go with them. They couldn't leave her here on her own with no husband to protect her, and Salma couldn't ask Makoud to take responsibility for her; he had done so much for them already. But what about Layla?

'We must talk to Makoud,' Simon said. 'We can't leave just like that.'

'But what do we tell him? I don't want to lie to my cousin; he's been so good to us.'

'Don't. Just tell him that we feel Malaqah is not for us, so we're going home.'

'He won't believe me.'

'Does that matter? What matters is that we don't drag him into our problems and we don't put him and his family in danger. We should never have come here,' he added, putting his head in his hands. 'It's all my fault.'

'You can't help it if your faith is so strong.'

'But I'm putting my salvation before my family. Is that a Christian thing to do?' he asked.

She didn't answer; instead she said, 'All right. We'll speak to him when we get home.' She had that awful sinking feeling in her stomach that always happened when she was about to do something she knew she would regret. How could they explain to Makoud why they were turning their backs on his hospitality, his friendship, and going home? How hurt he would be.

They walked through the narrow streets in silence. The late afternoon sun glinted on the cobbles; it lit up the sandy coloured walls of the city and threw long shadows across their path. It was a beautiful city made more so by the sunshine; she had warmed to it the moment she had stepped through its impressive West Gate. And now she was leaving it, her dreams in tatters. She couldn't let Simon know how badly she felt, not just for herself but for their daughters. What was there back in Ardales for them? For any of them?

A seagull let out a shrill cry as it flew low over their heads. She watched its slow grace as it flapped its way towards the sea.

'We'll speak to him before dinner,' Simon said. 'Best to get it over with.'

'You don't think we should talk to the girls first?'

'No. We'll tell them later.'

Makoud was about to close the shop when they arrived.

'Just in time,' he said. 'I'm glad you're back, Zara has been in low spirits today. It will cheer her up to see you.' He bolted the door and began to cross the narrow street to his home.

'Wait cousin,' said Salma. 'We need to speak to you.'

'Now? Can't it wait till we get inside?'

'No, we need to speak to you before we join the others.'

'Very well,' he replied. 'What is it? I've never seen you so sad before, Salma.'

'We are going back to Ardales,' Simon said. 'You have been so kind and welcoming, cousin, but we feel it is time to go home.'

'But this is your home now. I don't understand. I thought you were happy.'

'We are. We were. It's just time to leave,' said Salma, her eyes brimming with tears.

'Have you lost your job? What's happened to make you want to leave?'

'We can't tell you Makoud, but we aren't making this decision lightly. Believe me,' Simon said. He put his hand on Salma's arm. 'We will be sorry to go.'

Makoud smiled at them sadly, 'I will be very sorry to see you leave. So what will you do about Layla?'

'We hope she will agree to marry your son, but if she won't then she will come with us. We won't force her to marry but we have no intention of leaving her here, unprotected,' said Simon.

Salma suddenly noticed her older daughter had just arrived and was standing in the doorway, staring at her father. 'What are you talking about, Baba? What is so urgent that you want to hurry Layla into a marriage that she doesn't want?' Zara asked. 'And where are you going?'

'Well you'll know soon enough, so we might as well tell you now. All of you,' Simon said following Makoud into the house. He waited until Makoud had called his wives and Ibrahim had joined them before continuing, 'We are leaving Malaqah. We're returning to Ardales.'

The stunned looks on everyone's faces made Salma realise just how much they had become part of Makoud's family.

'But we've only just arrived, Baba,' Zara gasped.

'It's not safe here, my dear. Look what happened to Iqbal,' he replied, unconvincingly.

'But that had nothing to do with the rest of us,' Zara said. 'Iqbal was obviously moving in bad company. Why else was he in that part of the city, at that time of night?'

'Nevertheless, that is what I've decided,' Simon said.

'Well I'm not going with you,' Zara cried. Salma looked at her in alarm. Why had she raised two such defiant daughters? Surely for once they could be compliant and do what their parents wanted. 'In case you've forgotten,' Zara continued, 'I have a business to run. How else will we live? The alfarería is my only livelihood, Mama. I have to stay here.'

'But you will be all alone,' protested Simon. 'No, that's impossible.'

'I will have our cousins to support me. And Iqbal didn't work alone; he had two excellent alfareros who will want to continue working. If it doesn't succeed then I will return to Ardales, but not now, not so soon after my husband's death.'

Salma could see, even if Simon couldn't, that there would be no moving Zara. She was right; they had brought her here to make a new life and now they wanted to take her back again. Zara was the most practical of her daughters; she was strong. She would survive in the city; Salma was sure of that.

'Let's talk about how you would manage, later,' Salma said. 'There's the baby to think of as well, remember.'

'I think it's time we sat down to eat,' said Basma, looking completely baffled by the news. 'The food will be spoiled if we leave it much longer.'

Salma went out to the patio to help her bring in the plates and a large bowl of rice and fish stew. It smelled delicious, but she had no appetite. What was she going to do about her daughters? She couldn't bear to leave without them, but if she insisted on staying they could put the whole family in danger.

Umar was angry, as much with himself for taking so long to tell his father that he wanted to marry Layla, as he was with Ibrahim for beating him to it. Well at least Baba had said it was up to Layla; it was her choice. But what if she chose neither of them? She wanted love, not just security. He would speak to her and tell her how much he loved her. He knew he couldn't promise her the same security as Ibrahim, with his career as an apothecary laid out for him. What soldier could? However he could promise to love her forever. But would that be enough? Would her parents agree?

He went to the fountain and stripped off his uniform, washed himself until his skin stung and his hair gleamed. Once satisfied he dressed in his best and newest uniform then set off for his parents' house. His mind was whirling; what should he say to her? How could he convince her to marry him? And if she accepted him, where would they live? He didn't have living accommodation over the shop, like Ibrahim. Would she mind living with his parents? And what about Ibrahim? How would he feel to be rejected in favour of his older brother? Umar groaned. There was no point worrying about all these things now. The time for that was when, if, she accepted him as her husband.

His mother was outside on the patio, preparing a dish of dates and almonds, when he arrived.

'You again. I am beginning to worry that something is wrong; you have taken to visiting us quite a lot lately,' Basma said. 'Is there something on your mind that you want to tell me, son?'

'As-salama alaykum, Mama. Has Baba told you I'm thinking of getting married?'

'Oh, my boy, how wonderful. Two of my sons have at last decided to settle down. I am so happy to hear it,' she cried, throwing her arms around him.

'So Baba hasn't told you everything then?'

'What hasn't he told me? Your father never tells me anything. It was Ibrahim who told me he'd asked permission to have Layla as his bride. So, tell me, what else should I know about my own children?'

CHAPTER 29

Ben-Yahya could hear the commotion in the parade ground. What was happening? Were they coming to release him? He tried to pull himself up to see through the tiny opening in the wall of his cell, but he had no strength in his arms and fell back on the pile of filthy straw that was his bed. He lay there looking up at the sliver of light that crept through the opening and strained to hear what the crowd were shouting. The tone was angry. No, this wasn't a crowd about to release their prince; this was a crowd calling for blood. Did they mean him? Or was some other poor fool in trouble now? Did that mean he was to get a companion in this black hole that was his home? His neighbour in the adjacent cell had been little company, but at least Ben-Yahya had been able to hear his snoring at night and know that some living creature was close by, other than the multitude of rats that visited him every night. It was some time now since the prisoner had died and since then Ben-Yahya's feeling of isolation had intensified and he longed to join him. When he heard that Naja wanted him dead, and had even sent soldiers to kill him, his instinct had been to survive, and thanks to the gaoler he had. But it had been a mistake. He should have stayed in his own cell and let them kill him, rather than hide away pretending to be a dead man. He'd sooner be dead anyway than continue with this half-life. He knew he was never going to get out of here as soon as the gaoler told him that Naja had declared himself khalifa and appointed ibn Baqanna as his grand vizier. He had been stunned by the news, to think his friend could do that to him. He still couldn't understand his betrayal but he knew he would never be released now. As far as everyone was concerned he had died and his body lay at the bottom of the Middle Sea. The only way he was going to leave this dungeon was in a dirty jute sack, just like his old neighbour. Food for the fish, that was all the future he had to look forward to.

The clanging of heavy bolts being pulled back echoed along the passageway, followed by a sound he knew well: the slow, ponderous steps of his gaoler. Was it mealtime already? He never thought of his meals as lunch or dinner, or even breakfast; time had no meaning here in this dark nether land. Even his stomach didn't act as a guide because he was always hungry. Hunger filled his waking hours and even woke him from his sleep. It racked his body with longing and filled his dreams. At first, following the khalifa's orders, they had fed him well, but bit by bit the portions had got smaller until now he was fed slops, just like all the other prisoners, he was sure.

The footsteps grew closer. Was this the end he had prayed for? Had they found out about the trick the old gaoler had played on them? Were they going to drag him to his execution? Was this why the mob were screaming for blood? The footsteps stopped outside his door and he heard the elderly gaoler struggling to unlock it. He began to whisper his prayers to Allah, asking for forgiveness for his sins and praying that he would welcome him into Paradise.

At last the cell door swung open, and only when Ben-Yahya opened his eyes, did he realise that someone was standing behind the gaoler. The man, a soldier, an officer, entered Ben-Yahya's cell and bowed. 'Your Majesty, I have come to release you.' Ben-Yahya, who had tried to stand up when they entered, collapsed back on his pallet. Was this a dream? Had Allah answered his prayers so quickly? 'Your Majesty, let me help you,' said the officer, reaching across and lifting up Ben-Yahya in his strong arms. 'I will take you to the alcázar, where your mother is waiting.'

Mama was here. So it wasn't a dream. He really was going to be free. He tried to speak, to ask what had happened, but no words would come, only tears that flowed freely down his cheeks, washing away the grime of the prison.

Ben-Yahya staggered along behind the quaid, blinking at the fierceness of the sunlight. A squad of soldiers formed a protective cordon around him as they headed for the alcázar. How long ago was it that he'd taken this same walk, only to end up in the dungeons? It seemed like a lifetime. Betrayed by his own brother and then by his friend; he felt he could trust no-one. Gradually the warm sunshine began to ease the pain in his legs and back, and he pulled himself up as straight as he could manage. His mother, he could trust his mother; he had never doubted her. But he was surprised that she had come here from Sebta to save him. How she had managed to do that with no army and no money, he had no idea, but he knew she was a woman who would do anything for her family, for her sons. What had the officer called him? Your Majesty? If Ben-Yahya was going to be the next khalifa; he needed to look like one.

'Quaid. Take me to my quarters. I need to clean myself up before I see my mother. I cannot go into the zenana looking like this.'

'Very well, Your Majesty. I will have your servants prepare a bath for you and send word to your mother that you will join her later.'

'Thank you.'

A commotion near the main gate of the alcazaba made him stop. 'What's happening?' he asked. Then as a great cheer went up from the crowd, he saw Naja's head being hoisted on a pole by the gate.

'The traitor has been executed,' the officer replied. 'Come, Your Majesty, we must get to the palace. The people will want to see you later, when you are ready to speak to them.'

The quaid was right in his assumption; Ben-Yahya was not ready to face the crowd. In his weakened state, he was fearful of them; they had turned on Naja in an instant, could they not also turn against him? He must be prepared when he stood before them. They would expect a strong leader, not a man enfeebled by incarceration. No, he couldn't allow them to see him like this, dirty and half-starved, dressed in rags.

He tried to match his step to that of the quaid, but try as he might, he could feel the strength draining from his legs. He would not be able to go much further.

'We are almost there, Your Majesty,' said the officer.

They had arrived at the entrance to the alcázar. Suddenly there was only one thing on his mind, not the possibility of lying in the arms of a beautiful woman—he was too exhausted for that. Nor the thought of the delicious food that he knew would have been prepared for him—suddenly his shrunken stomach had no appetite. Now he was free, none of the delights he had lain in his cell dreaming about, mattered. All Ben-Yahya wanted right then, was to wallow in the luxury of a hot, scented bath, have the grime scrubbed from his body and let the stench of the dungeons be erased forever from his skin.

Fatima began to tremble when she entered the zenana; it seemed years since she had been forced to leave. Now she was back and the emotions that raced through her body were a mixture of pleasure and disbelief; she had never believed she would be able to return to her home.

'Sayyida, welcome back,' said her servants, rushing to meet her. They bowed before her and then immediately began to take care of her as though she had only just left. Rahil, her old maid was still there, older and more careworn but just the same kindly face. She carefully removed Fatima's outer garments and led her through to the bath chamber.

'We thought we would never see you again, Sayyida,' she said, her eyes shining with unshed tears. 'We are so very happy that you have come home. But now I will leave you with Zena, while I go and find you some clean clothes.'

Fatima didn't recognise Zena; she was very young, and she didn't remember seeing her in the zenana before. She would have preferred it if Rahil had stayed with her but she knew that each one had their tasks to do and she didn't want to disrupt their routine. She forced herself to relax and allowed the girl to remove her clothes and lead her into the warm bath. Fatima stretched out her legs and let herself sink below the scented water. She sighed; it was so good to be home. The musicians were playing a traditional tune that she remembered from her childhood; it soothed her and took her mind off the shouts of the crowd outside the palace gates. Suddenly there was an enormous cheer from the crowd. She sat up, pulling away from the ministrations of the young slave girl.

'What has happened?'

'I don't know Sayyida. Shall I send someone to find out?'

'Yes, quickly, child. Then get me out of here.'

While an even younger girl scampered off to see what the commotion was about, Zena helped Fatima out of the bath and wrapped her in a white robe.

'Hurry. I need to see what's going on.' Were they cheering because Ben-Yahya had been released? She prayed to Allah that it was so.

At last she was ready and hurried out of the zenana, just in time to meet the young slave returning.

'Sayyida,' she said, bowing as low as she could.

'Yes, child. What have you found out? Quick, tell me.'

'Sayyida, your son has been released from prison. He is with the quaid now and will come to see you at his first convenience,' the child said, obviously repeating the quaid's words exactly.

He was free. Praise be to Allah; she had succeeded in getting him released. Tears of joy cascaded down her cheeks; this was the moment she had been praying for.

'Are you all right?' the slave girl asked, nervously. 'Shall I get Rahil for you?'

'Yes, child. I need to look my best today. My son will soon be your new khalifa,' she said, wiping her tears hurriedly away. Her job wasn't over. She had to make sure that Ben-Yahya was crowned as soon as possible and that any threats to his safety were removed. 'What of the traitors?'

The slave looked distressed. 'I saw a head on a pole by the main gate,' she whispered. 'The people executed him.'

'Him? Who did they execute, child? Hurry find out whose head it is?'

Before the young slave scurried off to find out what she could, she whispered, rather hesitantly, 'Sayyida, there is a soldier outside waiting to speak to you. I think he is a foreigner.'

The Barghawata quaid. Of course. In the excitement of the moment. she'd forgotten all about the soldiers who had brought her to Malaqah. 'Send him in at once,' she ordered. How could she ever repay Abu Mansur for his help? She still didn't know his real motives for helping her—she was sure it was not out of respect for her dead husband as he claimed—but as far as she was concerned, his reasons didn't matter. For now all she could feel was gratitude towards the old man who had made this possible.

The Barghawata quaid bowed respectfully. 'Sayyida, all is well?' he asked.

'Yes, thank you, Quaid. My son has been released and at least one of the traitors has been dealt with.'

'Yes, Naja al-Siqlabi. I saw them dragging his body towards the main gate.'

'But what of ibn Baqanna?' she asked.

'He escaped, Sayyida, but don't worry he won't get far. Your soldiers are already searching for him.'

'He mustn't escape. He's an evil man,' she whispered. 'My son will never be safe while he lives. We must find him.'

'Yes, Sayyida. Do not concern yourself; they will find him. Now, you have no more need of me and my men, so I will take my leave. The khalifa's army will protect you now.'

'I am forever in your debt, Quaid. Please give this to your king as a token of my gratitude.' She pulled a large emerald ring from her finger and handed it to him. 'It was a present from my husband. He too would have been most grateful that Abu Mansur came to our aid, and helped to prevent the annihilation of the Hammudid line.'

The Barghawata quaid bowed. 'Ma'a salama, Sayyida. May Allah keep you safe.'

She watched as he left the room, and hoped she hadn't dismissed him too soon. The people wanted her son back on the throne, but did the viziers?

'Sayyida, Sayyida.' the young slave girl hurried into her room. 'The dead man is someone called Naja. The other one has escaped but everyone is searching for him. The officer said to tell you that you will be informed as soon as he is captured.'

'Thank you, child.' She turned to one of her personal guards. 'Tell the grand vizier, Labib that I wish to discuss some matters with him as soon as possible.'

All Fatima's fears disappeared when she saw Ben-Yahya walk into the zenana. This was the moment she had been waiting for; during two long years she had prayed to Allah to return her son to her. Now here he was, standing before her; it was a moment that she thought would never come. She had lost her beloved husband and her elder son, but Allah had returned little Ben-Yahya to her. She couldn't contain her joy, and her eyes filled with tears as she grasped him to her breast and held him tight.

'Mama, are you trying to strangle me?' Ben-Yahya gasped, pulling away from her gently.

'Oh, excuse me, my dearest. I am just so happy to see you alive and well.' She studied him carefully. 'Although you do look a little thin. Have they not been feeding you?'

Her son smiled at her. 'I am perfectly well. Now tell me how you managed to secure my release. What magic did you use? Or did you find a purse of gold to buy yourself an army?'

She laughed. 'Neither of those things. Come and sit down and I will tell you all. Then we must make arrangements for your coronation. The viziers will want to speak to you tomorrow.' She hesitated and then added, 'If you feel up to it, that is.'

'Of course. I am quite fine, Mama. I do not want to delay. I hear that my brother had talks with a mercenary; I need to find out what that's all about.'

'Tomorrow, my son. Today you need to rest and think about your future.'

She clapped her hands for the musicians to resume playing and then lay back to watch as her son began to pick at the feast she had ordered for him. Surely nothing could go wrong now.

CHAPTER 30

Salma was bent over her work, deep in concentration; she had persuaded Simon that they must stay at least until she had finished the book of poems by Solomon ibn Gabril. Reluctantly he had agreed, but made her promise not to take too long. It was a vain promise; how was she to know how long it would take? Each page was a work of art, each poem a world unto itself. As she laboriously copied his poems she was struck by the beauty of his language, words that conjured the images she drew out of the air. It was a pleasure. She stifled a groan when she thought about how much she would miss her work at the library.

'More work for the khalifa?' She looked up; Marwen was standing there, leering down at her.

'Some poems,' she replied, as politely as she could. He was always creeping up on her; it was if he expected, or wanted, to find her doing something wrong.

'Very nice. Pretty.' He leant closer and hissed, 'I think it's time you and your husband went back to where you came from. I know things about you which would make the khalifa see you in quite a different light.'

'I don't know what you're talking about, but neither Simon nor I have any intention of leaving Malaqah,' she lied.

'Really? Well, don't say you weren't warned. I'm giving you a chance to get away before your husband is arrested,' he continued.

'Is that a threat?' she asked, raising her voice so that some of the other scribes looked up to see who was disturbing the normal tranquility of the library.

'You've been warned,' he hissed and went back to his desk.

Marwen sat at the end of the scribes' room, facing them all, and now every time she looked up he was staring at her. She wiped the nib of her pen and put it down beside the manuscript. It was no good; she couldn't work like this. It was impossible to concentrate. One mistake and there would be hours of work to correct it.

'Where are you going?' called Marwen, as she put the manuscript away and stood up to leave.

'I'm feeling unwell. I'm going home,' she said. It was true; she felt sick at the thought of how many lives he could destroy. 'I'll come back later, if I feel better.' She could see from his expression that he was displeased, and that in itself cheered her. What she couldn't understand was why he hated her so much; she had no problem with any of the other scribes. On the contrary they all got on well together.

'I hope you feel better soon, Salma,' said one of the older scribes, as she walked past his desk. 'That book you're working on looks a real treasure.'

'Thank you. It's just a headache; I'll probably feel better after some fresh air.'

'See you tomorrow then.'

'Ma'a salama,' she said. She had to walk past Marwen's desk in order to leave the room, but she stared straight ahead of her, refusing to look at him.

'You will have to make up the time you've lost,' he said, loud enough for everyone to hear. 'You can't just come and go as you please, you know.'

She didn't bother answering him. She had to get out of there before she said something she would regret.

Instead of going to Makoud's house where his wives would bombard her with questions, she decided to go to his shop; as usual he was in the back preparing his weird and wonderful remedies.

'Salma, this is a surprise. But shouldn't you be working in the library?'

'Yes I should,' she said, and then began to cry. She hadn't meant to tell him about Simon; she didn't want him to think her husband was being selfish but she couldn't help herself. It all came pouring out.

'My child, sit down and tell me everything,' he said, pulling the curtain across so Ibrahim wouldn't hear them.

'First of all, who is this Marwen, and why is he so eager to ruin your lives?'

'He is the assistant librarian. And in answer to your second question, I have no idea. Neither Simon nor I have done anything to upset him, certainly not knowingly.

'You realise what it will mean if Simon's secret comes out?'

'Yes of course.'

'And how sure are you that this Marwen knows about Simon?'

'Well he said that if we didn't leave Malaqah then he would tell everyone about my husband. What else could it be?'

'Is this the first time he's threatened you?'

'Yes, but ever since we started working in the library he has been antagonistic towards me.'

'You? Not Simon?'

'Yes, it's me he hates, for some reason. He's only threatening Simon to get at me.'

'But you're planning to return to Ardales anyway, aren't you?'

'Yes, but I have work to finish first. I'm worried he will betray us to Yusuf before I have time to tell him we're both leaving.'

'I'll speak to Yusuf. I'll tell him that Marwen is making your life a misery. I'm sure he will sort it out. He owes me a favour.'

'You won't mention Simon to him, to anyone,' she said. 'Even the girls don't know.'

Makoud stared at her for a moment. 'What about Iqbal? Did he know? He was found very close to the Christians' church.'

'I don't think so. I could ask Simon; they quarrelled on the day he was killed.' She stopped and then said, her voice quavering, 'You don't think Simon had anything to do with Iqbal's death? He was very angry with him.'

'No, of course not, but it is a coincidence that he was found not five hundred paces from the church.'

'Baba, is everything all right?' asked Ibrahim, pulling back the curtain. 'As-salama alaykum, Salma. How are you?'

'Wa alaykum e-salam, Ibrahim. I've come to ask your father if there has been any progress on the wedding plans.'

Ibrahim smiled. 'Well I'm still waiting for Layla to give me a decision, but I think she might agree to be my wife. I hope so.'

'I've told him that they can live here, above the shop. I'll be retiring in a few years and then this will be Ibrahim's.'

'I will be so happy if she agrees to marry you, Ibrahim. I couldn't wish for a better son-in-law, said Salma.'

Makoud's son blushed as red as the curtain hanging behind him.

'She said anything to you, Salma?' asked Makoud.

'No, not yet, but she's stopped being angry that we didn't consult her first. So that's a good sign.'

'Indeed.' He took off his stained over-all and washed his hands. 'Ibrahim, I'm going out for a bit. I won't be long.'

'Shall we walk along together?' asked Salma. She felt less anxious now; if Makoud could gain them some more time then she could finish her work and present it to the khalifa before they left. Those beautiful poems deserved some fine calligraphy.

While Salma went back to Makoud's house, he headed straight for the library. Yusuf's son worked with Makoud's son-in-law in the shipyard. The two families had become very close since the kidnapping of Bakr and two of his men, one of whom had been Yusuf's only son. Together they had managed to rescue them, and because of that, the bond between them was still very strong. He knew Yusuf would help him if he could.

'As-salama alaykum, Makoud. I haven't seen you in a while. How are you? And your delightful family?' asked Yusuf, immediately getting up to embrace him.

'Wa alaykum e-salam, my friend. Well, we are well.'

'I'm sure you haven't come just to greet me, although you are always welcome to call in whenever you want.'

'As usual, Yusuf, you are correct. I need to speak to you about my cousin, Salma.'

'Salma, yes what a talented woman. You did me an enormous favour when you brought her here. The previous khalifa loved her work. She has such an eye for detail, and is a diligent, hard-working member of my staff. So why do you want to speak about Salma? Is she unwell? I saw she was not at her desk today.'

'This is very sensitive, I'm afraid. I've come to make a complaint about one of your librarians or scribes—I'm not sure what he does—who he has been making Salma's life very miserable.

'Marwen, my assistant librarian?'

'Yes. You know about it?'

'I had my suspicions. He's done this before. Whenever we get anyone he perceives as a threat to his position he tries to drive them away. Well he's not going to succeed this time. I blame myself; I should have dismissed him sooner, but getting experienced librarians is not easy these days.'

'So you'll speak to him?'

'Of course I will. Don't worry. I don't want Salma to leave us; she is invaluable.'

'Thank you, Yusuf. That is a weight off my mind. As I was the one to persuade her to come to Malaqah in the first place, I feel responsible for her.' He was tempted to say that Salma would probably leave anyway but that might lead to some awkward questions.

What a dreadful mess it all was; he would be so sad to see them return to Ardales, but he could see no other option. If not tomorrow, then one day Simon's secret would be discovered; they were all threatened by his foolish actions.

'Ma'a salama, my friend. And thank you.'

'Alla ysalmak. May Allah go with you,' said Yusuf.

Once his friend had left, Yusuf sent for Marwen. He should have tackled Marwen's hostility towards newcomers before, but Yusuf was not a man fond of confrontation. There had been an excellent young man, admittedly inexperienced but eager to learn, and he left after only six months. He should have done something then. Well he couldn't let it go on like this.

'Yes, sayyad? You wanted to speak to me?' Marwen asked.

Yusuf hesitated. How should he begin? There was no point in bringing up old cases; he would tackle this current problem. 'I did. It's about your behaviour, Marwen.'

'My behaviour, sayyad?' his assistant asked, trying to look surprised.

'Yes, it's unbecoming in a man of your age and position. You are my deputy. I expect more from you.'

'To what do you refer, sayyad? I am not aware that my behaviour is at fault in any way.'

'You know exactly what I'm referring to, your attitude towards the other scribes, and Salma in particular. Why are you so insecure, Marwen? There is no need to feel threatened every time I employ a new scribe.'

He saw his assistant stiffen at this insinuation. Yusuf had obviously hit a raw nerve.

'I must object, sayyad; my attitude towards the new scribe, Salma, is not in question. I have always treated her respectfully. Has she made a complaint about something I did or said?' He smirked at Yusuf, confident in the answer to his question.

'No, she has said nothing, but I am not blind, Marwen, and I am not deaf either; I hear what the other scribes are saying. The incident with the missing ink, for example, did that have anything to do with you?'

'It most certainly did not. I admit I am strict with her, and the others as well; but I am only trying to maintain the high standards we require.'

'Yes, yes, I know that, but sometimes you go too far. Today your manner was overbearing. I couldn't hear what you said to her, but it looked like a threat to me.' When Marwen didn't reply, he said, 'I won't stand for it. Do you understand? Mend your ways or I will be forced, regretfully, to ask you to leave.'

At these words the colour drained from Marwen's face. It grieved Yusuf to speak to him in that way but what else could he do? His assistant had become far too authoritarian, and not just with Salma. She'd suffered more because she was a woman;

Marwen had made it plain, on more than one occasion, that he didn't approve of female scribes.

'But sayyad, Yusuf, I have done nothing wrong.'

'I do not intend to discuss this any further, Marwen. But be advised; I will not tolerate this bullying any longer.'

Marwen looked down at the ground. Was it in humiliation or rage? Yusuf couldn't be sure. But one thing he was sure about was that his assistant would not take this rebuke without retaliating in some way. He would have to keep a close eye on him.

CHAPTER 31

The viziers were all waiting for him in the throne room; Ben-Yahya recognised a couple of them from when he was a boy, including the grand vizier, but the rest were new to him.

'Your Majesty,' they said, bowing before him. 'We are so pleased to see you back here, where you belong.'

Nobody apologised for locking him up for two years. Nobody said it had been a travesty of justice. Nobody commented on how thin and old he looked after his incarceration. It was as if his imprisonment had never happened. Maybe they hadn't been aware of his brother's treachery. No, they had known where he was and not one of them had tried to help him. He wouldn't forget that, no matter how much they fawned and pretended that they were pleased that he was their new khalifa.

'Indeed. Tell me, what is that old saying?' They looked at him in puzzlement. 'You know, the adage about if you know evil has been committed and do nothing then you are as great a sinner as the perpetrator?' Nobody replied, but he knew they had understood him. 'No matter. Let us get down to business. First of all, where is ibn Baqanna?' he asked.

There was some shuffling of feet, and then Labib said, 'He escaped yesterday, Your Majesty. We have everyone out looking for him. He won't get far.'

'Escaped? How is that possible?' He spoke quietly, bottling his anger at the casual way the grand vizier spoke.

'The people arrested the saqaliba, but ibn Baqanna fled before they could get to him.'

'Well, he must be found right away or there will be other heads adorning our beautiful gateway. Make sure that my message is clear. That man is a dangerous viper. Nobody is safe while he is free. Am I understood?'

'Yes, Your Majesty,' said Labib. 'We all know the extent of ibn Baqanna's cunning; he will stop at nothing to get what he wants.'

'The man is unscrupulous,' muttered one of his advisors.

'Shameless,' said another. 'And evil. He should never have been a vizier.'

'And to encourage that upstart to take the throne...' the treasurer said, but didn't have a chance to finish because Ben-Yahya raised his hand for silence.

'Well we agree on that at least. Now, what other matters should I know about right away?'

'There is one, Your Majesty. Your brother was planning to attack Morón. He had entered into a treaty with a Christian mercenary to gather reinforcements,' said Labib.

'A Christian? Since when have we been allies with the Christians?'

'We aren't, Your Majesty. Your brother wasn't in agreement with such a strategy, but he needed more men in order to mount an attack, so he had no alternative but to approach Roberto de las Iglesias.'

'He is better known as Jabalah,' added the general.

'What kind of man is he, this Jabalah?' asked Ben-Yahya. He wasn't ready to jump into a war with Isbiliya, especially if his army was as depleted as they were suggesting. He needed time to judge the situation for himself. If there was one thing he had learned during those long dark months in the dungeon, it was that he couldn't trust anyone. He looked around the room at the viziers attending him. He hardly knew these men; why would he believe what they said?

'Jabalah has accumulated a large army over time. He has become rich and powerful fighting for both Christian and Moorish rulers,' said Labib.

'Yes, but is he trustworthy?' asked Ben-Yahya. He saw his grand vizier look across at the general. 'Well?'

'No, Your Majesty. He is not. He has loyalty to neither Christian rulers nor Muslim, only to himself.'

'And whoever pays him the most,' added General Rashad.

'But why would my brother trust him?'

'He didn't, Your Majesty. He agreed to pay him ten thousand gold dinars, and he assumed that would be enough to buy his loyalty.'

So his brother was stupider than he'd thought.

'But why the hurry? If he were hell bent on attacking Morón, and I can't imagine why he'd want to, why not wait until his army was strong enough?'

'Abbad has sent troops to Morón and your brother feared he would use them to attack Malaqah,' explained General Rashad. 'We lost a lot of men in the battle for Écija and we would be unable to defend the city on our own if Isbiliya decided to attack.'

Ben-Yahya knew they'd been enemies of Isbiliya for years but he'd never paid much attention to the details of the campaigns when he was in Sebta, and during his imprisonment he'd received no news of the outside world, except for miscellaneous scraps of information from his gaoler. More often than not they were meaningless to him.

'What of our allies? Do we have any allies?' he asked.

'We had hoped that Garnata would support us, but they have refused,' said the general. 'They say they have domestic issues that take priority. Whatever that means.'

'There has been talk of some unrest in the city,' added one of the viziers. 'Some dispute between the Jews and the Muslims.'

'So tell me more of this threat from Isbiliya,' he said. He saw his counsellors look at each other; they seemed uncomfortable. 'I take it is a real threat?'

'Well, Your Majesty,' said General Rushad. 'In my opinion, it was over exaggerated. Abbad is not in a strong position at the moment; like us he lost a lot of men in the battle of Écija. But...' he faltered.

'But my brother didn't agree?'

'No, Your Majesty. I tried to explain to him that Abbad was a successful campaigner because he only fought the battles he knew he could win. He is like a wounded lion, who knows when to lie low, but that made Hasan all the keener to attack.'

'And these troops in Morón?'

'Very few, Your Majesty. Nothing to worry about.'

'Very well, we will make no hasty decisions on this matter. We will send an ambassador to Morón to talk about trade and gauge the mood of the city. It may be that my brother misread the situation. I do not intend to waste ten thousand gold dinars on a campaign that may not even be necessary,' Ben-Yahya announced. He saw a look of horror pass over the grand vizier's face. 'Well, Labib, what is the problem?'

'Your Majesty, you don't understand. Jabalah is already on his way to Morón.'

'Then send word to him that the attack is cancelled, and if he proceeds he won't get paid. We can't waste men and money on a campaign against one of our neighbours, when we don't even know their intentions. I do not intend to start my reign with a useless and bloody battle. You might as well realise now, gentlemen, that I am not my brother. I do not intend to squander money on pointless wars against our brother Muslims. We will fight when it is necessary; when we are under threat of attack and only then.'

'But, Your Majesty…' said Labib.

'No buts, and as for the ten thousand gold dinars, that can be used to beautify our city and enlarge our libraries. I intend to build up the cultural reputation of Malaqah to rival that of Qurtubah of old.'

'With respect, Your Majesty, Jabalah is not a man to be trifled with. He will be angry when he hears of your decision.'

'What are you saying, Labib, that the khalifa of Malaqah must bow to the wishes of a mercenary? I sincerely hope not.'

'Of course not, Your Majesty, but I wanted you to know that he might try to sack our city,' the chastened grand vizier said, looking at the ground.

'How many soldiers can you muster, General?'

'Many are already on alert, Your Majesty, ready to march to Morón. I believe we have some thirty thousand men in all.'

'Good. Make sure that your men know of our new plans but do not stand down the army until I tell you. We will be ready, just in case this Jabalah decides to attack us. Labib, speak to the ambassador and tell him of my decision; I want him to leave for Morón as soon as possible.'

'Your Majesty, what of the people living in the suburbs? They are mostly Genoese and Jewish merchants; their trade with the Maghreb is important for the economy,' asked the treasurer. 'If Jabalah attacks the city, they will certainly all be killed.'

'General Rashad, arrange for them to be ready to move into the city if we hear news of an impending attack.'

'Yes, Your Majesty.'

'And now I want to talk to the treasurer about the state of the city's finances. The rest of you may leave for now. We will meet again tomorrow morning and you can give me your reports. And you'd better have some news of ibn Baqanna.'

It was risky, he knew, but if Jabalah did decide to attack Malaqah, he would not find it a simple task. Their city was easy to defend with its strong stone walls and regularly spaced square towers; there was the Middle Sea to the south and the river Guadalmedina to the west. As soon as they received news that Jabalah was heading their way then he would mobilise the army and give the order for the people living in the suburbs to be brought within the city walls.

He leaned back and waited while his viziers left one by one, until he was alone with the treasurer. So this was what it was like to be Khalifa, to have power over everyone, to make unchallenged decisions, to be the Supreme Commander. He could feel the adrenalin running through his blood; it was exhilarating. Now he could understand why his brother had no hesitation in getting rid of anyone who threatened to take it away from him. Only one small fear niggled away at the back of his mind. Ibn Baqanna. That man had as many lives as the fabled cat. He could never rest easy until he was found.

CHAPTER 32

Simon waited outside the university for Salma to appear; they always walked to and from the library together. It was the only time they could be alone and talk without someone overhearing them.

'You're late this evening,' he said, kissing his wife on both cheeks.

'As-salama alaykum, dear husband. I'm trying to finish the manuscript before we leave.'

'Have you much to do?'

'One more poem, then it's done.'

'Good. I'm anxious that we don't delay. Tonight we must speak to Layla. She has to understand that she either agrees to marry Ibrahim or she leaves with us for Ardales. I will not allow her to stay otherwise; it would be wrong.'

'I agree. We cannot tell Zara what to do, but at least we can make sure that Layla is safe. I do hope she sees reason and marries Ibrahim. She could do far worse,' said Salma.

'It's our fault. We led her to believe that love was the most important thing, that it could conquer anything,' said Simon. 'We failed her.'

'But love is the most important thing in life. From love comes everything else, happiness, faith, family.'

'In an ideal world, maybe. But Layla has to open her eyes and see that love is not always what it seems; especially at her age. She's looking for passion, a man to sweep her up into his arms, a character from one of those songs she's always singing. There is more to marriage than passion.'

'Yes, but what sort of marriage would it be without love, husband? How can we deny her what we have in abundance?' Salma took his hand and smiled up at him.

His heart stirred within him as he gazed at her, so lovely still despite her grey hair. This was the woman he had risked his immortal soul for, and he did not regret it. All he regretted was that he had placed so many others in jeopardy, people that he loved and should be protecting.

'Come, let us get home and see what that independent little princess has to say for herself.' He wanted Layla to be happy but he also wanted her to be safe. If only she could understand, but to make her do that he would have to confess the truth to her and he couldn't bring himself to do it.

'Oh, there you are,' said Makoud, greeting them with a broad smile when they arrived at his home. 'Basma is not happy; she said this is the third time this week you've been late for dinner.'

'I'll go and help her,' said Salma, hanging up her djellaba.

'No, wait. First I must tell you that I have spoken to Yusuf,' he said. 'He was not unaware of Marwen's behaviour; apparently he makes a habit of bullying newcomers. You are no exception.'

'I find that hard to believe. Not that he's bullied others; it's his nature, that of a weak, insecure man who relishes the little power he has. But I don't believe I am no exception. You haven't seen how he looks at me, such hatred in his eyes,' she replied.

'Well, no need to worry. Yusuf promised me he would speak to him and tell him in the strongest terms that he must desist from harassing you.'

'That would be good. It might give me the time I need to finish my work in peace. Thank you. It can't have been easy telling your friend he has no control over his assistant.'

Makoud laughed, 'Well I didn't actually put it in those words, cousin. But Yusuf was happy to help.'

'Did you tell him about our plans for leaving?' asked Simon.

'No. I thought it best that you told him when you were ready. After all you may change your mind,' he added. Makoud still could not believe that Simon had been so foolish; he just prayed that Salma was right when she said he had stopped visiting the church.

'No, we won't change our minds,' said Simon.

'About what?' asked Layla, coming in carrying a bowl of rice and vegetables.

'Going back to Ardales.'

'Well I am not going with you. I'm staying here with our cousins,' Layla said, putting the bowl down on the table with such force that the rice spilled over the edge.

'Do you be careful, child,' snapped her mother. 'You can't always have everything you want, you know, there are others to consider.'

Layla flounced back to the kitchen without a word.

'She is welcome to stay with us,' said Makoud. 'She could finish her course at the university and then she might be ready to think of marriage.'

'Unless she is betrothed, she is coming with us,' Simon said firmly. 'Make her understand that.'

Makoud couldn't stop smiling; every time he thought about it, his face automatically creased into the biggest smile imaginable. One of his sons was going to marry at long last; he would become a grandfather again. He could hear his wives bustling about the house; they had not stopped talking about their plans for the wedding, who would be there, which of them should make the wedding dress, who should henna the bride's hands and feet. This would go on for weeks. Luckily all he had to do was talk to the imam.

'Ma'a salama, I'm going to work,' he called. Normally one, or both of his wives came to see him off, but today they were too busy to even reply. It was good to see them working well together; there had been a time when he thought he might have to divorce one of them because they were always at each other's throats. Thankfully things had settled down into an amicable working relationship. And now with a wedding imminent, they were equally happy. Abal loved Ibrahim as much as his mother did; he even called her Mama at times. How could they both not be happy that he was marrying the woman he loved.

He pulled the gates closed behind him and walked the short distance to the shop. There was only one cloud on the horizon, Umar; he hadn't been home since the time he found out Ibrahim had asked Layla to marry him. How would he react when he knew that she had accepted him? Well he would know soon enough; he planned to visit his eldest son at midday when he knew he would be resting.

Salma had finished the book of poems she'd been copying for the khalifa, but she hadn't told the chief librarian. She would have liked to have shown it to the poet before she gave it to the khalifa, but Simon told her that Solomon had left Malaqah. He was in Garnata now visiting his patron, Samuel ibn Naghrila, the grand vizier, and then his intention was to go to Zaragoza. He wasn't returning to Malaqah in the near future, apparently. She hoped he was safe. Rumours were flying around the city that things were not good in Garnata, Makoud's friend's son and his family were talking of returning to Malaqah because of some animosity against the Jews. She was disappointed that Solomon would never see her work because she had tried so hard to make her designs complement his beautiful poetry. But as Simon reminded her, it was enough that the khalifa would see it.

'We must tell the chief librarian that we are leaving,' said Simon. 'I am more worried than ever after hearing the news from Garnata. If people are turning on the Jews then they might also turn against Christians. We mustn't take that risk.'

'We can't leave now, not yet. Let's wait until after the wedding. Surely you want to see Layla get married?'

'Of course I do, but I don't want anything to happen to our family. People are becoming more suspicious of foreigners, and especially ones married to Muslims. I really think we should leave right away.'

'But they're getting married next week. Surely nothing can happen before then. We'll leave the night of the wedding; I promise you. I'll tell Yusuf.'

She could see Simon was not happy, but he nodded briefly and said, 'Come on. It's time we went home before Basma gives our supper to the dog.'

When Makoud explained to the sentries at the gate that he needed to see Umar, there was no hesitation in letting him into the Dar al-Jund. He'd been there before, and it took no time at all to locate his son, who was in the stables with his favourite mare, Basil.

'Baba, as-salama alaykum,' he said, putting down the brush he was grooming her with.

'Wa alaykum e-salam, my son. How are you? It's a while since you visited us; your mother is worried about you.'

'What nonsense is that, Baba? I'm a soldier. I sometimes don't see her for a year or more. Anyway, I only saw her last week; so how can she be worrying about me when I am safely here in the alcazaba?'

'And bored, by the look of it.'

'Not just me, all the men are frustrated that the new khalifa has decided not to attack Morón. We were ready, at the point of leaving any day, when the order came down.' Umar lowered his voice. 'The new khalifa is not a man of action. He prefers to spend his time in the gardens talking with poets and philosophers.' His tone was bitter with disappointment.

Makoud knew his son well enough to understand that this was more about Layla than the lack of military action. After all, a soldier's life was as much about waiting, preparing and training as it was about fighting. Umar had never complained before.

'Anyway, why are you here?' his son asked, picking up a horse comb and combing Basil's mane.

'I have some news for you.' Makoud said. His son knew what he was about to tell him and continued grooming the mare. 'Your brother is getting married next week.'

Umar spun around and stared at him. 'Next week? Why so soon?'

'Layla's parents are going back to Ardales. We are hoping to have the wedding while they are still here.'

'I don't understand. I thought they had settled in Malaqah. They both have jobs here. Have you fallen out with them? Is that it?'

'No. Nothing like that. It's their decision.' He might as well tell him what happened. 'They had planned to take Layla with them, but when I told them about Ibrahim's offer, they decided it was an opportunity she couldn't miss.'

'Just like that? They think Ibrahim would make their daughter a good husband?'

'Yes. They're very happy about the match.'

'And Layla? Did she agree?'

'Of course she did. Nobody's forcing her to marry your brother.'

'So she preferred marriage to my boring brother rather than return to that backwater town of Ardales?'

'Umar. I know you're disappointed, but I had no option. When you spoke to me, your brother had already asked for her hand in marriage. What else could I do?'

'You could have told Layla that we both wanted to marry her, and let her choose for herself.'

Makoud shook his head. 'That's not how it's done. You know that. Stop sulking; you will soon find someone else. Now that you've actually expressed a wish to marry, I will find you the perfect wife.'

'I had found the perfect wife. Just too late, it seems.'

'You will come to the wedding?' It was more a command than a request. 'Ibrahim will be very upset if you don't. I haven't told him that you wanted to marry Layla; I didn't see the point.'

'Do I have a choice?'

'No. I want you there to support your brother. It's your family duty.'

'Very well, Baba. I will come to the house tomorrow and congratulate them.'

'Thank you son. Remember your family is the most important thing in your life. We must all stick together, no matter what.' He smiled at Umar; he hated to disappoint any of his children but what else could he do? Either way someone was going to get hurt. 'Now I must get back to work,' he said. He wanted to hug Umar but his son had already turned his back on him and was brushing Basil's already gleaming coat. He felt sad for him, but he would get over it. Once the wedding was done Makoud would visit the matchmaker and see who she had to offer that Umar might favour.

CHAPTER 33

Dirar was unhappy. It was nothing to do with Gideon or his family; they had welcomed him with open arms. 'The family of Makoud is like my own family,' he had said. 'You will always be welcome here.'

He knew Gideon, of course, but he was much older than him so that they had had little social contact when he was living in Malaqah. Gideon was a Jew. Not a good match for his sister. He remembered how his sister, Aisha, had had a crush on him; one night, sobbing at the end of his bed, she had told him she and Gideon were in love, and because of that, Gideon had been sent to Garnata to run part of his father's business. He'd obviously soon forgotten her, because now he had a wife and two children.

Dirar didn't know any other Jewish people; there hadn't been a single family in Ardales. Even in Malaqah he didn't mix with the Jews; most of his friends were fisherman and all were Muslim. So it came as a bit of a shock when he realised that Garnata had such a large Jewish population; he had never really paid much attention to the dhimmis in Malaqah but here it was hard to ignore them.

But none of that was the reason for his wretchedness. The truth be told, he was homesick for Malaqah. He never realised that Garnata was so far from the sea, or that it was such a bitterly cold place in the winter, with the snow on mountains that seemed to reach the sky, and that in summer the heat was blistering. He longed for the temperate climate of Malaqah, with its cool sea breezes, and the constant sound of the Alborán sea, sometimes roaring far into the night, sometimes murmuring as it lapped against the shore, but always there, omnipresent. He missed the smells of his city, the salty fresh tang of the sea itself, of newly caught fish, and the pungent odour of the seaweed covered rocks, where they searched for mussels on the days when the fishing had been poor. Most of all he missed being out with the other fishermen, their companionship and the challenge of the sea; he, who'd never even been in a boat before he came to Malaqah, found that he felt completely at home at sea.

'Have you eaten?' asked Gideon.

'Yes, thank you.'

'We'll be off then.' Gideon slung his djellaba over his shoulders and picked up a heavy stave. Just recently he had adopted the practice of always being armed and never going out alone; it was too dangerous, he said. Dirar felt that Gideon saw him as some sort of protection because he was Muslim, so it was Dirar who found himself having to go out and buy supplies or arrange for shipments of their cloth while Gideon spent more and more time working inside the warehouse than out on the streets.

'Dirar, you need to take this bale of cloth to the seamstress near the alcazaba. One of the sultan's wives wants new winter djellabas for her maids; this woollen cloth will be ideal for them. It won't take you long.'

'Very well, Gideon.'

He knew where the seamstress lived; she had a very pretty daughter. If he was lucky the girl might be in the shop and he would get to speak to her. He picked up the bale of cloth and set off through the narrow streets and up the hill towards the red fort that everyone called the Alhambra. The seamstress lived in a small house near one of the inner gates.

His head was so full of what he would say to the woman's daughter, if he was lucky enough to see her, that he didn't notice them until he received a sharp blow on his back.

'Hey what's going on?' He shouted, dropping the bale of cloth and staggering round to confront his attacker.

'Shame on you, working for a Jew,' shouted one of them, more boy than a man.

'Yes, why is that?' asked his companion, delivering a well-aimed kick to his ribs. 'You're a Muslim. Why don't you work for a Muslim?'

Dirar groaned and tried to stand up, but the other one pushed him back, so his head hit the cobbles with a loud crack. He lay still, feeling the blood trickle down his neck.

'What's going on here? You two, leave that man alone or I'll call the muhtasib.'

'Filthy Jew lover,' the older one shouted, as he ran off down the alleyway, closely followed by his companion.

'You all right, son? You've taken a bad blow to the head. Here let me look at it,' said the man.

Dirar pulled himself upright; his head was spinning and his ribs hurt every time he breathed. 'I'm fine. I must deliver this package,' he said, looking around him for the bale of cloth. It was gone. His attackers had taken it.

'Can't see any package, son. I think you should go home; you don't look too good to me. Do you want me to help you?'

'No, no, I can manage. Thank you.' Dirar staggered to his feet. He didn't want anyone to know where he lived.'

'Well you go easy. Here put this on your head to stop the bleeding,' he said, giving him a square of white cotton which had seen better days.

'Thank you.' Dirar pressed the cloth against his head and winced at the pain. 'Ma'a salama.'

'Alla ysalmak, son. Take care now.'

As Dirar hobbled back to the Jewish quarter and the warehouse, he began to worry what Gideon would say about the stolen bale of cloth then he realised that this was unimportant compared to what he had just witnessed. People were attacking not only Jews but anyone who had anything to do with them. He couldn't believe it. Nothing like this had ever happened in Malaqah.

The disturbances had sprung up quite suddenly. There had been some grumbling and rumours that the Jews had too much power, and that the Muslims were being cheated of what was rightfully theirs, but nobody had paid much attention. After all, the previous grand vizier, Samuel ibn Nagrilla, had been both loved and respected, despite being a Jew, but people had taken a dislike to his son, who had taken over his father's role as grand vizier to the sultan of Garnata. A rumour was even spreading that he intended to kill the ruler, Badis ben Habus, and claim the throne for himself. Why hadn't Dirar taken it more seriously? He knew Gideon was nervous about the situation, but he never expected he would be attacked; he was a Muslim.

'What in Jehovah's name has happened to you?' asked Gideon, looking at him in horror.

'Two ruffians attacked me. It could have been worse but an old man chased them away. I'm sorry Gideon, but they took the bale of cloth that I was supposed to deliver to the seamstress.'

'Don't worry about that. But attacking you because you work for a Jew is very worrying; things are starting to look bad.'

'I can't understand it,' said Dirar. 'Nobody hates the Jews in Malaqah. Everyone gets along well together.'

'We've never had a problem before. I'm surprised too, that people can be so easily swayed by the words of one man,' replied Gideon.

'One man?'

'Yes, his name is Abu Ishaq. He's written a poem which provokes hatred against the Jews, and worse still, condones their slaughter. What was it he wrote?' Gideon paused, searching for the exact words, then continued, 'Do not consider it a breach of faith to kill them, the breach of faith would be to let them carry on.'

Dirar gaped at him.

'There's more, but I can't remember it all. But copies are being plastered all over the city; I'm surprised you haven't seen them. It's not safe for us here anymore.'

'But this is your home.'

'No, my family is in Malaqah, you know that. But, we'll talk more about this later; in the meantime get off home and tell my wife to clean you up. I'll be home as soon as I've finished here. I've made up my mind. It's not safe here any longer.'

The next day Dirar woke to a bitterly cold but bright morning; the Jewish quarter was empty and still. The only sound was the call of the imam, echoing across the city, calling all Muslims to prayer.

'Why don't you go to the mosque?' asked Gideon, walking briskly towards his warehouse.

'I prefer to pray at home,' Dirar replied. 'I went a couple of times, just after I arrived here, but I didn't feel welcome; I don't think they like outsiders in this city.' He thought back to his experience the day before. His ribs were still very painful, and the cut on his head stung, but otherwise he had recovered from his ordeal.

'You could be right. And if more people find out that you're living in the house of a Jew, they will like you even less. You could be in danger.' Gideon lowered his voice and then said, 'The mood is getting very ugly. I'm worried what is going to happen, so I'm thinking of taking my family and going back to Malaqah.'

'Really? What about the business?'

'I'll take most of the stock with me and shut everything else up.'

'Is it really so serious?'

'I think it might be. You could stay here if you want, and look after everything.'

Dirar looked at him; he didn't like that idea at all. The only thing that made his stay in Garnata bearable was his growing friendship with Gideon and his family. Without that there was nothing here for him.

'No, I'll come with you. You will need my protection.' They both laughed. Even the two of them would be no match for bandits, and the mountains around Garnata were rife with these thieves and cutthroats. 'So when do we leave?' asked Dirar, his spirits rising at the thought of going home.

'I don't know. Let's see what we learn in the next few days.'

When Makoud arrived to open up his shop, he was surprised to see Avi standing outside; his friend rarely visited during the day. They had a habit of meeting in one of the local tea shops occasionally in the evenings to play a game of chess, but never during working hours; Avi was always too busy.

'As-salama alaykum, Avi. What brings you here? Are you after some medicine?'

'Aleichem shalom, my friend. No I'm not in need of your potions, unless you have something that will allow me to fly.'

'Fly?' Makoud laughed. 'No, but I'm working on it. Why so early and where do you want to fly to?'

'No magic carpet for me?'

Makoud shook his head. 'I can offer you some tea.'

'No thank you. I can't stay but I have some news for you. Good or bad, I'm not sure.'

'Come, sit down and tell me what's happened.'

'I received a message from Gideon this morning. He sent it by one of the homing pigeons that we use for anything really urgent. So I knew he was worried.'

'What did it say?'

'He thinks that he and his family are in danger. Anti-Jewish feeling is growing. Dirar was attacked a few days ago because he was working for a Jew.'

'Dirar? Is he all right?'

'He didn't say, but I expect so.'

'So they're leaving Garnata? And Dirar too?' asked Makoud; he was beginning to feel worried now. But Hasan was dead, so there should be no danger for his son, anymore.

'Yes, all of them, the whole family are on their way.'

'This is very unexpected.'

'No, it's surprising but not unexpected. He wrote to me a few weeks ago and told me how people were not happy with the new grand vizier, and are using his failings to blame all the Jewish community. He was worried then that it was all going to turn nasty.'

'But the Jews have lived in Garnata for decades; you told me so yourself. Didn't you say that many had escaped from Qurtuba and settled there; you told me it was the Jews who founded the city. I don't understand why, all of a sudden, people have turned against them,' said Makoud.

'I know. I can't understand it either. I have heard that there's a poet who is stirring up ferment; his latest poem is extremely anti-Semitic and provocative. I just pray that they all get out of the city safely.'

'We will both pray for that my friend, and that they arrive here safe and sound.'

CHAPTER 34

'My Lord, there's a messenger to see you,' one of his knights said, pulling his horse to a standstill in front of Jabalah.

'Well send him to me, man.'

Diego was one of the few knights that he respected; he had fought in King Fernando I's army for many years before joining forces with Jabalah. It was a good job he still had some men he could rely on to control this rabble of untrained peasants that he called his army. Four days march remained before they reached Morón, and it was hard work keeping them together. Only the promise of rich spoils after the battle was over kept them motivated and maintained discipline. He nudged his horse forward into a trot; the sooner they arrived in Morón, the better. Immediately behind him rode some six thousand cavalry and the rest of his knights; most were Christians. These were men he could depend on, unlike the fifteen thousand or so infantry who trudged behind them. None of them had been trained, but many were experienced fighters; they were a rough lot, a mixture of Spanish serfs and French fugitives, but all were brave and hungry for the spoils. Those that wore armour had taken it from the dead on the battlefields—and most of their weapons—, others declared they didn't need any armour. He'd heard that Morón was a prosperous city, with plenty of gold for everyone; these Moors were rich beyond measure. That in itself was enough to keep the men from deserting.

He was deep in thought about what a victory at Morón would mean for his reputation, when a young Moor, riding a very pretty bay mare, was suddenly trotting by his side.

'Sayyad, I have a message for you from Malaqah. The khalifa is dead. Murdered by his own wife,' the young soldier said.

'What's that? Dead you say? I'm sorry to hear that. So who will be commanding the Moorish army now?'

'Forgive me, Sayyad, that is why I am here, to tell you that the new khalifa does not intend to attack Morón. He says you are to return home.'

'What treacherous lies are these?' Jabalah cried, pulling out his sword and striking the youth to the ground. 'Is this a trick?'

'It's the truth,' the boy managed to gasp, blood gurgling from the wound in his throat.

'Diego,' Jabalah shouted, turning away from the dying messenger and seeking his second-in-command. 'Diego.'

'Yes, my Lord?'

'Did you know about this? Did you hear the news this infidel has brought me?'

The knight looked at the still figure on the ground. 'No, my Lord. I take it it wasn't good?'

'Good? It's a betrayal. That's what it is. Damnation. The new khalifa of Malaqah has no intention of attacking Morón. We are on our own.'

'That is bad news, my Lord,' Diego replied, looking back at the restless men waiting behind them. 'The men are impatient to fight. Their blood is up.'

'As is mine.' Jabalah wiped the blood from his sword and spat on the ground. 'Wealth has made these Berbers soft. They have no stomach for warfare anymore.' He stared at his army; already the soldiers were questioning the delay. They would be hard to control when they heard the news. 'Say nothing to the men at the moment,' he whispered to Diego. 'I need a moment to think. Give the order to continue.'

What the hell was he going to do now? Did the people of Morón know they were on their way? If they didn't, then they soon would; news of an advancing army would travel fast. And what had been Hasan's plan? All he knew was that they were to meet close to the border between Malaqah and Morón, and issue a one-to-one challenge to the city. This single face-to-face combat was the prequel to the battle to follow; the strongest man in Jabalah's army would fight the strongest man their opponents could find. Once your enemy lay dead at your feet, the order to charge was given. It was an ancient way of motivating the troops. But what then? How well was the city fortified? Were they even sure that forces from Isbiliya were in the city? Hasan had been very vague about everything except the money he would pay him. Jabalah didn't want to take on Abbad's army without a clear strategy and the men to back it up. Abbad I was a ferocious warrior; tales of his exploits abounded in the bars and taverns. It was even said that the ruler of Isbiliya used human skulls as flower pots, and kept the heads of his defeated enemies in leather cases; the man was a barbarian.

Jabalah had been a general in the army of Fernando I of Castille and had many glorious victories during his career; he'd been cheered by grateful crowds from Valencia to Portugal. It was him the people saluted for freeing them from the Moors, not Fernando. Jabalah was their hero. Not for one moment had he regretted breaking away from the king; he'd become sick and tired of risking his life for the miserly amount Fernando paid him, so he'd turned to richer rulers. It was all very well for Fernando to proclaim they were fighting for Christendom. Al-Andalus was where the money was. The Christians either had no gold or kept it well hidden. It had been a good decision; now he had a personal army—true some of the recruits lacked discipline — and he was rich, with a fortified castle in the north of the peninsula and a lovely wife. He wasn't going to risk all that by attacking Morón without any backup. He may not have the education of these Moors but he was a good strategist; he never lost more men than was necessary and they always came out on top. No exceptions.

'Diego,' he shouted.

The knight galloped over to his side. 'Yes, My Lord?'

'Get the army to turn round; we're heading for Malaqah.'

'The men won't like it; my Lord. They're hungry to fight.'

'They'll like it well enough when I tell them we're going to sack the city. I warrant there's gold enough for all of us behind their walls. A city full of merchants and an overflowing treasury, it has to be worth attacking.'

'But their walls are strongly fortified. We'd never break them down. We don't have enough equipment to set up a siege.'

'I'm not talking about a siege. We don't have time for that. We won't need to break the walls down. Nobody will be expecting us, least of all the new, young khalifa; they will be completely unprepared, and by the time they realise what is happening we will be inside the gates. We were invited to join them in battle, so we will. Send one of our scouts ahead to see what is happening. But tell him to be careful; I don't want to alert their new khalifa that we are on our way.'

'Yes, my Lord. I have just the man,' Diego grinned at him. 'The men will be happy to fight. I doubt if they care if it's against Morón or Malaqah; they're all Moors to them.'

'This will show the new khalifa that he can't mess about with Jabalah. If he won't pay me my 10,000 gold dinars then I'll just have to help myself. By the time we've done with his city, he'll be sorry that he ever crossed me.'

'My Lord, the scout has returned,' said Diego.

'So what news? What did he find out?' asked Jabalah.

'It is easy to enter the city, he says. There doesn't seem to be many guards and everybody is going about their business as normal. He doubts that they suspect we are going to attack.'

'Good. How far away do you think we are now?'

'Two days march. Not more. We cross the mountains and the city will lie before us.'

'What is it? I can see you have something to add. Spit it out man.'

'The scout returned with someone.'

'What sort of someone?'

'A moor, my Lord. He asked to be brought to you. According to the scout he was returning from Malaqah when he met him; he was on the hill above the camp. At first he didn't know what to do; he thought the man was a spy and was about to kill him, but then the man said he needed to speak to you. It was a matter of life and death. What do you want to do with him, my Lord?'

'Bring him here. Let's see what is so important that it brings him all this way.'

The man they brought before him was dressed in fine robes that had seen better days; the hem of his djubbah was stained with mud; what had once been elegant leather slippers were worn and split from walking over rough ground and his djellaba had a ragged tear in it. He was not a soldier, that much was clear. His manner and bearing suggested a man who'd once had power. Now he looked like a hunted criminal. So who was he and why did he want to speak to him?

Jabalah threw himself onto some cushions and stared at the man, whom he left standing although he was obviously exhausted. At last he asked, 'Where are you from?'

'As-salama alaykum, sayyad. I've come from the city of Malaqah to speak to you.'

The man looked longingly at the cushions but Jabalah ignored him. He wanted him at a disadvantage, at least until he knew what this was all about. 'Did the khalifa send you?' he asked.

'No sayyad. I have come because I have a proposition for you.'

This was strange. Something was not right; why was this scruffy old man offering him a proposition? 'And what is that? Something so important that you claim it's a matter of life and death?'

'I know that the khalifa called off the campaign against Morón; I met some of his militia men returning to their farms.'

'So?' This old man was tediously slow, but he wouldn't hurry him; he'd let him carry on until he heard something useful.

'I know Malaqah well. I know how to get men in there undetected. I can help you to destroy the city,' he said, smiling confidently at Jabalah.

Yes, this was a man used to intrigue, a man accustomed to power. 'And why do you think I would want to destroy Malaqah? The khalifa is my ally.'

'But you know he won't pay you now. He wants to use that money to impress people with his libraries and mosques. You will have no money to pay your men. You need to sack the city; it's the only way to get the money.'

'How do I know this isn't a trap?'

'Why would it be a trap?'

'If you have just come from Malaqah, then you can tell me how well it is fortified,' Jabalah said.

'It is a well fortified city as you know, but as we are not at war, everything is as normal. People are free to come and go as they please during the day; at night there is the usual curfew. It would be easy to smuggle in a few of your men during the day and then, after dark, they could kill the guards and open the Antequera Gate. Nobody would be aware of the attack until it was too late.'

'It sounds a reasonable plan, if what you're telling me is the truth.' This man must have a strong grudge against the city—a place he claimed to know well—to betray its people in that way. But that in itself didn't worry him; he'd come across lots of men who'd sell their own mother for a handful of silver. 'Well, if I'm to believe you, then I need to know who you are. What is your name? You have the air of someone who has held the reins of power in his hands.'

The man smiled, obviously pleased to be seen in this light. 'I am ibn Baqanna, sayyad. For many years I was the loyal servant of Khalifa Idris I; I was his grand vizier. But you know how it is, each new ruler wants to change the people who serve them. I was relieved of my duties for no fault of my own. I am an old man now and need somewhere quiet to enjoy my remaining years.'

Jabalah stared at him. Of course. He'd heard of this ibn Baqanna; his infamy was widely known, a man not to be trusted. So what had happened that had sent him scurrying out of his hole seeking revenge? He didn't believe he was someone who would relinquish the post of grand vizier without a fight.

'It's an interesting proposition. But what's in it for you, ibn Baqanna?'

Again the confident smile as he replied, 'Well I'm sure you will reward me generously, sayyad. Malaqah is a very rich city; there will be gold for everyone.'

'Yes, as I said, an interesting proposition. Now I think it's time you rested and ate something, while I discuss this with my officers,' said Jabalah. 'Diego take ibn Baqanna to the officers' tent and look after him. Then come straight back here.'

'Thank you, Sayyad. I am rather tired,' ibn Baqanna said.

By the time the knight returned, Jabalah had already decided what to do.

'Diego. Send one of the scouts to find out all you can about this man, ibn Baqanna. Something is not right. Why would an ex-grand vizier be wandering about the countryside looking like a vagabond? And where has he been these last few years since Idris died? Find out what you can as quickly as possible. Tempting as his proposition is, I am not leading my men into a trap.'

The more Jabalah thought about it, the more he was convinced that there was something else behind Ibn Baqanna's story. Somebody was after him; he had all the signs of a hunted man. Someone like him would have made many enemies over the years; Jabalah had not only heard he was a man not to be trusted, but also someone whose ruthlessness made things happen. Even those whom he served were said not to give him their complete confidence. So why should he?

The next morning Diego presented himself in Jabalah's tent just after dawn.

'Well, what news? I hope it's useful. The men are getting restless. The news has got out that we're not attacking Morón after all, and they're not happy. I need to make a decision soon about whether we attack Malaqah or not.'

'My Lord, I have found out something very interesting. Our friend is hiding from the new khalifa. Ibn Baqanna is accused of locking up Ben-Yahya, the new khalifa, and attempting to put a slave on the throne. He narrowly escaped with his life. The slave was executed but they have been searching for ibn Baqanna ever since.'

'So I was right. He is a hunted man. Well that makes quite a difference. How much do you think the new khalifa will pay for this man?'

'A lot, my Lord. He wants him dead. But more than that, he wants him returned to Malaqah so he can be executed. His head will adorn the main gate as a warning to any other possible traitors.'

'I would imagine so. How long was the khalifa imprisoned?'

'They say two years. His brother gave the order,' said Diego.

'So he's thirsty for revenge. Perfect. Maybe we can get our 10,000 dinars without losing a single soldier.'

'My Lord?'

'We'll send a message to the khalifa and tell him that we have ibn Baqanna, and for the price of the money he owes me, we will return him to Malaqah. What he does after that is up to him.'

Diego smiled. A rare occurrence as the knight was very formal around him; he'd seen him laughing and joking with his men, but when he spoke to him he always addressed him as my Lord. Jabalah quite liked that. That's what a soldier should do, adhere to the chain of command.

'I take it you approve, Diego?' he said.

'Yes my lord. I will send a messenger right away. But what of ibn Baqanna?'

'Have him locked up. I don't want him wandering off now we have such big plans for him. The man is worth his weight in gold.' He laughed. This was working out much better than expected. 'And make sure the men know they will either get paid or we will attack Malaqah.

Ben-Yahya had called a meeting of all his counsellors, including the treasurer. They gathered in the throne room, muttering and grumbling at being summoned at such an early hour.

'Gentlemen,' he said and smiled to myself as the room instantly fell silent. 'I have news for you. Before daybreak I received a message from our friend, Jabalah. As we expected he is not happy that I've called off the attack on Morón. I understand. He has an army hungry to fight and expecting to be paid.'

'So we attack him?' said the general.

'That is one option. But if we lose, the city will be sacked.'

'And if we win?' asked the general.

'If we win we will have lost men in battle and our army will be all the weaker for it.'

'So what do we do? Just hand over the 10,000 dinars your brother promised him?' asked Labib.

Ben-Yahya could see that nobody was willing to agree to that.

'Yes, and get nothing in return,' added the keeper of the Royal Mint.

'Well, there is something he has offered in return for paying him the money he was promised,' said Ben-Yahya.

'Promised by a dead man,' said Labib.

'That's as maybe, Grand Vizier, but I think you should wait to hear what I have to tell you.' The grand vizier bowed his head and muttered something which Ben-Yahya decided to take as an apology. They were all watching him now, eagerly waiting to hear the news. 'Jabalah has arrested ibn Baqanna, and at this very moment has him under armed guard. His proposal is that, in return for 10,000 gold dinars, he will bring him here to Malaqah and hand him over to us.'

His court exploded into a cacophony of noise as they took in this news. At last, the keeper of the Royal Mint said, '10,000 gold dinars is a lot of money, Your Majesty.'

'Yes it is, but I want you all to understand that while that man lives we can have no rest. If we are to have a stable government; if I am to have any kind of peace of mind, then we have to get rid of that serpent. He betrayed my brother and I when we were children; then, even after my uncle was dead, he contrived to put someone else on the throne, rather pass it to the rightful heirs. After my brother was so cruelly murdered, he put a slave on the throne and left me to rot in the dungeons. He hates me and all my family. And I would not be at all surprised if he had something to do with my father's death as well. He is power hungry and a traitor to his country, and as you all know, our laws say that traitors must die. How can Malaqah have stability if that man lives? How can we have peace? Do you want yet another change of ruler?' He stared at them, as they stood in silent agreement. 'I want him brought here in chains, so he can be dragged before the people of this city, so they can watch his execution and everyone can learn that Ben-Yahya gives no mercy to men who betray him and his country.'

He looked about him; he knew he had their agreement. It was time they realised he was no longer the child who had been exiled to Sebta. He was Khalifa.

'Your Majesty, maybe you could offer the mercenary a lesser sum, say 7,000 gold dinars? After all he hasn't had to fight, and his army is intact,' suggested the keeper of the Royal Mint.

'No,' Ben-Yahya shouted. 'No. I want no mistakes. If it costs the treasury 10,000 gold dinars, then so be it. I want that man here so I can watch him suffer. I want him standing in front of me. I want to look into his eyes and see his black soul.' He paused, trying to control his anger. 'There's to be no more discussion on this. Labib draft a reply to Jabalah and say we accept his offer, but he must deliver ibn Baqanna alive. I will not pay him a single dirham if the man is dead. Is that understood?'

'Yes, Your Majesty. I will attend to it.'

'Right away.'

'Yes, Your Majesty,' the grand vizier replied, bowing and backing out of the room.

'You are all dismissed. General, let me know the moment ibn Baqanna arrives.'

'Yes, Your Majesty.'

Ibn Baqanna knew he had made a terrible mistake. He should never have trusted Jabalah; he had heard of his reputation. The man had no loyalty to anyone. He thought he could persuade him to attack Malaqah and then ingratiate himself with him. After all even mercenaries needed someone like him, someone who understood the political manoeuvrings of most of the taifas in al-Andalus. He could have become invaluable to him, but now it seemed he'd never get the chance to demonstrate his worth. The man was too greedy and too idle. Instead he was to be sold to Ben-Yahya like a common slave, for a mere 10,000 gold dinars; he could have helped Jabalah to gain far more riches than that if only he'd given him the chance. Now he had to suffer the humiliation of being dragged before that boy; he couldn't bear the indignity of it.

He tried to stretch his aching limbs but the ropes that bound him were too tight; they cut so deep into his flesh that he could hardly move.

The guards sitting by the entrance the tent watched as he writhed on the floor.

'Lie still, you stupid bastard. There's no way you can get out of that,' said one of them. 'You're bound like a lamb for the slaughter.'

The other guard laughed. 'Yes that's exactly it. All trussed up and ready for the execution.'

'Can't you loosen these ropes a little,' ibn Baqanna pleaded. 'I'm an old man. I'm not going anywhere.'

'That's where you're wrong. You're going to hell; that's where you're going.' Both men laughed. 'Now shut up or I'll make you.'

Ibn Baqanna lay still and closed his eyes; his mind was racing. Surely there was some way he could escape from this.

CHAPTER 35

It was not yet daybreak when Gideon and his family set off down the hill towards the city gates. Their breath floated in the cold air as fine puffs of white smoke that drifted before them. Dirar stamped his feet on the hard ground in a vain attempt to warm them. Gideon's wife was weeping silently, and her tears gleamed like tiny jewels on her cheeks; she carried the smallest of the children in her arms. Next to her waddled her mother, an overweight, jolly woman who never stopped chattering to whoever had the time of day to listen to her. That morning however, she was silent, deep in her own thoughts, and heartbroken at having to flee from the city of her birth. None of the family wanted to leave Garnata, but Gideon had insisted it was necessary. He led the way, with two mules laden with their belongings and some of the finer bales of cloth—most of the cheaper fabrics had been left in the warehouse. Dirar brought up the rear, with Gideon's son perched on his shoulders and a stout stave in his hand. There was nothing about their attire that advertised the fact that they were Jews; in Garnata the laws relating to dhimmis had been relaxed and it wasn't necessary for them to wear the yellow stars and sashes that they were obliged to wear in other parts of al-Andalus. Their clothing was plain and simple, and covered by thick warm djellabas to keep out the cold. The only change was that Gideon had removed his skull cap and replaced it with the traditional Berber red and green ghifara.

They walked in silence until they reached the south gate, where a sleepy sentry stopped them.

'As-salama alaykum,' Gideon said.

'Where are you off to so early in the day?' grunted the sentry.

'Taking some goods to the coast to sell. Had to get an early start.'

'Well you be careful going through the pass; there have been some reports of bandits in the area,' he added, apparently not that interested in them. 'You should've left the women at home.'

'Thank you. We'll be careful.'

The guard shook his head in bewilderment. 'Well don't say I didn't warn you.' He pulled the heavy iron gate open and let them out.

'Who are they?' asked his companion, coming out from the sentry house and rubbing the sleep from his eyes.

'Some idiots going down to the port.'

'They'll be lucky if they make it.'

'Just what I thought. Like sitting ducks,' replied the sentry.

Gideon was hurrying ahead, his wife and mother-in-law desperately trying to match their short steps to his long strides.

'Did you hear what they said, Gideon? They think we're walking into a trap.' Dirar knew the pass the soldiers were referring to. In order to reach the coast they would have to go through a narrow gorge, the steep slopes of which were covered in thick bushes and rocky outcrops, excellent cover for anyone waiting to attack passing travellers.

'What else can we do? If we cross the plain we would be safer, but at some point we would have to head down to the coast. The mountains around Malaqah are just as infested with bandits as here.

'So we have no choice?'

'Not that I can see. We have to trust in God to keep us safe. After all we have both Allah and Jehovah looking after us now,' he said with a grin.

Dirar tried to smile, but he didn't feel very happy about it. 'So it's go through the pass and risk the bandits or stay in Garnata and hope we're not massacred by the mob? Not much of a choice.'

'Come on. I never took you for a coward, Dirar. Bandits are more interested in stealing from travellers than killing them.'

'I think they'd be happy to do both,' muttered Dirar.

'When we get to the port, we'll take a ship to Malaqah. I don't think my mother-in-law will be able to walk all that way.'

'I agree.'

The road was rough, not much more than a goat track in places, and on more than one occasion the mules looked as though they would lose their footing and tumble down the ravine to the fast flowing torrent that had carved its way through the mountains, but stalwart creatures that they were, they trudged on and on, with the travellers stumbling behind them. Nobody complained, not even the children. Everyone was intent on not making any noise. On this deserted path who could be sure if anyone was watching them or not, if at any minute a group of bandits would spring from their hiding place and attack. Dirar felt like a coiled spring; able to jump into action at any moment. He loosened his grip on the wooden stave to relax the muscles in his arm for a moment.

'Are we nearly there, Baba?' a small shrill voice asked, the sound echoing through the silent valley.

Gideon held up his hand for them to stop. Had anyone heard the child? While they waited, his mother whispered in her son's ear, trying to reassure him and keep him quiet. They listened, straining for the slightest sound, but all they could hear was the screech of the buzzards overhead. When no-one appeared, Gideon signalled for them to move forward. With hindsight Dirar realised that they should have brought at least one other man with them; there were just the two of them to defend two women and two children. Not good odds, especially as neither Gideon nor Dirar were accomplished swordsmen. For a fleeting second he wished his brother Umar was with them; all he and Gideon had in the way of weapons were the two wooden staves and an antiquated dagger, which from its heavily bejewelled handle was more for ceremonial use than action.

Ahead of them the path twisted and turned with regular monotony, making it impossible to see if anyone was ahead, lying in wait for them. Suddenly the mules stopped.

'What's wrong?' Dirar whispered, moving closer to Gideon; he was beginning to feel nervous. He tapped the leading mule on its haunches, but it refused to budge.

'I don't know; it won't go any further. Climb up onto that rock and see if you can spot what's around the bend. I'll wait here with the others.'

'All right.'

Dirar lifted the boy off his shoulders and seated him on one of the mules. 'Not a sound, mind,' he whispered to the frightened child, and took hold of the stave. What was he going to find? And what did he think he could achieve with the stave? A sword would be far more useful.

He clambered up the rock and peered over the edge. He gasped, unable to believe his eyes. Beneath him, crouched behind the rocks were his brother Umar and four men. What, in the name of Allah, were they doing there? And why wasn't Umar wearing his uniform? He slithered back down the rocks and went straight up to Gideon.

'You're not going to believe this, it's my brother. He must think we're bandits; they're lying in wait for us.'

'Well in that case you had better go first; I don't think your brother knows me, and I wouldn't want him to mistake me for a robber.'

'Umar? What are you doing here, brother?' Dirar shouted as he rounded the bend.

'What in damnation? Dirar. Is it really you?' He turned his men and said 'Stand easy, men. This is my little brother, the one we've been sent to get out of trouble, again.' He emphasised the last word.

It was true, Umar had got him out of trouble on more than one occasion. 'Who sent you, brother?' he asked, hugging Umar as hard as he could. How good it was to see him. 'And why the disguises?'

He could now see that underneath the dung coloured djellabas that they wore, were the smart red and black uniforms of the jinetes.

'Baba, who else? He heard there was unrest in Garnata and told me to come and rescue you. Unofficially of course, hence the disguise.' He pulled the djellaba open, so Gideon could see he wore his uniform underneath, and the sword tucked into his belt. 'I'm very glad we met you on route; I'm not sure I had much of a plan for getting into the city. We are already inside the taifa of Garnata, and that wouldn't go down well with the Sultan if he knew the khalifa's soldiers were here.' He looked at Gideon and added, 'We must hurry. I need to get you and my men back into the taifa of Malaqah before we can rest. I don't want to provoke an international incident.' He regarded the weary travellers and said, 'It's all right; I've brought two spare horses. I think the women and children had better use them. You can get up here with me Dirar, where I can keep an eye on you.

Gideon, you and the children can ride one horse, and the two women can get on the other. Is that all right?'

'What about the mules?'

'One of my men will lead them.'

Gideon's mother-in-law looked petrified. 'It's all right, Mama. I'll hold on to you. It will be just like riding a donkey,' said Gideon's wife.

Dirar saw the shock on Umar's face as she compared the beautiful war horse to a donkey, but he said, 'Yes, you will be fine. This one has a very sweet temperament.'

The old woman didn't look very reassured, but she allowed her son-in-law to help her up onto the horse and sat there clinging to the saddle, while his wife clambered up behind her.

Dirar leapt up onto the mare, and stared at his brother's broad back; he could hardly believe that Umar had come to get them. It was like magic; he had wished for him and suddenly there he was.

The last few days had been like a nightmare from which he was only just waking up. And it wasn't over. They had barely gone an Arab mile when a band of about a dozen men leapt out in front of them, brandishing an assortment of swords and cudgels. Bandits. So the sentry has been right.

'Just hold it right there,' shouted a burly man, who was obviously their leader. He wore the tattered green uniform of a soldier from Garnata. 'Don't move, any of you. Throw down all your belongings. Hurry up. Money. Jewels. Weapons.'

While he stood there on top of a rock, glaring at them and waving his sword in the air, the others approached slowly.

'Come on, get a move on. Throw down your money,' said one of the men.

They were getting closer. Dirar didn't move. Why wasn't Umar doing anything? Surely he was going to attack them; they were better armed than that rabble.

'Get the mules,' ordered the chief brigand. 'There'll be plenty in those bags. And the horses.' His eyes gleamed as he looked at them. 'That's a prize well worth having.'

One of the men grabbed the reins of the leading mule from the soldier. It was as though that was a prearranged signal between Umar and his men. Immediately they leapt into action. The man leading the mules pulled out his sword and ran it through the bandit. Umar and the other three soldiers spurred their horses into action and rode straight at the others, slicing and slashing at them until, before Dirar had time to draw breath, they were all lying dead at their feet. He looked to where their leader had been standing on the rocky outcrop. There was no sign of him.

'Everyone all right?' called Umar, wiping his sword and replacing it in its sheath.

The women were stunned. The children were crying, and Dirar and Gideon stared helplessly at Umar. It had all happened so fast.

'The mules,' gasped Gideon.

'Don't worry. We'll get them for you,' said Umar, nodding at one of his men. 'They won't have gone far.'

Dirar couldn't stop staring at his brother. He had never seen him in action before, and Umar never said much about what happened when he went on a campaign, so he had no idea how quickly he could respond. 'What do we do with the bodies?' he asked, eventually.

'Drag them over to the gorge and drop them in. But take their weapons off them first,' Umar said.

Dirar looked towards the gorge. Suddenly a flash of light in the rocks caught his eye. The rising sun was reflecting on the sword of another of the bandits, and standing next to him was a man with a bow in his hand. He was aiming straight at Umar. 'Watch out, Umar,' Dirar shouted and threw himself at his brother, knocking him off his horse. They both tumbled into the road and rolled down into a ditch.

'What the devil are you up to now?' Umar bellowed at his brother. 'Are you trying to kill me?'

'Keep down. There's an archer up there, in the rocks,' he explained. Just then one of Umar's men, spun round and fell on top of them, an arrow jutting from his neck.

Umar pushed the soldier off him and crawled to safety. Dirar knew the jinetes carried bows as well as swords, but Umar's bow was attached to his saddle and his mare had run off down the road after the mules.

'Do you want me to get your horse?' he asked.

'No need.' Umar placed his fingers in his mouth and whistled. A few minutes later, Basil came trotting back.

While Umar and one of his men fired arrows at the two bandits, the remaining soldiers clambered up the mountainside. Within minutes, one of the bandits was dead and the other had fled.

'Right, how about you get rid of the bodies?' Umar said, picking up the dead soldier and putting him across the back of his horse.

Dirar was still shaking, but he and Gideon did as his brother instructed. At closer inspection, the bandits, who had seemed to be so menacing a few minutes earlier, were nothing more than a few undernourished youths, their sightless eyes staring up at them.

'How fortunate your brother came along to find you,' said Gideon. He smiled ruefully, 'I don't think we'd have stood much chance against those bandits with our wooden staves.'

'And the dagger. Don't forget the dagger,' said Dirar. He felt quite light headed, but Gideon was right; things could have gone very differently without Umar.

'Dirar,' Umar called. He was standing by his mare, and wiping the mud from his uniform. 'Thanks, brother. That could have been me, lying there,' he said, pointing to the dead soldier.

CHAPTER 36

Umar knew he would have to decide what he was going to do soon; his father had told him that the wedding was planned for the following week and Simon and Salma were leaving Malaqah straight after it . If Layla wasn't married by then she would be forced to leave with them. He didn't know which was worse, to never see her again or to see her living in his brother's house as his wife. He loved his brother but he loved Layla more. If he had to choose between them, he would have no hesitation in choosing Layla. He didn't want to be estranged from his brother, but this was something he couldn't back down from. Ibrahim had told him he was looking for a suitable wife a while ago, long before he met Layla. He was sure that his brother would be able to find someone else and be just as happy, while Umar knew he couldn't live without her.

There was no point is saying anything more to Baba; he had said categorically that he would not get involved and it was up to Layla whom she chose to marry. But at the moment she didn't know how Umar felt about her. Hard though it would be for him to expose his feelings to her in this way, he knew that if he truly wanted her for his wife, then he would have to speak to her as soon as possible.

He would wait for her outside the entrance to the university; she was due to come out very soon. He squatted in the shade of a large carob tree, hoping that nobody he knew would come past; he was well aware of how incongruous he looked in his soldier's uniform, squatting like a street beggar.. A few of the students looked across at him as they came out of the university; they seemed to be surprised to see him there, but just hurried on without saying anything. He was used to the way some people behaved towards him, with a mixture of respect and fear. The students were no different.

Layla was surprised to see Umar waiting for her when she came down the university steps.

'As-salama alaykum, Umar. What are you doing here?' she asked.

'I wondered if I could talk to you, Layla? Maybe we could walk somewhere quieter.' The square was filling up with chattering students; like caged birds just set free, they grouped and regrouped with their friends, laughing and talking about their day.

'Of course.' She turned to her companions and said, 'See you tomorrow.' The girls looked at him quizzically, obviously wondering who he was. 'I must speak to my cousin,' she added.

They walked in silence for a moment, but once they were out of earshot of the other students, she turned to Umar and asked, 'Is something wrong? Has something happened to my parents? They have been behaving very strangely just lately.'

'No, nothing like that, Layla. As far as I know, they are fine.' He took her arm and guided her towards the city walls, through the West Gate and along the riverbank. A flock of birds flew overhead, heading for north Africa and warmer climes.

This was very mysterious. Why was Umar here? And what was so urgent that he had come to find her? Layla was beginning to feel worried.

Once they were out of sight of the city, he suddenly stopped and looked at her. He took her hand in his and said, 'Layla, I know you don't want to marry just yet. It must have come as a shock to you when Ibrahim proposed; you had your heart set on going to the university and living your life a little before thinking of marriage—I saw how happy you were when you came out just now and I can understand that you want more from life than being a wife and a mother. However I have to tell you that I've also asked my father if I can marry you.'

'What?' Layla couldn't believe her ears. 'Are there no other eligible women in this city?' she asked, with a laugh.

Umar smiled, 'None as lovely as you.'

'Well, I'll tell you what I have told them all, your brother, your father and my parents, I'm not ready to get married,' she said. 'You said it yourself; I want more from life than to be somebody's wife.'

'So the wedding has been cancelled?' he asked, his heart skipping a beat.

'Yes, I just told you, I'm not ready to be wed.'

'I know that, and I understand. But I want you to know that I'm in love with you and I want you for my wife.' Layla felt her heart give a skip; he was in love with her. Suddenly things seemed different. If he could love her, then maybe she could love him in return; some of those childhood memories came flooding back to her. 'I know Ibrahim asked you to marry him, and I know you haven't made up your mind yet, which is why I am speaking out now. If you love Ibrahim and want to marry him, then I will go away and never bother you again. But before you make that decision, I want to tell you that I have loved you since the moment I set eyes on you in my father's house. I can't stop thinking about you.' He hesitated. 'If you're not ready for marriage, I can wait. However long it takes, I will wait. I just need to know that you will be mine, one day. I will prove to you that I will make a good husband. I promise. I know I'm just a soldier, but I am paid well; I will be able to give you a good life.' He looked away, nervously, looking worried that he'd said too much.

'Give me a little time and I will think about it,' she said.

'That's all I'm asking, my dearest one.'

The nervousness was gone, and it seemed as if the mist that had been swirling about her and clouding her mind had lifted.

As they headed back, no longer in a hurry to get home, Umar said, 'Tell me why you came to Malaqah, Layla. What are your dreams?' And she began to tell him.

CHAPTER 37

Marwen was still smarting from Yusuf's words. How could he take Salma's side, a woman who had only been working there a few months. It angered him to think that the chief librarian should favour her over Marwen, who'd worked diligently for him for almost twenty years. Threatening him with dismissal was too much; he wasn't going to stand for it. He would speak to the muhtasib; he knew him well. He would soon get rid of her duplicitous husband, one way or another. He had heard the other scribes gossiping about Salma's younger daughter, who was to be married the following week. If her father was exposed before that, then it would jeopardise her future as well; but what did he care.

'Marwen, I have a job for you,' said the chief librarian, appearing suddenly in front of his desk. 'Leave that for now; I want you to catalogue some books. They are long overdue.'

Marwen reluctantly followed Yusuf to a remote part of the library where they kept books and manuscripts that had been copied but not organised into the appropriate categories; it was a task normally undertaken by the very junior librarians. He bristled with rage. 'You want me to catalogue all these?' he asked. 'Surely this could be done by someone else, not the assistant librarian?'

'No, I'd like you to do it. It shouldn't take you more than a week or two,' said Yusuf.

'But...'

Yusuf was not listening; he had already left the room, leaving an angry Marwen surveying the mountain of dusty manuscripts.

Makoud was surprised to see Yusuf come into his shop; he couldn't remember when he had last visited him, probably the time when his son was missing.

'Ahlan, dear friend. What can I do for you?' asked Makoud.

'Ahlan wa sahlan,' Yusuf said. He looked harassed, as though he had been in a great hurry to get there. His djellaba flapped open and the white turban he always wore was loose. Absentmindedly, he tucked the loose ends in place and said, 'I had a visitor this morning. The muhtasib.'

'So that's why you're looking so flustered, my friend. What did he want?'

'He wanted to see Simon.'

'Simon, whatever for?'

'He wouldn't tell me, so I'm afraid I had to lie to him. I said I had sent Simon to Garnata to collect some rare books for me,' said Yusuf.

'So where is he really?'

'After the muhtasib left, I found him in the kitchen preparing some ink. I told him the chief of police was looking for him and suggested that it was better if he worked at home. So I suspect that's where he is.'

'And you have no idea what the police wanted?' asked Makoud.

'None. I expect it was more of Marwen's doing. He and the muhtasib often play chess together; it wouldn't surprise me if he didn't feed the police chief some lies about our new translator.'

'Would he really do that?' He had never met this Marwen, but he didn't like the sound of him. 'So Simon knows the muhtasib is looking for him?'

'Yes, I told Simon he had a few days grace until he returned. Now I must leave you and return to the library, my friend. I want to keep a close eye on Marwen at the moment. He's angry that I rebuked him, and when he's angry he can be dangerous.'

Makoud watched the chief librarian as he headed back towards the university; he had brought troubling news with him. There was only one reason the muhtasib wanted to speak to Simon; he had found out about him visiting the church and it was probably Marwen who told him. But how did he know about it?

Well the situation was clear now. No matter how much he regretted seeing them leave Malaqah, that was what they had to do. No-one was safe while Simon remained in the city, even though, as Salma had said, he was no longer attending the church. The damage was already done; too many people knew his secret. Simon and Salma would have to leave for Ardales immediately.

Makoud had provided them with a donkey to carry their belongings, and Basma and Abal had prepared them enough food to feed an army. Now the whole family had gathered at Makoud's home to wish them a safe journey.

Salma tried and failed to hold back her tears. They had all been so kind and hospitable to them, and even though she and Simon were turning their backs on that kindness, they continued to shower them with good wishes and advice for the journey. If only she could confide in them so that they would understand, but the fewer people who knew their secret the better.

'Don't cry, cousin. Your daughters will be safe here. I will visit Zara every day and make sure she is well. And Dirar has said he will help her in the alfarería until he finds a new fishing boat; so she won't be without friends and family,' said Makoud, embracing Salma.

'Thank you, Makoud. I'm sure she'll be fine.' Her eldest daughter had blossomed since Iqbal's death; she was a different person now. Salma knew she would manage well enough, and if not, then she could come home to them. It was Layla she was worried about. She had hardly spoken to them since she had said she wasn't ready to get married; it was as though she was punishing them. Salma couldn't bear to leave with any ill feeling between them. She had pleaded with Simon to stay just a few more days longer but he wouldn't change his mind. She looked across at her younger daughter; she was deep in conversation with Makoud, and for once she looked happy. Maybe she had accepted the inevitable. It was a frightening time for every young woman, to marry a man she hardly knew and leave her family and friends, she knew that. But that was the way of the world.

'Mama, Makoud and I have been talking,' Layla said. Salma's heart gave a skip. She was going to marry Ibrahim, after all. She looked around the room. Umar and Dirar were there, but no Ibrahim. Where was he? It seemed rather strange that he wasn't there to wish them a safe journey. Maybe he was angry that Layla had called off the wedding, or with them for threatening to take Layla with them, but what option did they have? If she refused to marry him there was no alternative.

'You are marrying Ibrahim?'

'No, Mama,' replied Layla, with a smile.

'Oh, so you're coming with us to Ardales?' she asked, beaming at her daughter.

'No, Mama. I'm staying in Malaqah.'

'Now don't be stupid, child. We have discussed this; if you don't get married then you must come with us. I know it isn't what you planned, but believe me, it's for the best,' said Simon.

'I think what your unruly daughter is trying to tell you,' said Umar, breaking away from the conversation with his youngest brother, 'Is that she has agreed to marry me. With your permission of course.'

Salma stared at him in amazement. Layla was going to marry a soldier. She couldn't believe it. 'Makoud, is this true?' she asked.

'Yes, cousin. I told you we would let Layla decide and she has chosen Umar. Both my sons had asked for her hand in marriage.'

'We have agreed that it would be best if Layla finished her course at the university first, and then we will get married,' said Umar.

'So you're not getting married next week?'

'No, Mama. We are going to wait. We don't see that there is any great hurry.'

'But we agreed. You would marry Ibrahim or you would accompany us back to Ardales,' Salma said.

'No Mama, we agreed I would become betrothed and I have. I told you I would only marry for love, and Umar loves me.'

Her daughter didn't say that she loved Umar, but by the way she was looking at him, it was obvious that she did. Salma didn't know what to think and even less what to feel. Selfishly she wanted Layla to go with them to Ardales, but why should her daughter's dreams be taken away from her, just because hers were?

'I am heartbroken that I won't be here to see you wed,' she said eventually. 'Is your father in agreement with this delay?' She looked straight at Umar.

'Yes. My father agrees we can wait. There is no problem, and maybe you can come back for the wedding next year,' Umar said.

'I don't like this, Layla. You are twisting things to get what you want. We can't leave you here, unprotected.'

'I won't be unprotected, Mama. I have Umar and his family.'

'But where will you live? It's unseemly to live in the house of your betrothed.'

'With Zara of course. She'll need the company, and I can help her with the new baby. Anyway Umar has to spend a lot of time at the Dar al-Jund.'

So her daughters had it all planned between them. She sighed. What could she do? Simon would not wait even one more day, and it was unthinkable that she should stay here without him.

'Very well, child. I hope you know what you're doing. And you too, Umar. As you can see, my youngest daughter has a strong will.'

'Yes, mother-in-law. Don't worry; I will look after your daughter.' He smiled at Layla as though she were the only person in the room.

'Salma, come my dear; it's time to leave,' Simon whispered. He looked sad. 'Layla, look after yourself, child. If you ever want to come home, you know where we will be.' He took her in his arms and hugged her, blinking back the tears.

'Ma'a salama, Baba. Thank you, but Malaqah is my home now.' She took Umar's hand and smiled up at him. She looked happy; maybe it would work out for her after all.

Salma and Simon walked slowly towards the West Gate. Neither of them spoke. Salma knew that Simon was as unhappy as she was at having to leave their two daughters behind, but it was inevitable. All daughters married and left home at some time. Salma was sad, but she was also pleased that Layla had found someone she could love; she would have preferred her new son-in-law to have been Ibrahim, with a solid career and his own living space above the shop, but Umar was a good man and he was obviously very much in love with her daughter. She hoped Layla understood the perils of being married to a soldier, even a decorated nazir.

'Sad to leave?' Simon asked.

'A little,' she lied. How could she tell him, the man she loved, that he had destroyed her dreams, that she had been so happy working in the library, that now she wouldn't see her grandchildren grow up, that she would miss the friendship of Makoud and his wives? The thought of returning to Ardales, where all everybody spoke about were the weather and how well their crops were growing, depressed her.

As they passed through the market, she glimpsed the soothsayer they had met on their first day in the city, and as clear as it they were spoken aloud, she heard her words, once more, 'Don't worry, despite your broken dreams, life will go on.'

Salma stopped and looked back at the city, her hand going automatically to the bag over her shoulder; inside it were her writing materials, a number of sheets of parchment and a book of poems. She had stolen them from the library. She knew it was wrong, and she would be punished if she were caught, but she had to take a tiny moonbeam of her dream with her. She couldn't leave it all behind. She had to believe in the soothsayer's prophecy.

CHAPTER 38

Ben-Yahya stood on the ramparts of the city's walls and surveyed the scene below him. Jabalah and his men spread across the land beyond the river like a plague of locusts. What an unruly band of men. So this was his great army. He didn't doubt that the men could fight, but were they disciplined? They did not resemble his own well trained soldiers in the slightest, dressed as they were, in a motley range of uniforms and with no regimentation whatsoever. Thanks be to Allah that he had the foresight to move all the inhabitants of the suburbs inside the city walls; despite his agreement with Jabalah, he didn't trust the mercenary's soldiers to keep to it. The pickings would have been too easy to resist for men like that.

'There he is,' said Labib, who stood beside him. 'They are bringing him across the bridge now.'

'Where is the general?' General Rashad had the task of delivering the ransom money to Jabalah because he'd known ibn Baqanna for many years; he would be able to identify him at once. Ben-Yahya had to be very sure that they had captured the right man.

'He's crossing now.'

They'd agreed that Jabalah and the general would meet on the bridge and make the exchange. He had ordered twenty of his best soldiers to accompany him, and just inside the city walls another two hundred were waiting, armed and ready, in case the warlord tried to double-cross him.

'Is that Jabalah on the bridge? he asked.

'No, it doesn't look like him. He's back there, see, where his standard is flying, at the head of the army.'

'So he doesn't trust me, either,' said Ben-Yahya, with a sharp laugh.

'He's far too canny to walk into a trap, Your Majesty,' said one of his officers.

Just then the general came into sight. He stopped in the middle of the bridge, the soldiers grouped around him with their lances in their hands, and behind them the donkey with two sacks of gold slung across its back.

'Where is ibn Baqanna?' asked Ben-Yahya, craning his neck to see more clearly.

'I think that's him, slung over the back of a mule. He looks as though he's tied hand and foot.'

'So we can't see if it's him?'

'Don't worry Your Majesty,' said the officer. 'General Rashad is checking now.'

The general marched up to the inert body and pulled the head up to identify him. He then turned and waved; this was the signal they had agreed he would make if he were satisfied that it was ibn Baqanna.

At last he had him; ibn Baqanna had been captured. Ben-Yahya felt the adrenaline pumping around his body; now he would have his revenge.

The dishevelled, dirty and bruised ibn Baqanna was dragged before him. What a pitiful sight he was. No longer the proud, overbearing man who wore ermine-edged djellabas and carried himself like a king, that Ben-Yahya remembered from his childhood. Then everyone had regarded him with awe. Now he was a worthless traitor. As ibn-Yahya looked down on the wretched man prostrate at his feet, he knew he should feel some compassion for him, but all he felt was hatred.

'Your Majesty,' the prisoner croaked. 'There has been a mistake. You know I would never betray you. I am not a traitor, please believe me. Your Majesty, I beg you, just give me a chance to explain.'

'Silence. I have not had you brought here to listen to your lies. I have brought you here to see for myself the man who had everything: power, wealth, the trust of the khalifa, but it was never enough; to see for myself the man who connived and plotted and ultimately betrayed all those who trusted him. You know only too well the fate of traitors. Now that fate is yours,' said Ben-Yahya, his face twisted from the hatred that burned inside him. 'Take him to the public square and execute him. I want everyone to witness the end of this perfidious worm of a man.' He stood up letting his robes billow out about him and watched them drag ibn Baqanna away. Fear had silenced his pleas for mercy and a hush fell on the room, broken only by the heavy footfall of the soldiers.

Ten thousand gold dinars was a lot of money to pay Jabalah, but it was worth every single dirham to be rid of that viper. Ben-Yahya had avenged his father's death; he had avenged his family's exile to Sebta, all those long years in a foreign country, cut off from all they knew and loved, and now he had his revenge on the man who had colluded to keep him from his rightful place as Khalifa of Malaqah.

He stopped as he heard the cheers from the place of execution; at long last, ibn Baqanna had met his fate. It was over. Now Ben-Yahya could turn his attention to being Khalifa, free from worry, at least until some other usurper crept out from the shadows. But that was the way of the world; there was always someone who wanted to take the power from those who had it.

The sunshine beckoned to him and he wandered out into the still air; the noise from the crowd was diminishing. The excitement was over. By now ibn Baqanna's head would be adorning a pole next to that of his old friend and tutor Naja al-Siqlabi, traitors both. But he wasn't going to think any more about them. It was over. He had his revenge. Now he planned to enjoy his freedom. He stopped by the pond and watched as a male peacock strutted past him, flashing his iridescent feathers at this intrusion. He blinked; his eyes were still not accustomed to the brightness of the light and the density of the colours around him. All these things he had taken for granted before his incarceration; now he was constantly amazed at the beauty of the world. It was as though he had been blind and now could see.

He plucked a rose from a bush and held it to his nose; how sweet was its perfume. Gradually two years of stench and filth began to fade like a bad dream, as he stretched his arms and gazed up into a cloudless blue sky. Today the sea was calm and lapped gently against the walls of the alcazaba. Gulls whirled and dived above his head, screeching as they searched for scraps left by the fishermen.

'Ben-Yahya, what are you doing?' his mother called. 'The librarian is here to see you.'

'Tell him I'll see him out here; it's such a beautiful day.'

Jabalah reined in his horse and turned to look back down on the city below him. It was a jewel on the coast, with its wide harbour, its magnificent fortress and the hills and forests sheltering in from the north winds. Of all the cities in Spain that he had visited, this was the one he coveted the most. The khalifa was weak; that was made obvious by his haste to back out of the agreement to attack Morón. Young and weak, and ruling that beautiful city, how long would he last? How long had the previous khalifa lasted? Two years? And the one before that even less. This one wouldn't fare any better.

Not today, but one day, he would be back, and it wouldn't be for a miserly ten thousand gold dinars; no, he wanted it all. The smaller taifas, once numerous, were gradually falling under the control of the more powerful ones. Al-Andalus was a country teetering on the brink of collapse; it was a perfect time for a man such as himself. Yes he would be back.

'Is everything all right, my Lord? asked Diego.

'Yes, everything is fine. I'm just thinking of our future.' He wheeled his horse round to face north. 'But for now, it's time to move on.'

AUTHOR'S NOTE

Jabalah's prediction was partly true; Ben-Yahya reigned until 1047, when he was deposed by his cousin, Muhammad I al-Mahdi. It continued in that way, with another four khalifas ruling the country before Malaqah was conquered by its one-time ally, Badis ben Habus of Granada in 1057.

The persecution and massacre of the Jews in Granada, mentioned in chapter 33, actually took place on 30th December 1066, twenty-four years later than stated in the novel. Muslim mobs stormed the royal palace, killed the Jewish grand vizier, Joseph ibn Nagrilla, and massacred four thousand Jewish citizens.

The character of Jabalah was loosely based on Rodrigo Diaz de Vivar, a Castilian knight and warlord known as el Cid, a name given to him by the Moors, meaning my Lord, and not far removed from the Arabic *sayyid*. He lived from 1043 -1099.

GLOSSARY

Alcaiceria textile workplace, especially silk
Aleichem shalom peace be upon you (Jewish greeting)
alfarero potter
Ahlan welcome
Ahlan wa sahlan. the reply to welcome
Alla ysalmak response to goodbye
ammu uncle
Arab mile between 1.8 and 2 kilometres
As-salama alaykum Hello
Atarazanas shipyards
Baba father
Barid postal service
Barrio district
Calendula used as a disinfectant
Churros a sweet fried batter
Dar al-Jund soldiers' quarters
Dar al Wuzara house of the viziers
al-Darrabun night watchman
dirhams silver units of currency
dinars gold units of currency
Djubbah a simple tunic
Djellaba a hooded cloak
Djinn a mythical being from the spirit world
Ghifara a crocheted cap
Hammudid dynasty rulers in al-Andalus 1016 AD - 1056 AD
Iddah period of mourning: four months and ten days
Imam holy man
insha'Allah God willing
Jarrah jug
jihad holy war

Jinete horseman

Ma'a salama goodbye

Medina a town

Mojama dried tuna

Muhtasib officer in charge of municipal muhtasib

naquib officer in charge of a contingent of up to 2,000 men

nazir sergeant in charge of a squad of 16 men

Omayyads the rulers of al-Andalus 970 AD - 1031 AD

Puerta gate

Qadi religious judge

Qarib a wooden ship, strong enough to go out into the ocean but also close inland

Quaid officer in charge of a corps of 10,000 men

Quran the central religious holy book of Islam

rababah Arabic stringed instrument

saqaliba a slave from northern and eastern Europe

Sayyad master or sir

Sayyid lord

Sayeda madam

Sayyida queen, queen mother or mistress

Sayyida al-Malika, mother of the khalifa

Seedo nickname for Grandfather

Shaitan the Devil

Shatrang check-board banner

Souk market

Taifa an independent Muslim-ruled principality

Teta nickname for grandmother

Tisbah ala-kheir goodnight

Wa alaykum e-salam Peace be upon you

Wasit alzaway marriage broker

Zenana the innermost apartments where the women in the harem live

Thank you for taking the time to read THE PRISONER. If you enjoyed it, please consider telling your friends or posting a short review. Word of mouth is an author's best friend and much appreciated. Thank you, Joan Fallon

CONNECT WITH JOAN FALLON ONLINE AT:
http:// www.joanfallon.co.uk
https://www.facebook.com/joanfallonbooks